The
Fine Art
of
Murder

The Fine Art of Murder
Copyright © 2016

Published by Blue River Press
Indianapolis, Indiana
www.brpressbooks.com

Distributed by Cardinal Publishers Group
Tom Doherty Company, Inc.
www.cardinalpub.com

ISBN: 978-1-68157-023-5

Editor: Kelsey Schneiders
Senior Editors: Diana Catt & Brenda Stewart
Interior Design: Dave Reed
Cover Design: Rebekah Hobbs

Printed in the United States of America

Contents

Authors and Entities

Acknowledgements

The editors, **Brenda Robertson Stewart** and **Diana Catt**, would like to thank the members of Speed City Indiana Sisters in Crime for their enthusiastic support for this project. We had an excellent response to our request for fictional short story submissions and for factual inserts about artists in Indiana. We send special thanks to Travis DiNicola for writing the introduction, and to the wonderful team at Cardinal Publishers Group—especially Morgan Sears, Kelsey Schnieders, Ginger Bock, Adriane Doherty and Tom Doherty—for their support and belief in our group and our latest endeavor. Again, we send our special congratulations to all the members of Speed City Indiana Sisters in Crime for the successful completion of another project to showcase the creative talents of this group of writers.

Introduction

Twenty-some years ago, when I was looking for a quote to include in my graduate thesis (on why art museums should use this "new" technology called the "internet" to expand their education and marketing outreach) I found the following by philosopher Nelson Goodman:

"The only moral effect a museum has on me is a temptation to rob the place."

If the words "art thief" don't give you a little thrill, if the thought of how to bypass a museum's security system has never once crossed your mind, and if you've never, ever, thought about the perfect place to hang your own Picasso, then perhaps this book isn't for you.

But you have thought these things, haven't you? You've been tempted.

My thesis advisor strongly advised me not to use the quote. He didn't think it was appropriate in an academic paper. I thought it was hilarious, and appropriate. Eventually, I convinced him of the merits of including it, my thesis was approved, and I graduated with a Masters in Art Education.

The reason I wanted to include it in the thesis is because in the early 1990s most art museums did not want to be on the internet for fear of having their work "stolen." Curators spoke at conferences and wrote in forums speculating that digital images of their collections could be copied (stolen!) and appreciated outside of the museum walls. Directors feared that people would stop coming to museums if they could access their collections online. These were the same fears that museums had early in the twentieth century when critic Walter Benjamin argued that art created by human hands has an aura that can't be reproduced mechanically. A photograph of an artwork is not the artwork. Museums did not shut their doors.

Photographs were one thing, but now anyone could "steal" a digital copy of any work in a museum, without even going to the museum.

And they did.

And it didn't hurt the art.

And the museums didn't have to shut their doors. And today, every art museum in the world has their collection available on-line.

At some point the museums realized that it was a good thing that people wanted their own copies of art they loved. It wasn't a crime, and it didn't keep them from coming to see the real thing.

But this book you are holding is about crime and art. And, it is about the real thing. Because people don't kill for a copy.

That temptation, to possess the original, is also real. It can be overwhelming. That temptation leads to motivation—motivation to steal, and motivation to murder.

Art and mysteries. Two of my favorite things.

I blame my mother. They are two of her favorite things as well.

I grew up surrounded by art and by murder mysteries. Every vacation led to a museum and at least a few bookstores. Prints of Picasso, Klee, Rothko, Monet, Duchamp, and Matisse covered the walls. Copies of Christie, Spillane, Rendell, Hammett, James, and Highsmith filled the shelves. One year, for her birthday, of course I bought her a replica of the Maltese Falcon statue.

The stuff that dreams are made of: Art & Murder. The Fine Art of Murder.

And those dreams, those temptations, have led me here. I've made a career of them.

As the Executive Director of Indy Reads, Indianapolis's adult literacy program, I also founded the bookstore, Indy Reads Books – where we sell a lot of mysteries to support our program. In my other role, as the co-host of WFYI Indianapolis Public Radio's "The Art of the Matter," each week I get to talk with artists about their work. I pay my bills because of art and murder mysteries. My mother is very proud.

This is why I so gladly agreed to write this introduction for the Speed City Indiana Chapter of Sisters in Crime. What could be better than mysteries with art? Having them written by Indiana authors with most of them set in Indianapolis! There are even references to my NPR station, my Mass Ave neighborhood, and my favorite minor-league baseball team, the Indianapolis Indians. How could I say no?

This is a great collection of stories. Hardboiled and cozy. Abstract and impressionist. Like any good museum collection, there is something here for everyone. This book is filled with temptations. I hope you enjoy reading them as much as I did.

Now, I've got to go help my mom find a perfect place to hang her new Picasso.

M. Travis DiNicola, April, 2016

To Catch a Thief

Andrea Smith

My friend, Noah, slides into the booth and sits facing me. His smile is so broad it stretches the lines in his weathered brown face.

"Vera Ames, little girl, you look more delicious than my sweet potato pie," he bellows above the din of people chatting and enjoying his southern fare.

I purse my lips. I'm fifty-four, a long way from being a girl. "Don't waste your charms on me."

His eyes sparkle with mischief. "Just speaking the truth, pretty girl. You're always so put together. Now if you didn't have that big ol' husband and I was ten years younger, I—"

"Would still be ancient, you eighty-two-year-old flirt," I say without cracking a smile.

Noah slaps the table and we both collapse in laughter.

When you've been friends for thirty years like Noah and me, teasing comes as naturally as breathing. We've been an unlikely team of sorts since we organized to keep my sons' and his granddaughter's school from closing. My hubs was working and going to grad school. I had left my corporate manager's job to open the Beauty Emporium. Noah sent clients my way when only a handful of customers would take a chance on my skills. His beloved wife, Ella, was one of the first ladies to sit in my chair. She had thick, gorgeous hair and the sweetest personality anyone could want in a client. I was there for Noah when she passed away after fifty years of marriage, six sons and so many grandkids and great-grandkids I doubt Noah even knows the number. Now we're trying to keep the struggling Community Art Center afloat.

Which is why sitting here laughing with Noah, inside I feel like a first-class heel.

A backstabber.

A snake.

I'm not just here for his comfort food and laughs.

I'm here to betray my friend.

I sip my strawberry iced tea hoping to ease the dryness in my mouth. It doesn't help. When I run my tongue over my teeth, it feels like sandpaper.

"Mary," Noah calls to one of his servers. "Folks at table twelve been waiting too long for their order. They don't want me coming back to the kitchen. Tell 'em to step it up."

Mary nods and scurries off.

"You don't miss a thing," I say.

Noah leans forward. "Like I told you when you opened that fancy beauty salon, no one will take care of your business like you. You have to be watchful at all times. Especially during your rushes."

There's always a rush at Noah's restaurant, *A Taste of Heaven*. It's so popular, celebrities, athletes, and politicians make it a must stop when they breeze through Indianapolis. Photos of Noah with his famous diners decorate the restaurant walls.

"You sounded a little stressed on the phone. What's making you so anxious about tomorrow?" Noah asks.

The server brings my crab cakes. They smell divine, but I'm going to have to fake an appetite for them. "Don't you mention this to a soul because it hasn't been confirmed yet. The auctioneer says it's possible Cecil's mosaic might sell for one million dollars."

I watch Noah's expression for a hint of anything unusual.

He whistles. "Are you serious, little girl? That kind of money could turn an honest person into a thief."

That comment pricks my spirit but I tell myself I'm probably reading too much into it. "Remember, Cecil pledged fifty percent of the profits to the art center. With that kind of a donation we can finish the renovations and increase the number of scholarships."

"Mighty generous of that young man. Was it only five years ago he was a skinny kid who barely spoke a word? Then you got him enrolled in art classes at the center, and overnight he's doing custom work for rich folks. Shows you not everybody forgets where they came from when they make it. Your crab cakes okay? You're barely touching your food."

I pick up my fork and stab at the crisp patty. "Oh, they're wonderful as usual. I, uh, had a huge breakfast and didn't realize I was so full. You know Hamp, always over-doing it in the kitchen. Maybe he should come work for you."

Noah laughs. "Send him on. Be glad to teach him a few things. Course it's not as important as what he does, finding medicines to treat diabetes and such."

I summon the guts to ask what I think might be revealing. "The value of the mosaic has me wondering if Allied's security plan is good enough. I—"

"Worry too much," Noah says waving at the air. "They do all right on the basketball tournament. Nothing's ever gone wrong there."

I scoot a piece of crab cake around on my plate. "You don't think we need to make any changes for tomorrow night's exhibition? It'll most likely cost us more, but if the mosaic sells for that price, we'll be able to absorb it easily."

Noah shakes his head. "Seems fine to me, but if it'll make you feel better, you've got my board vote to make whatever adjustments we need."

I'm grateful. "Appreciate that. I'm going to have a sit down with that Brian Townes at Allied. Maybe he can ease my mind."

* * *

When I call Allied Security, the assistant tells me Townes is in a meeting and she'll have him get back to me. Since I can't see him right away, I head to my salon to make sure no one has given a client a bad haircut or made them wait too long for service. Most of my stylists have been with me long enough where I know I can be away without chaos breaking out. But Rhonda, my receptionist, has only worked for me for a month and I'm monitoring her closely until she gets proficient with my system. Sure enough, Rhonda is wearing an anxious expression when I step through the door.

"Oh, Ms. Vera. So glad you're back."

"Is something wrong?" I ask, hoping nothing's gone horribly haywire with the new digital scheduling and payment program my son, Nathan, installed for me.

She gives a nervous giggle. "Just have a couple of questions about entering repeat appointments. Had a few requests like that today." She picks up her notepad. "I wrote down everything that needs to be entered and I checked to make sure there were no time conflicts."

I'm relieved she thought to do that. I'm showing Rhonda how to enter repeating appointments when the last person I want to see right now buzzes the door.

"I'll be with you in a minute," I say when I let him in.

He nods. "Take your time, ma'am."

I cringe. I've gone from being a little girl to a ma'am. I'm guessing he's in his forties, yet he says ma'am as if I could be his mother.

"Think you got it now?" I ask Rhonda.

She nods, and after a furtive glance at our visitor, buries her face in the computer screen. Exactly what I would do if I didn't have to talk to him.

I head for my office with him lumbering behind me. After he eases his long legs into my black leather chair he tells me, "Unfortunately, I have more bad news. We've picked up increased chatter about the impending theft of the Davis piece now that word is out it's selling for one million dollars."

I narrow my eyes at him. He's not a bad looking guy, clear skin and a muscular frame beneath his custom-tailored suit. It's his full-of-himself attitude that's unattractive. "Tell me, Agent Summers, how is it this *chatter* isn't telling the FBI's Arts Crime team exactly who might be planning to steal it?"

"Sorry, there are certain details I can't divulge about our operation, ma'am," he says in a too-patient tone.

I think if he calls me ma'am one more time, I may end up under investigation.

"I realize it's difficult to accept your friend is a thief—"

"It's not difficult," I interrupt. "It's impossible. I didn't believe it yesterday when you came here asking for my help and I don't believe it now. The Noah Gardner I know is an honest, hard-working family man. A war hero. He's not about to ruin the art center he's worked so hard to help build."

His body stiffens as if he's bracing himself for me to become unhinged. "We didn't make up Noah Graves. A.k.a. Nick Gardner. A.k.a. Noah Gibson. That's just a few of the aliases he's used. Arrested three times in the fifties and only got caught when he made the mistake of bringing in a partner who lost his nerve and spilled his guts to the cops. They were waiting for Noah at the gallery he was about to hit and he did a year in jail. We suspect the list of thefts he pulled off is longer than we'll ever know."

I take a deep breath. "You really believe he would go back to that life? At his age? He's not stupid—or suicidal."

Agent Summers gives me that patient look again. "Last week we finally caught a ninety-one-year-old bank robber we've been chasing for years. He took up his life of crime when he turned seventy."

Summers pops up from the chair and strolls his smug self out of my office.

I need to verify what he's just told me about Noah. In my dealings with law enforcement, I've found some have a tendency to jump to conclusions before getting all the facts. I leave the salon in the capable hands of my head stylist, Thelma, hop in my Prius and head for IMPD headquarters to see Officer Janice Billings. I got to know Janice when I helped one of her lazy detective colleagues solve the murder of one of my employees. The detective didn't seem to care that an innocent young man had been killed and wasn't conducting much of an investigation. So I did the investigating for him and nailed our delivery driver for the crime. Janice had helped by giving me details her colleague wouldn't share. She's become a friend—actually more of a kindred sister.

"You said this was urgent when you called. Which detective are you *helping* this time?" she asks with a chuckle.

"FBI," I say, squaring my shoulders.

Officer Billings's green eyes widen.

I shrug. "Is it my fault law enforcement is so incompetent they have to ask a middle-aged black woman for assistance? Present company excluded, of course. The FBI insisted I work with them because the man they claim is planning to steal the mosaic we're showing tomorrow sits on the art center board with me. I've known him decades. There's absolutely no way he would do anything like this. I'm hoping you might, you know, run a check, as they say, on Noah's background and let me know if what they claim is true."

"I can't butt into a federal investigation."

I stare at her. We both know she can get around that little detail.

Officer Billings gives me a sly smile. "However, that doesn't mean you, coming to us in your capacity as chairperson running an event that city officials will be attending, can't ask for my advice."

Like I said—kindred sisters.

Officer Billings picks up her pen. "What's his full name?"

I tell her Noah's personal history as I know it and she bounces out of the room, her ginger ponytail swaying with each step. While she's gone I call Allied Security again and get the same story. Townes is still in a meeting. I make a mental note to recommend we never use Allied again once this is over. If I didn't respond to my clients, I wouldn't have any.

"You're not going to like what I found, Vera," Officer Billings warns when she returns.

"Don't sugar coat it," I say.

"Arrested for art theft three times when he was in his twenties. Like the FBI file says, he was sentenced to a year for the one job. They didn't recover the stolen artwork, which isn't unusual. Only a small percent of stolen art is ever found."

My heart sinks and I'm unable to find my voice for a response. Finally, I get out, "What I don't understand is what Noah is doing now to make the FBI suspect he's planning to steal the mosaic. This agent just claims they've got chatter. I can't believe Noah would risk the life and business he's built to go back to being a thief."

"Is his business in trouble? Woman problems?"

I can't help but laugh at the last question. "At his age the only problems he has with the ladies are in his imagination."

"I can look further if you like, check his financials to see if there's an issue with money that might be driving him back to his old ways," Officer Billings says.

I think for a minute. I don't want to accept that Noah may have been wearing a mask all these years.

With a sigh, I nod. Hating myself for it.

* * *

I trudge back to my car and my cell phone buzzes as I start the engine.

"Hey, love. Are you at the salon? Is my tux ready? Coming

home for dinner? As my mother used to say, I put my foot in this garlic chicken."

Hamp's rapid fire questions almost make me smile. I answer the same way. "No. You can pick up your tux anytime tomorrow morning after ten. I'll be home but I need to make a stop first."

"Uh oh. What are you up to now?"

Hamp knows me so well.

I'd told him about the FBI asking for my help so I give him the short version of what I learned about Noah. "It doesn't look good for him but I just know there's more to this than what the FBI is saying."

"Maybe you should trust the experts on this one, love. I know Noah is like a father figure to you. Sometimes we're too close to people to see what needs to be seen."

I straighten my shoulders with indignation as if Hamp can see the gesture. "Oh, you're Doctor Phil now?"

I have to admit Noah does remind me of my dad, who died when I was only fourteen. He was hard working too, and always full of smiles for mama and us girls. Maybe it's why Noah and I get along so well.

"They don't have to be right," I say.

Driving across the city to Castleton is the last thing I want to do. Traffic is always a mess on the northeast side, and this time of year, two weeks before Christmas, it's like being in New York City. Since it seems Brian Townes at Allied doesn't plan to return my calls anytime soon, I have no choice but to make the trip. It takes me thirty minutes to get there because sure enough 82nd Street is clogged like an artery. My mood is sour when I pull into the office complex where Allied is located. Before I can get out of my car, a familiar figure comes out the front door.

I blink to make sure I'm seeing clearly.

Noah.

I watch him walk to his truck. For some reason he looks more stooped than I've ever noticed. This man who still works ten to twelve hours a day running his restaurant usually looks younger than his years but right now he looks every day of them. There must be a good explanation for why Noah would come here and not call me to tell me what he was up to, I try to convince myself.

After he drives off, I gather my sense of purpose and go into the building. A twenty-something woman with strawberry curls at the reception desk offers me a seat and a promise to get Brian Townes after I tell her who I am and that I'm not happy I haven't been able to reach him all day.

The little display of attitude does the trick as a few minutes later Townes finally shows his face. Last time we'd met was when he'd presented his security proposal to the board. He was in a suit and tie. Today he's dressed in casual khakis and a jacket with an eagle logo on the chest. His comb-over isn't doing the job, and you can see his bald spot peeking through. Were he to come to my salon I would advise him to just embrace Michael Jordan smoothness. Truth is, men are vainer than women. He'll probably hang on to those blond strands until they scream for freedom.

"Mrs. Ames, so good to see you again," he says and gives me one of those spaghetti handshakes I loathe. A person shaking your hand like that is either a fraud or thinks you're carrying a virus. He shuttles me into a small conference room.

"Excuse me for dropping by without an appointment, but I called several times," I say.

"Been a real full day," is all he offers. Then adds, "I just had a visit from your colleague, Mr. Gardner. He doesn't think we have enough people assigned to the show. I went over our plans and reassured him we'll be fine."

"That's exactly why I'm here. If you don't mind repeating yourself tell me why you think your current plan is sufficient?"

Townes punches his palm with his index finger as he ticks off, "Tapped into the center's surveillance so we've got eyes on it from here twenty-four seven, we'll have twice the number of staff on site for the event tomorrow, and we'll have our top crew delivering it to whoever buys it at the auction. Trust me, there's no need to be concerned. I'm on call every minute. Nothing is going to happen to that masterpiece with me in charge."

I'm reassured after meeting with Townes and anxious to compare notes with Noah. Back in my car, I call Noah's cell phone. I get no answer, so I try the restaurant, and a staff member tells me he went to pick up supplies. I'm about to check in at my salon when my phone vibrates. It's Officer Billings.

"You're not going to like this, Vera. Your friend is carrying enough debt to sink a ship. Mainly student loans for his grandkids, it looks like. He has two second mortgages on his house and one on the business. It appears he's barely making it on what the restaurant is bringing in."

Just like that, my sense of relief vanishes.

* * *

My new jitters send me to the art center as I need to see for myself that the mosaic is secure. The center closes at five on Thursdays but, as executive director of the board, I have keys, security codes, and access at all times. It's almost six when I get there in the winter darkness. The center is located in a secluded area surrounded by gorgeous landscaping and sculptures. It's usually inviting and pleasant. Tonight, not so much. Tonight it makes chills run through me.

I park in the front lot, glad the exterior and main exhibit area lights remain on at all times. With a glance over my shoulder, I slip in and punch in the security codes so the alarm doesn't go off. Then I reset it.

The click of my suede Louboutin pumps on the tile floor echo in the empty hall. The main reception area is already set up for the hors d'oeuvres and champagne bar. I take a left turn to head to the Marian Broadnax exhibit room where Cecil's work is being displayed and use my key to let myself in.

My chest swells with pride seeing it again suspended from the ceiling in all its glory.

No Place Like Home. Cecil's tribute to his home state. The painstakingly assembled pieces of colored glass shimmer in the room. The pieces represent significant events and places in Indiana black history. As magnificent as it is, I still can't process that it could sell for a small fortune.

A sound snaps me out of my musing. My heartbeat picks up speed. *Calm down, Vera,* I tell myself. It's probably nothing. But now I'm sure I hear footsteps. Who could have gotten in without the alarm going off? A smaller exhibit room adjoins this one; I run in there and crouch down behind a sculpture.

"Well, look. They left the room unlocked for us," a male voice says.

"Let's unhook this baby. Time to get paid," another male voice says.

Fear crawls through me as I pray they don't sense my presence and that my phone doesn't go off. I hear them cackle with glee after they've gotten the mosaic down. I hear the door open and close.

My first thought is to call the police. Who am I kidding? By the time they get here, the thieves will be long gone. I peek from my hiding place and, not seeing anyone, tiptoe to the door and crack it open. They've moved fast and the hall is empty. I figure they wouldn't have parked in the front where their thievery would be on display so I race to the back entrance and, sure enough, through the big windows I see two white men loading the covered mosaic into a plain white truck. I'm angry and grateful at the same time. Angry at the thieves, grateful Noah isn't one of them.

There's only one way out of the art center complex to College Avenue, the closest street that runs north and south, and the thieves have to go past the front lot, where I parked, to get to it. My breath is coming in spasms as I sprint to the front entrance, reset the alarm with trembling fingers, and race to my car to wait for the truck to appear. When it does, I crank the engine and pull out of the lot. I hang back as I've seen the detectives on my favorite shows do, to make sure they don't suspect I'm following them. While we're moving, I call Agent Summers and get his voice mail. I leave as detailed a message as I can. I make my second call and have to leave a message there too. Geez, doesn't anyone answer their phone anymore?

We end up at a warehouse on Kentucky Avenue. They pull into the driveway and rumble to the back of the building. I sit across the street from the front entrance pondering my next move and hoping for a call back.

My hand flies to my mouth as I see Noah's truck pull up. He parks a few feet from the front entrance, gets out, and slinks up to the warehouse door. "Oh, Noah." I don't feel anger at him now, just a profound sense of disappointment.

I watch Noah ring the bell and disappear inside when someone I can't see lets him in. I wait. Praying one of my calls will be returned. Finally, I can't take it any longer, and before I know it, I'm out the car, crossing the street and pushing the doorbell myself. A husky black guy with a scraggly beard and menacing scowl snatches it open. There's something familiar about the jacket he's wearing.

"Hi," I say in my most pleasant, most innocent voice. "Is this the Dixon Company? I'm supposed to meet my contractor here."

"You've got the wrong place," he says and moves to close the door.

I put my hand on it and peek around him as much as my five feet two inches will allow. "This is the address he gave me. Do you mind if I get out of this wind and call? Not safe for a lady to be standing out here by herself."

He hesitates as if trying to decide if he can be mean to this middle-aged woman, so I strike and slide around him. "It'll just take me a minute."

He tries to block me. "Lady, you can't. . . ."

Too late. I'm in and weaving around the boxes that clutter the floor. I see Noah in the corner of the room with the two other rats who'd stolen the mosaic.

"There he is," I say. I start walking fast in their direction, although I have no idea what I'm going to do or say when I reach them. The menace is on my heels.

"Hold it, lady." He reaches for my arm, but I speed up.

"Noah!" I call, trotting toward him.

Noah looks pained when I reach them.

"Who's she?" one of the rats asks Noah.

Noah looks sheepish. "Never saw her before."

Menace has reached us now. "She says the old guy is her contractor but he told us the boss sent him."

That's when it hits me where I'd seen those jackets with the emblem of an eagle. They're just like the one Townes was wearing.

Before I know it, the words fly out of my mouth, "Now I know why the security alarm didn't go off. You're with Allied. Instead of protecting our art like you're paid to do, you're stealing it."

One of the rats grabs my arm. "The boss will be real happy to see both of yous."

"Yous?" I mock.

"Oh, yous don't like how I talk?" the killer of English sneers. "Maybe yous like this."

They snatch us by the arms and handcuff our hands behind our backs.

"Wannabe cops?" I snark.

"Put 'em in storage," the menace orders.

The rats push us down a corridor and shove us into a dimly lit room. We land on the damp concrete floor with a thud. I drop my handbag and its contents scatter.

"You all right, little girl?" Noah asks, his voice quivering.

I manage to sit up. "I guess." I scan the room and all I see is box after box. No sign of the mosaic. I wonder where they stashed Cecil's masterpiece.

"Want to tell me what you're doing here?" we ask each other at the same time.

"Ladies first," Noah says.

"Elders." I sniff.

He takes a deep breath. "When I saw how worried you were this morning I decided to visit Allied about the security plan. I know what things to look for, eh, based on my past experience. While I'm there, Townes gets a call about a delivery for this evening. That bothered me. I mean, what is a security company going to be delivering? He mentions the warehouse and the address to whoever he was talking to and I decided to check it out."

Relief washes over me. I've never been so happy to be right about a person. A confession is in order though. "If I don't tell you this, Noah, it will eat up my insides. The FBI came to me and said you were planning to steal the mosaic."

"FBI?"

"The agent told me about your record and wanted me to keep an eye on you. I agreed because I knew in my heart you would never steal from the center. That you'd never do anything like this. I was desperate to prove them wrong."

For what feels like hours instead of seconds, all I hear is Noah's labored breathing. I can sense his hurt. Finally, he says, "I did some things as a young man I regret. I came back from Korea trained as an engineer. Could fly any kind of plane and couldn't get a job. It was rough for a black man back then. Only job I could get didn't pay enough to take care of a cat. I had a wife. Babies were coming fast and they had to be fed. I fell in with the wrong folks and believe me I paid dearly for it. A year in hell."

My mind flashes back to the stories I'd heard about my father's struggles during those years. I can imagine what Noah had to fight. "FBI says you were good at what you did."

Noah chuckles. "Little girl, I was the best."

"They also say the art you stole was never found. What happened to it?"

He's silent again. Then he says with a touch of self-satisfaction in his voice, "Let's just say it made for a nice down payment on a restaurant."

I shouldn't, but I smile at that.

"Are we just going to sit here and wait for them to kill us?" I ask. "Can you use your skills to get us out of this mess? You know like on that old television show, *MacGyver*?"

He tries to twist his arms. "I might be able to pick these cuffs if I had something small and straight."

"I have hairpins in my purse." I scoot over to where the contents of my purse had scattered. I use my foot to shuffle through the items until I find the little plastic case of hairpins. I stomp it with my stiletto heel and smash it open. "Can you reach them?"

Noah crawls over on his knees and works to pick up a hairpin. It seems to take forever but finally he says, "Let's see if I still got the touch."

I have to ask Noah the other question nagging at me. "FBI said they had chatter pointing to you as a suspect. What have you been doing to make them think you were planning to steal the mosaic?"

"Shoot. Almost got it in the lock. Haven't been doing anything except working my business and the art center."

"It makes no sense for the FBI to single you out," I say. "You hadn't talked to any of your old acquaintances?"

"Folks I used to work with are either dead or too feeble to even think about our old business. When you have a record there's always a target on you. In this country folks never let you forget your past. You're always the first one they point the finger at when they need an arrest or a scapegoat. Black man's burden. How'd you find this place?"

I tell him how I was checking on the mosaic when the thieves showed up.

"Got it!" Noah almost shouts.

I shake with nervous joy.

Noah comes over to me and works on my cuffs. Shortly, my hands are free, and I scoop up the contents of my handbag, stuffing some items in my coat pocket. We make our way to the door, me on my tiptoes so as to not make noise in my heels. Noah flattens his ear against the door.

"Can't hear a thing," he says.

At that moment the door is snatched open and the menace is scowling at us.

"How the hell did you get out of those cuffs?"

Before I know it Noah throws himself at the menace, hitting him at the knees and making him pitch forward. Without thinking, I sink the heel of my pump into his backside. He topples, taking Noah with him.

"Run, Vera!" Noah yells.

I'm frozen. I can't leave him.

"I said run!"

Finally, I take off, slowing down when I get to the end of the hall that leads to the warehouse floor. Townes has arrived and is huddling with his thieves.

I crouch down and quietly zigzag around the big crates and boxes toward the door. My heart is pumping fast. I make it to the front door when it opens and Agent Summers steps in.

"Thank God, you got my message!"

His expression is hard, not one of someone who has come to my rescue. He's alone and he doesn't even have his gun out.

Light bulb moment. I start to back up.

"Yeah, thanks for the heads up. You kind of screwed up our plans but that's okay."

"I get it now," I say. "Nice little scheme you have. You use Noah's record to set him up. Who would believe an eighty-two-year-old felon, right? You and Townes steal the mosaic and split a nice bundle."

Summers smirks. "We already have a buyer for the pretty piece."

"You don't even care about destroying an innocent man."

Now Summers laughs. "Old coot has lived his life."

"You don't get to decide that."

"Lady, I'm the law. Haven't you noticed we can do what we want?"

He steps toward me. "Over here," he calls to his thieving partners and snakes his hand out to grab me.

But I have something for him. I pull my fragrance bottle from my pocket. "This is my bestseller," I say and spray him right in the eyes.

"Argh. Jesus!" He grabs at his eyes and stumbles, giving me a chance to sprint around him for the door.

I fling it open and run smack into Officer Billings, who's brought plenty of backup. The officers barrel in and turn their weapons on Townes and his goons who were rushing over to take care of me—or so they thought.

"I wouldn't move," Billings warns Summers, who's doubled over and still unable to see.

I almost collapse with relief.

"Sorry we're just getting here," Billings says. "When you called I was in the field taking up the slack for another detective. You know how that is."

"It's what we ladies do," I say.

* * *

I want to pinch myself.

Agent Summers, Brian Townes, and their thieves are locked up in the Marion County jail, and it's standing room only at Cecil's exhibition. Even the mayor is here. "We're thankful to all of you for supporting this event," Cecil says. "The Community Art Center is where I held my first paint brush and did my first sculpture. Therefore, it's my great honor to announce the mosaic was auctioned for one and a half million dollars—"

The crowd gasps.

"—All of which will be donated to this wonderful center to give aspiring artists the same opportunity I had. And I want to say a special thank you to the lady who made this possible, the president of the board of directors, Vera Ames."

I'm so tickled I'm blushing beneath my chocolate skin.

"How about that," Hampton, looking absolutely yummy in his tux, says to me as we sip the champagne and watch guests swarm Cecil to offer their congratulations.

Noah clears his throat. "I need to make a toast, young blood. To the fierce woman who believed in an old man. Who's the daughter I never had."

My heart is about to burst. I kiss the bruise on his cheek—a souvenir from our little caper—and lift my glass. "To the man who replaced the father I lost too soon."

Noah's eyes mist up.

So do mine.

Marie Goth (1887–1975)

N. W. Campbell

Marie Goth's life was filled with art. Once she was old enough to hold a pencil, her father, Charles, encouraged her to write and draw. Her passion led to her career as one of Indiana's most successful portrait and still-life painters.

While a student at Manual High, Goth won an Indianapolis art contest. Her father's cousin, Otto Stark, a Hoosier Art Group painter, directed the arts at Manual. He invited Goth to be his assistant, which she did until 1909. She studied art at Herron and spent a summer at the Cincinnati Art Institute. In 1909, she won an Art Students League scholarship and moved to New York, where she lived at the Three Arts Club on West 85th Street until 1919. This rich environment allowed her to develop aesthetically among musicians, dancers, and fellow visual artists.

Goth painted portraits, luminous wristwatch faces, and instrument dials for income. She fell in love with a young artist, Varaldo Cariani. The two lived and worked together throughout Cariani's life. In 1919, Goth returned to Indiana. Cariani followed her, but they never married. In 1923, Marie came to Brown County at Alberta Shulz's invitation. Soon, Goth's sister, Genevieve, joined her. The two sisters built a cabin. Genevieve married artist Carl Graf, and Varaldo built a studio nearby. Marie Goth lived and worked there for the rest of her life.

James Whitcomb Riley is one of her best-known portraits. *Florence* won the Julia A. Shaw prize of the National Academy of Design in 1931. In 1975, she died, leaving six hundred thousand dollars to the Brown County Art Gallery, stipulating that her works and those of Genevieve, Carl Graf, and Varaldo Cariani be displayed there.

That Ugly Painting

Joan Bruce

"Where'd you get that ugly painting?" Mandy Malone, my best friend since first grade, shouted from the middle of my tiny living room on Sunday morning.

"At an estate sale last Friday while on my way to work," I said, stepping out of my bathroom. "Do you like it?"

"No, it's ugly."

"No, it's not."

"Yes, it is. How much did you pay for it?"

"Twenty dollars," I said. "It's an abstract. It's supposed to be unusual. I think it looks great." I eyed it hanging there on the wall between my two small windows.

"You were robbed," Mandy said, turning away from the painting. "Wait a minute, you're not wearing that outfit to go shopping, are you?"

"Huh?" I said, glancing down at my black mini-skirt to see if Mandy had spotted a stain. "What's wrong with it?"

"Candi DeCarlo, you're over forty. Women our age don't dress like that when shopping at the Fashion Mall," Mandy said. She was wearing a beige silk blouse and floral print skirt that reached down to her ankles. "You might wear that if you're looking to get lucky on Saturday night at Ray's Hideaway Lounge, but not to go shopping in Indianapolis. Put on a pair of slacks instead."

"Whatever." I sighed before turning on my four-inch heels and stomping off to my bedroom. "When did you become my mother?" I muttered under my breath.

* * *

It was nearing six o'clock when Mandy dropped me off in front of my duplex on Elm Street and sped away in her shiny, black Jaguar.

I trudged up the rickety outside steps that led to my second-floor apartment. It'd been a productive shopping trip. Lots of fifty percent off sales. My hands were full of shopping bags.

Once on the landing, I dropped the bags and rummaged through my hobo bag looking for my keys. As I stuck the key into the lock I noticed one of the panes of glass in my front door was busted. I twisted the doorknob and the door opened in my hand. Damn. Somebody'd broken into my apartment! I dug through my bag for my pepper spray. Somebody was about to become a blind man.

"Anybody here?" I shouted as I stepped through the front door.

That was dumb, Candi. Nothing like letting the burglar know you're home.

Fortunately, nobody answered. I headed straight for my bedroom to see if the burglar had taken any of my clothes or costume jewelry, but nothing appeared to be missing.

When I stepped back into the living room, I noticed my new abstract painting was missing. Snatched right off the wall. Who'd stolen it? I reached for the cell phone in my bag and called Mandy.

"Somebody broke into my apartment while we were shopping and took my new painting," I yelled into the phone after she picked up.

"Who knew Bartonsville still had a good Samaritan?"

"That's not funny, Mandy," I said. "I really love that painting. What should I do?"

"I suppose you could offer a thousand dollar reward for its safe return, or file a missing painting report with the police."

* * *

It was just after three on Tuesday afternoon when Mary Donovan, a dispatcher with the Bartonsville Police Department, walked into Tips & Toes for her regular nail appointment.

"Heard your place was burglarized the other night," she said, plopping down in front of my nail station.

"Yeah, they stole my new painting right off the wall," I replied.

"I also heard you bought it last week at Agnes Murphy's estate sale."

"Yup. So, have you guys found it yet?"

"No, but I talked to Chief Cobb briefly before coming over here," Mary said. "Your case is more complicated than he first thought."

"What do you mean?"

"The Chief's first homicide when he worked for the Indianapolis Metropolitan Police Department involved a reclusive art collector named Russell Thompson. The Chief and his fellow detectives believed two men broke into Thompson's house on North Meridian Street a dozen years ago, stabbed him to death and made off with his most valuable paintings."

"Did they ever find the murderers?" I asked.

"No, it's a cold case, but the Chief says he always had a gut feeling about who did it."

"I don't understand. What's that got to do with my missing painting?"

"Among the suspects were two guys from the Bartonsville area, but IMPD couldn't prove they stabbed Thompson."

"Wow," I said. "Does the Chief also think those guys stole my painting?"

"I can't say anything more," Mary said. "I've already told you too much. Let's try a different color on my nails today."

* * *

After Mary left with her new tangerine nails, I started thinking about the two Bartonsville guys she mentioned that were art thieves and murderers. Who were they? I must have known them. I knew practically everyone in town. And, finally, were they the ones that broke into my apartment and stole my abstract painting? I needed some answers and fast. I missed my painting.

I called Mandy to ask for her advice. "What are you doing?" I asked when she picked up.

"Ravishing the boy toy who showed up on my doorstep a half hour ago," she replied. "What do you think I'm doing?"

"Let's see, its eight o'clock," I said, after glancing at my Betty Boop watch. "You're probably taking a bubble bath and sipping a glass of champagne."

"Bingo. You win. Why are you calling me? You know I hate being disturbed while I'm enjoying my bubbles."

I apologized and then told Mandy what Mary Donovan had said about the two Bartonsville guys suspected of murdering an Indianapolis art collector and how they may have stolen my painting.

"That's highly unlikely," Mandy said when I finished. "Why would two guys who are used to stealing valuable paintings want your ugly thing?"

Mandy had a point. I only paid twenty dollars for my painting, but it wasn't ugly like she kept claiming. It held a lot of sentimental value. It's the first time I've bought a painting somewhere other than Walmart.

"Remind me again where you bought that ugly painting?" Mandy said.

"At Agnes Murphy's estate sale."

"I remember her. Sweet old lady, but she had this worthless nephew named Peter Shaw. He hung out in the same motorcycle gang with my first husband, Butch Muldoon. They called him Dead Eye Pete because he wore a black patch over his left eye, and he could shoot a gun really well."

"Sounds charming," I said. "Did Dead Eye have any close friends?"

"Yeah, a cousin," Mandy said. "Weird Willy Watson. Sounds like a professional wrestler, doesn't he? The story goes that Willy earned his nickname for doing crazy things when he drank too much or smoked pot."

"Think they still live in Bartonsville?"

"Doubt it," Mandy replied. "Last I heard Dead Eye and my ex were cellmates at Pendleton. Each doing ten years for beating up a liquor store clerk one night. I don't know about Willy. Why?"

"I want to ask him if he stole my painting."

"Candi, you're crazy. Even if you find Willy, he's not going to admit to stealing your ugly painting. Instead, he's liable to hurt you for asking. Stay away from him."

* * *

I decided to ignore Mandy's advice. Despite her warning, I needed to check out Weird Willy on my own, so after work on Wednesday night, I came home, changed into the shortest miniskirt and tightest sweater I could find in my closet, and drove to Ray's Hideaway Lounge. I figured Willy might hang out there.

"Well, look who's here," Ray Ives said as I strutted into his bar. "You're looking mighty fine tonight, Candi. What brings you out on a weeknight? Can I get you a drink?"

"I'm looking for a guy," I said as I sat down on a barstool and waited on Ray to fix me a strawberry daiquiri. "Weird Willy Watson."

"What do you want with that troublemaker?" Ray asked, setting the daiquiri in front of me.

"I need to ask him a few questions," I said, sipping my drink. It tasted wonderful.

Before Ray could reply, someone spun me around on my barstool and planted a juicy, wet kiss on my lips. It was my ex-husband, Bobby DeCarlo. Damn, he still looked as good as he did back in high school.

"What are you doin' here, Candi?" he asked, wiping pink lipstick off his lips. "Still looking for the man of your dreams?"

"No, I don't need another guy to ruin my life," I said. "I was asking Ray if he knew Weird Willy Watson."

"I know that dude," Bobby said, sitting down next to me. "We've worked on a couple construction jobs. He's a decent carpenter. Saw him last week outside the courthouse. Wondered if he was in trouble with the law again."

"Know where he lives?"

"Wait a minute, Candi, you're not thinking of hooking up with him, are you?" Bobby asked. "Willy's bad news."

"No, I only want to talk to him."

"Yeah, I know where Willy lives, but it's going to cost you."

"You're not getting another kiss," I said. "Ray, grab Bobby a beer and put it on my tab."

"You don't need to buy me a beer," Bobby said, as he grabbed the bottle from Ray. "I was hoping you'd like to do something else tonight if you catch my drift."

"Bobby, I'm not interested in you anymore," I said. "Remember, we're divorced."

"I know. . . . I know," he said, taking another long swig of his beer. "Remind me again how all that happened."

"Simple. You liked spending more time with your girlfriends than you did with me. Now, are you going to give me Willy's address?"

I took a pen out of my bag and reached across the bar for a

paper napkin so Bobby could write down directions. When he finished, I slapped a ten on the bar and shouted to Ray, "Bring Bobby another beer, and keep the change."

"Thanks, Candi," Bobby said as he slammed his empty beer bottle on the bar.

* * *

Once outside, I glanced at my watch. It was nearing nine o'clock. Probably too late to pay a visit to Willy's house. Besides, I had a busy schedule tomorrow at Tips & Toes and needed to go home and get some beauty rest.

Thursday turned out to be a bust at work. A couple clients called early to cancel their afternoon appointments. I hate it when that happens. It means fewer tips in my pocket.

I hurried home from work, ate a small salad from the Grab 'n Run, and then stood in front of my clothes closet, trying to decide what to wear to Willy's place. How about an outfit like I wore last night to Ray's Hideaway? No. Willy might get the wrong idea about my visit. I settled for black jeans and a loose-fitting top.

* * *

Willy lived at the Heaven's Gate Trailer Park on the east side of town. I knew the place very well. My mom, my brother, and I lived there for a short time while I was growing up. It's a dump. I steered my F-150 down the main gravel road. Willy's mobile home was next to a bright yellow trailer with at least a dozen wind chimes, just like Bobby had drawn on his map. After parking out front, I walked up to his front door and knocked.

"Come on in, the door's open," I heard a voice calling from somewhere inside the trailer.

I stepped through the doorway. Willy was sitting in a broken-down, faux leather recliner in the middle of his living room. He wasn't anything like I imagined. Willy had to lose weight to get to three hundred pounds. He was wearing a dirty white T-shirt and wrinkled black pants, and he had big holes in his smelly-looking athletic socks.

"Well, well," Willy said, a big smile forming on his face. "Who are you, darling?"

I was ready for his question. On my way to his place, I made up a story about why I was there.

"I'm Candi. Your landlord hired me to find out what he can do to make the trailer park a better place to live."

"Looking to raise my rent again, is he?" Willy said. "How much time you got to listen to my complaints?"

"A few minutes," I said, pulling a small notebook and pen out of my bag. "Go ahead whenever you're ready."

Willy was like the Hoover dam suddenly bursting at its seams. He spent the next fifteen minutes talking non-stop about everything that was wrong with the trailer park. It included the unpaved roads, potholes as big as moon craters, and weeds growing alongside the road as high as some of the trailers. I didn't expect a guy like Willy to even notice his surroundings.

I sat across from him on the edge of his couch and pretended to write down his every word. Actually, I scribbled circles in my notebook while casually glancing around the living room for any sign of my painting or any other artwork he'd stolen.

Willy had moved on to the trailer park's faulty septic system when the front door opened and in walked a tall, heavy-set woman with a cigarette dangling from her lips.

"What's going on here?" she screamed after spotting me. "Who's this bimbo, Willy? One of your little girlfriends?"

"No, Melissa, Candi's doing a survey for our landlord," Willy tried to explain, but his friend wasn't in any mood to listen.

She hovered over me like a linebacker glaring down at a quarterback he'd just sacked. "If I were you, missy," she said in a deep voice, "I'd get the hell out of here now while you're still in one piece."

Melissa didn't have to tell me twice. I jumped off the couch and was out the door in a flash. As I made my way back to my truck, I could hear Willy and Melissa yelling at each other inside their trailer.

Love was sure complicated at times.

* * *

Before going to work on Friday morning, I dropped by Ralph's Diner for my usual—a cinnamon swirl and Diet Dr. Pepper. I'd just taken the first bite of the swirl when I heard my name.

I turned around on the lunch counter stool. Chief Dan Cobb was standing beside me. I swear, he's the best-looking single man in Bartonsville.

"Hi, Chief," I said while trying to swallow the doughy swirl stuffed in my mouth. "What brings you here this morning?"

"Looking for you," he replied as he sat down on the stool next to me.

Oh my God, Dan's finally going to ask me out!

"Were you at William Watson's place last night?"

I grabbed my Diet Dr. Pepper and took a long swig.

How'd he know that?

"I'm waiting, Candi," the Chief said, tapping his fingers on the lunch counter.

"Yeah, I may have been there. You know, I used to live in that trailer park."

"You went there to see if Watson stole your painting, didn't you?"

"Maybe," I finally replied. I hate it when Chief Cobb grills me like a common criminal.

"I know because Mary told me all about her conversation with you the other day. I don't know how you learned Watson's name, but when my officers arrived at his place last night to break up the domestic dispute, Watson's girlfriend, Melissa Sharp, said the fight began over some girl named Candi. And, you're the only Candi I know in Bartonsville."

Darn. I should have used a fake name to go along with my fake story.

"So," I said, taking another sip of my Dr. Pepper.

"So, I don't want you investigating burglaries on your own. Watson is a dangerous guy and so is his girlfriend. She tried to bite one of my officers. Besides, you may have tipped him off about being a suspect in your burglary and possibly that cold case murder that Mary mentioned."

"Sorry, Dan. I didn't mean to do anything wrong. I simply want my painting back."

"Visiting Watson's place wasn't the right way to go about it. Do you understand?"

"I said I was sorry."

"So, did you talk to Watson while you were inside his trailer?"

"Yes," I replied. "I pretended to be taking a survey about repairs needed at the trailer park."

"Did you see anything unusual while you were there?"

Wait a minute. Dan's wanting me to be a snitch for him. So now it's okay that I went there?

"Nothing at first, but before I left, I noticed an empty picture frame propped against the wall next to Watson's recliner," I said. "But it wasn't mine, so I didn't accuse him or anything. I wanted to get out of there before his girlfriend broke me in two."

"That's interesting," Chief Cobb said. "I'll get back to you."

* * *

My boss, Madge Parsons, leaned down beside me on Saturday afternoon as I was applying a set of acrylic nails for my eighty-year-old client, Lonnie Sparks. "A strange-looking woman up front wants to speak to you right away," Madge whispered in my ear.

I looked up and spotted Weird Willy Watson's girlfriend, Melissa.

What's she doing here?

I asked Lonnie if she could wait a few minutes. She was in no hurry.

As Madge and I walked towards the front, I asked her to stand next to the phone and call 911 if Melissa followed through on her earlier promise to break me into tiny pieces.

"What can I do for you, Melissa?" I asked.

"We need to talk. Alone."

"The laundry room," I said, pointing to the rear of the salon.

Once in the room, Melissa insisted that I close the door. I was reluctant at first, but since she'd asked in such a calm voice, I figured she wasn't planning to hit me right away.

"I need to clear up a few things with you," she said.

"If this is about Willy, I'm not one of his girlfriends."

"No kidding," she said. "You're not his type. He likes big, full-bodied women like me. Not skinny babes like you."

I wasn't sure how to react to Melissa's comment. I'm a hot babe.

"What were you really doing at our place?" Melissa asked.

"My neighbor said you didn't stop by her place with any survey. She also knows you work here. Tell me the truth. Why were you talking up Willy?"

I looked at Melissa and could tell she was being sincere, so I told her how I suspected that Willy broke into my apartment on Sunday afternoon and stole my favorite abstract painting. I tried saying it as nicely as I could so she wouldn't go ballistic. She didn't.

"Funny you mentioned that," Melissa said. "Willy's been acting strange lately."

"How so?"

"He got a call from his cousin, Peter Shaw. Willy told me later that they talked about some artwork. Then, Willy went to check on some paintings at this old woman's estate sale. He never goes to auctions."

"Melissa, I think Willy and Peter murdered an Indianapolis art collector a decade ago and stole some of his valuable paintings. They must have hidden them at Agnes's house."

Melissa looked stunned. Then she turned and stormed out of the laundry room. "Wait till I get my hands on Willy," she shouted.

"Stop, Melissa," I yelled at her, but she was already at the front door. Confronting Willy on her own didn't sound like a good idea to me. I went back to my nail station to finish Lonnie's acrylic nails. Then, I called the Police Department and asked for Mary Donovan. I told her about Melissa's visit.

"I'll have Chief Cobb check out Watson's place," Mary said. "I agree. It sounds like his girlfriend could be in danger."

After hanging up, I glanced at the clock on the back wall. It was nearing four o'clock. I tidied up my station before telling Madge I needed to leave early to run an errand.

As I drove up to Willy Watson's trailer fifteen minutes later, I noticed three police cars parked out front with their red lights blazing.

I stepped out of my truck and walked towards Watson's trailer. "What's going on?" I asked a neighbor who was standing there.

"I think the cops are going to arrest Willy," the woman replied. "If you ask me, it's about time they nailed him for all the terrible things he's done to Melissa in the past."

A few minutes later, two officers walked out of Willy's trailer carrying several paintings. They opened the trunk of their cruiser and carefully placed them inside. A third officer brought out Willy in handcuffs and not-so-carefully placed him in the backseat of his cruiser. Finally, Chief Cobb and Melissa appeared. The Chief said something to her before speeding away in his own car.

All this time, I stood behind the woman I'd been talking to so Chief Cobb wouldn't see me and yell at me later for being there.

Once the cops left, I walked up to Melissa. She was still standing in front of her trailer with her arms crossed.

"What happened, Melissa?" I asked.

"You were right, Candi," she said. "Willy and his cousin did steal some paintings a long time ago. He also admitted to breaking into your apartment."

"Did he tell you why?"

"He didn't get the chance," Melissa said. "The cops pulled up right then and arrested him."

"Did you happen to see my painting?"

* * *

On Sunday afternoon, I was watching a made-for-TV movie on the Hallmark Channel when my doorbell rang. It was Chief Cobb.

"What are you doing here?" I asked after opening the front door.

"I've got something for you," he said, reaching behind his back and pulling out my abstract painting.

"Where's the frame that goes with it?" I asked.

"It's still part of our evidence," he explained. "After stealing the collector's paintings, Willy and his cousin realized reputable collectors weren't interested in buying stolen property, so they hired a neighborhood kid to paint some blank canvasses. They placed them in front of the collector's originals and hid them at Agnes Murphy's place. When she passed away, Willy tried to retrieve them at her estate sale, but he apparently missed the one you bought."

"Thanks for returning it," I said, hugging my painting. All I needed now was to buy a new picture frame at Walmart.

Paul Hadley (1880–1971)
David Reddick

To mark Indiana's centennial in 1916, the Indiana Daughters of the American Revolution held a statewide contest to create a state banner.

Paul Hadley of Mooresville submitted the winning design. A yellow torch, symbolizing liberty and enlightenment, was at the center of the design. Thirteen stars representing the original states formed an outer circle around the torch while an inner circle of five stars represented those states that became part of the Union following the country's Declaration of Independence. A large star representing Indiana was positioned above the torch.

Hadley was born in Indianapolis on August 8, 1880 and attended Manual Training High School where he studied art with Otto Stark, a member of the Hoosier Group. Following graduation, Hadley studied at the Pennsylvania Museum and School of Industrial Design. His early career was spent designing stained glass for a company in Chicago.

He moved to Mooresville following the death of his father, and was responsible for helping to design the family's first home there. Hadley was an accomplished watercolorist, and operated a studio in Indianapolis for many years before spending ten years as an instructor at the Herron Art Institute.

In 1955, the Indiana General Assembly made Hadley's design the official state flag. Previously, it had been recognized only as the state banner. The Legislature also added the word "Indiana" above the large star. In 1966, the town of Mooresville was officially proclaimed the home of the state flag, and the town's new middle school was also named in honor of Hadley.

For the state Bicentennial in 2016, a state historical marker honoring Hadley's design was erected in downtown Mooresville.

Hadley died on January 31, 1971, and is buried at Crown Hill Cemetery in Indianapolis.

Murder Confit

Marianne Halbert

Evangeline's long-dried bloodstain lay a few feet from me, permeated into the plywood, caked and dark. Dull compared to the glossy sheen of the duck confit sauce that was now splattered and soaking into the floor.

"You're positively *mad*," Lester breathed. He said it to Keither, but then his eyes roamed the room, looking for confirmation. I knew 'mad' could mean angry. Really, *really* pissed off. I knew it could also mean insane. Out-of-touch. Delusional. When Lester used it to describe Keither, I think he meant bat-shit-crazy. But when I looked at the revolver trembling in Keither's hand, looked in his smoky eyes, to me, it definitely applied in every possible way.

"Keither," Lester said, "you called us all out here today under the pretense of a celebration. You were going to start painting again," and he looked at me. I'd almost felt invisible for a few minutes, and even that small gesture made me self-conscious of the stains across my white shirt, the Crème Brulee clinging to the short spiral curls of my dark blonde hair. "Christ," Lester continued, "you even ordered all your favorite foods, the ones you and Evie used to get." He looked at me again. "Scared the poor delivery girl to death when you pulled that gun out. And this turns out to be a fishing expedition? To garner a confession from one of us? I may be your agent, but I'm not a fool."

Keither's gaze was fixed on him.

Erbie was at the bar, silver forked tongs dropping ice cubes, clunk, *clink*, into his tumbler. He'd brought his own supplies, ice and booze. Perhaps as a house-warming gift, or just insurance that he'd be able to numb himself. Standing this close to his sister's portrait, to that stain, couldn't have been easy.

Arthur took a small step toward Keither. Besides Keither, he was the only artist in the room, and as he stretched out his hand, I could imagine him molding his metals, bending them at will. Arthur towered over the rest of us, and the word *Gumby* flitted through my mind. His face seemed to have turned a shade greener ever since the gun had made its appearance. He was lanky, but had a broad forehead, and his shiny silver hair was pulled taut in a long ponytail. It seemed as though each hair might just pop out of that broad forehead, straining his long neck the way he was, Adam's apple bobbing up and down before he found his voice. Arthur spoke then, his voice just a pitch too high to convey confidence, but steady enough for sincerity.

"Look, chap, we're all broken up over Evangeline. We all loved her." Then remembering I was in the room, he glanced at me. *All of us except, of course, the girl who delivered the duck confit,* was what that look said. Almost as an afterthought he added, "In our own way."

"Some of us more than others," Hector snickered. He was studying the painting of Evangeline, tracing the birthmark on the small of her back with a lover's caress more than the art critic's eye he was known for. He still seemed to be taking all of this as a joke, in spite of the gun. Not like Erbie, Evangeline's brother, whose slender, delicate hand was pouring black label bourbon over the ice, merely disinterested in the drama unfolding. Ignoring us the way he might ignore a couple arguing on the train home, or several ants underfoot, fighting over a crumb.

Arthur, on the other hand, Keither's oldest competitor in the art-world, *was* taking it seriously, but only in the therapeutic, *let me help you through it* sort of way, instead of the *barrel the guy down, cuff him, ask questions later* sort of way. Except I couldn't picture a therapist's Adam's apple bobbing while his soothing tone hypnotized his patient. In fairness to Gumby, I don't suppose many patients point pistols at the good doctor during their sessions.

Lester, Keither's agent, was the only one losing it. Lester may have been the only one to know sometimes if you cuff 'em too late, well then, it's just Too Late. He brushed his hand up over his forehead, probably a life-long gesture from when he'd actually had hair to sweep off his face, and I was thankful that he didn't have a comb-over. He was the least attractive man in the room, so it didn't really matter. With the stains, with a man holding a loaded gun, a *mad* man at that, and probably a murderer among us, a comb-over shouldn't have mattered at all right then. But I was nineteen. So in spite of a slight pot-belly, legs a bit too short to aesthetically support his torso, and a mostly bald head, Lester never gave in to the comb-over and I was grateful. Lester, who had known Keither longer than anyone in the room. Longer even than Evangeline, who in her own way, was in the room with us. Yes, Lester, the only one, besides me, who knew Keither wasn't only angry, wasn't just bluffing, he was Mary-mother-fucking-out-of-his mind with grief.

"She wouldn't have left me," Keither insisted. "She wouldn't have committed—" And there was a moment—five seconds, maybe ten—when someone could have overtaken him. He was trying to spit out the word. Suicide. His eyes squeezed shut, his knees buckled. His arm, the one holding the gun, drooped. But Erbie was too busy pouring his liquid bronze over the ice, Hector too busy trying to come up with a witty retort. Lester, Arthur, and I, well we weren't busy or ignorant, but for our own reasons, we didn't overtake him. Then the moment passed.

Keither circled the room.

"For months, for the last five friggin' months, I didn't question what they said. She'd written it in her own blood." His voice sounded so anguished. *"Poison. Pain.* Only we all know she wasn't poisoned. Her wrist was slit on glass shards. So what the *fuck* did she mean." It wasn't a question. I mean it was, but not really. More of a challenge. He was desperate to believe someone in this room knew what Evangeline had meant when she'd written it.

Hector stood near the painting hanging on the half-finished wall behind him. Exposed two-by-fours, no drywall, just the large gray outer stones for a portion of the wall, then nothing but the two-by-fours, and the open air beyond. I wasn't standing close enough to know if a breeze caused his goosebumps, but his muscles flexed, stretching his evergreen polo tight over his chest and tan biceps. Ever the critic, he proceeded to criticize. "Well, there's the obvious. She knew you'd be the one to find her. Your love was *poison,* you caused her *pain."* Sandy blond curls almost fell across one eye. His eyes never seemed entirely open, squinting, glaring, maybe genetically that's just how they were, but I didn't like looking at them, in spite of how blue they were. The little bit I could see, that is, with him glaring that way. "Guess bleeding out the way she did, she wouldn't have had the time for an essay on the subject, or even complete sentences."

The bottle almost caught poor Lester's bald head. Maybe it was fate that his legs were so short, but it soared just over him and made straight for Hector's blond curls. Hector must've caught sight of it, squinty eyes and all, and lucky for him his reflexes were quick. He ducked and it shattered against the stone wall, little shards of glass showering his curls. The liquid bronze didn't look so bronze on the stone. It just looked dark, and where some had sprayed in little droplets, it gave the illusion that it had rained, on the inside of the stone wall. Evangeline continued to look away on the canvas above. Everyone turned toward Erbie, who was already kneeling, looking for another bottle of booze, to replace the one he'd thrown.

Lester ran his hand over his head again. This time it appeared he was making sure it was all still there. "Jesus. Keither, enough's enough. You start building this mansion on the mountain for Evangeline, now it's become some kind of half-built shrine to her. I thought after five months it would be finished, but it hasn't changed since the day . . . since that day. There are still builders' tools scattered around here, like they dropped 'em and ran." He was stating what we all had to be thinking. It was surreal. The front gate, the long driveway, the façade of the mansion. Then to enter it and see tile floor that suddenly stopped, a wall completely open to the elements. There was even a staircase in the corner that went up and ended midair, leading to nothing. Lester's voice was trembling, but I could see him struggling with it, struggling not to lose it, and I was pulling for him.

I was gaining some respect for pot-bellied Lester. He didn't back down. Maybe he had known Keither so long he didn't think Keither would actually kill him, or maybe he realized if this wasn't resolved soon, it might be resolved badly. But Lester didn't back down. "You don't even have working utilities. No phone, no plumbing."

For the first time, Keither seemed genuinely apologetic, at least toward Lester. "I found something today. You know, I'd proposed to her the night before she died. She was giddy. Not at the thought of us being engaged, rings and paper didn't bind us, we both knew we'd be eternal. She thought of the fun the critics would have with it," and he tilted his head, dark waves spilling over his shoulders and rested his gaze on Hector. "Artist and artist's model wed. 'What fun it would be,' she'd said. And she wanted to commission a piece, a wedding present for her. She knew how I liked to use a variety of elements in my work, not just the paint, but tangible, three-dimensional objects, of personal meaning. A collage. I didn't realize until today that she'd gotten started so quickly on finding the items for this new piece. Not exactly something old, something new. But something from everyone in this room. Everyone who had an impact on our lives in that moment of time."

I hadn't noticed the box until then. There were a number of boxes throughout the entryway, the foyer, the studio. They'd all struck me as so benign, holding drop cloths or wood screws. But he shoved one near his feet, pushing it like an accusation toward us.

He pointed the gun at Hector. "I found a list in there. Her handwriting. Your name's on it and crossed off, so I figure something of yours is in the box. Take it out."

Hector moved away from the stone wall, a few delicate splinters of glass dropping from his curls. He seemed a little relieved. "That's it? You and your sleuthing skills couldn't figure out my contribution?" He approached the cardboard box, and pulled back the lid. He reached in and retrieved a newspaper clipping. "My rave review of 'The Eve of Waning.' I should have titled it 'Folderol and Gimcrackery.' Why the public raves for your collage of worthless trinkets escapes me. You know," he chuckled, "she offered to sleep with me if I gave you a good review in the *London Times*. And here it is. Although the little tease never did make good."

"There's motive," Erbie slurred. "Might not be just the duck cooked in its own fat today. Right Hector? Or should I say Critic Confit?"

"Francophile," Hector spat.

"Philistine," Erbie mumbled.

Erbie shuffled in Hector's direction. His loafers were soft, almost silent on the floor as he moved away from the bar. "You may be one of the most well-respected art critics in the Western Hemisphere, but my sister. . . ." it came out *sisser* thanks to the bourbon, "was too smart to pimp herself out to a guy like you."

Arthur offered to go next. He knelt down, his silver ponytail streaming down his back like a river between his mountainous shoulder blades. He sifted through the box, carefully. For a moment I thought he wouldn't find anything, but then he pulled out two small black wire circles, hooked together. He palmed them, then opened his hand, held his arm out toward Keither.

"What is it?" Lester asked. Keither hadn't moved, but he was studying it, no recognition showing on his face.

"Rings of course." Arthur smiled. "Critics compared us, art-houses wanted us to be rivals, but our work is completely different. I work in metals. You never have. I used a wire-cutter to snap this small bit off a hanger used in one of my earliest pieces—"

Now recognition dawned on Keither's face. Recognition, and disbelief. "It's not from the hangers—"

"The ones that held her wedding dress and his navy uniform. The ones I used in 'Parental Ascent.' I only used part of the wire for that piece, saved some for me, and some for, shall we say a special occasion."

"It could be him," Hector said, brushing more glass from his hair. Maybe Hector was beginning to take this seriously after all, now that he'd been tagged with a motive. "You two were rivals, different styles, sure, but we compared you all the time, and let's face it, the rich can only put so much artwork in their homes. Your profit was his loss, and everyone knew Evangeline was your muse. Without her you'd fall apart. You *have* fallen apart. How much art have you sold since her death, Arthur?"

"This is no time to be pointing fingers at each other," Lester said. "Keither, the fact that this box exists doesn't prove anything, she still may very well have—"

"It's him," Hector said. He'd switched suspects pretty fast.

"What?" Lester said. Trying to act dismissive, but some worry over any possible suspicion was obvious.

"She was going to have Keither fire you," Erbie mumbled. "You knew it, and having a grieving artist as a client, an artist who might make a comeback is better 'an having no client at all. He was so successful, you put all your million dollar eggs in one basket-case."

"That's ridiculous. She wasn't going to have Keither fire me."

I felt sorry for Lester. At first, because of how his voice had changed, stuttering on the words *ridiculous*, and *me*, begging for confirmation, but mostly, because of how his eyebrows went up when he looked at Keither's face. Keither's expression said it all, but Lester pressed him, "*Was* she?"

Keither seemed uncomfortable. "She thought you were pushing too hard for me to do what was commercially profitable—"

"And that's a *bad* thing?" His stout arms raised above his bald head. "It paid for this house. It paid for her *ring*—"

"She knew I wanted to pursue some of my own projects. I had creative needs that wouldn't have made much money."

"So suddenly you want to be the starving artist? Die broke and let our grandkids appreciate your genius?" Lester was so hurt, I don't think he even realized he'd quashed Hector's possible theory regarding motive. Lester hadn't known he was on the way out.

"Lester, it was just talk, nothing definite," Keither said.

"Just talk," he huffed, his short legs marching toward the box. "No wonder she was able to fool Einstein over here into writing a good review, she sure fooled me that morning into thinking this really meant something to her." He rummaged, more roughly than the others had, and a faint tinkling of glass emanated from the box. "Here, here, happy engagement." He crumpled the paper and threw it at Keither's chest, where it bounced off harmlessly and landed at his feet. Lester walked away, bellied up to the bar, and sat there, too hurt to even bother making a drink.

Keither retrieved and unfolded the paper. "The bill of sale. From the first piece you sold for me." His eyes narrowed as he tried to make out something on the paper. "Twelve years ago. Has it really been that long?" he whispered.

"How many more names on the list?" Hector asked. "Are we all there?"

"Two," Keither said.

"Two? Then who's missing?" Arthur said. "Erbie, let's get this over with."

I also wanted this night to end.

"No one is missing," I said. They all turned to me, all with surprise, except for Keither, who of course knew my name was on the list.

"But you're just the delivery girl," Hector said.

And he was right. Just the girl who worked at a restaurant, delivering fine food to customers who could afford it. Sashimi grade ahi with ginger wasabi, and Crepes Suchard the day they broke ground on the mansion. I recalled how they had spread a blanket, and were half-way through a bottle of Dom when I arrived, sunlight shimmering off of their golden-stemmed champagne glasses. Knowing that she would disrobe before he painted her. Watching how his arm draped her waist, and how she laughed and pushed him off so she could pay me.

The following week, the foundation was coming along, and he wanted to paint her in the open field, windflowers and mountains as the backdrop. That afternoon I brought them grilled Portobellos in a garlic vinaigrette, salmon Caesar, and espresso mousse. I hesitated when I saw her posing, her skin so exposed. So perfect. Keither, oblivious of the paint covering his hands, some swiped on his brow, so focused. They didn't even notice me. I left the food and sent a bill.

At least once a week it went like that, for nine months. And each time I would linger an extra moment or two, watching them, their passion for the art, for each other. I stepped forward now, toward the cardboard box. That put me closer to a breeze coming through the open wall, and I caught a whiff of the duck sauce from my shirt, and vanilla from my hair. I knelt down by the box. Only a champagne glass, a tube of paint, and a small piece of paper remained. I took the paper out.

"A receipt from the night you proposed. She called me that morning, asked if I still had a copy." I'd kept a copy of all their receipts. A memory lane of stolen moments. "Duck confit. Broccolini. Crème Brulee. For two."

Understanding dawned on the men in the room. Understanding about why Evangeline would want the receipt, but they couldn't have understood how much I belonged in this studio. How intimately I'd known her. When Arthur had said we all loved her, he was right. Each of us, in our own way.

Keither seemed agitated. All of us were done except Erbie, and it didn't seem we were any nearer to a motive, or a killer. I'm sure Hector resented her for using him, Arthur may have realized that without her, Keither would no longer be a competitor, and Lester could be feigning surprise over her suggestion that he be fired, but it was clear Keither hadn't zeroed in on any of them. He was trembling with frustration.

"Erbie, come over here," Keither demanded.

Erbie was leaning up against the half-built wall. His eyes looked tired.

"What's the point Keith? The cops ruled it suicide. I can tell now you don't really believe any of us could have hurt her."

"Erbie, what did you bring her?"

Erbie shrugged his slender shoulders, and shuffled in his soft loafers toward the box. "Alright, alright." His feet stood still once he got there, but his head wobbled gently from side to side as he tried to focus. "Paint and a glass left. A glass, from my mother's collection." There was a note of melancholy in his slurred words. "I brought two glasses to Evangeline, to use how she wanted. To celebrate, to put in the painting, wha'ever."

Keither narrowed his eyes. "*You* brought her the glasses?"

We all knew there was only one in the box. The other had broken five months ago, and a large, sharp piece of it had slit the artery of Evangeline's wrist. In the serious, vertical kind of way.

Erbie nodded, and a sob escaped his throat.

"What about the paint?" Keither asked, waving the gun in Erbie's direction.

"What about it? She wanted you to do a painting, she got paint. Not exactly shocking."

For the first time that evening, I heard a certainty creep into Keither's voice. "Evangeline would never have bought that paint for me."

Erbie looked offended. "It's the same kind you always used, she knew that—"

"It's the wrong size." Something changed in the air just then, and I could sense everyone bracing for a revelation. "I only bought titanium white in the large tube, and she knew that." I couldn't tell if Keither was more excited that he may be onto something, or more horrified that it may have been her own brother, her blood, who killed her. I knew Erbie was lying about bringing her the gold stemmed glasses. I'd seen her and Keither use them before. I looked at the stain on the floor, the large, dark, dried pool, and the words beside it. Poison Pain. I imagined an artist adding oil to pigment, and longed to interpret Evangeline's desperate message. To go back to the moment when the letters flowed. There had to be more she was trying to say, but what? The words ran through my head again and again. *What was she trying to say?* I looked at Evangeline's scrawls, written in her own blood, and couldn't help notice the confit sauce in the shape of a cross, or, a letter. . . .

"Not poison pain," I whispered. Keither looked at me, looked down to the words on the floor. He didn't understand and flew toward me, gripping my arm.

"Poison *paint*," I said. "She died before she could finish. No time." *For an essay, or even complete sentences.* Erbie would have known how Keither worked. He wasn't a neat artist. The art was always brilliant, but during the process, Keither was covered in paint. His hands, forearms, face. Terre verde, raw sienna, titanium white. Keither must have been making the same connections I was, and he grabbed the tube out of the box and opened the cap. He approached Erbie with the gun in one hand, paint in the other.

"Why don't you paint a picture, Erbie?"

Erbie waved a drunken arm at Keither.

"Why did you do it?" Keither demanded, the gun inches from Erbie's face. "Why Evangeline?"

"It wasn't supposed to happen like that," Erbie slurred. He seemed to be talking to Evangeline, looking at the portrait. She refused to look him in the eye. "I haven't managed my share of our inheritance very well." Then he turned to Keither, as though it were all his fault. "If you two got married, then I was out of the picture if anything 'appened to her. As her husband, all of her inheritance would go to you." He raised his glass, "so you had to go." He drained the glass, and his head drooped. His voice trembled when he spoke again, feeling sorry for her, and for himself.

"She wasn't supposed to know, or get hurt, but she figured it out and we argued. She had already set those glasses in the box, and when I'm angry, I have a tendency to break things."

Keither looked like he was going to be sick, but he steadied himself. He kept his eyes on Erbie. "Lester, do me a favor. Use your cell phone to dial the police. We have a confessed murderer."

Erbie shoved Keither, and ran toward a door at the end of the room. Keither looked horrified, and shouted, "Erbie, no! Stop!" but it was too late. Erbie had already flung the door open and was stumbling through it, arms flailing, and I saw him disappear. His scream carried through the open doorway, faded, then cut to silence.

We all stood there looking at each other, stunned. Arthur's voice had gone back to its normal, low pitch.

"He had way too much to drink tonight."

I think when Arthur said that, he didn't realize what he'd put in motion, but Lester's wheels were turning and we all followed his momentum.

"Yes, *way* too much," Lester said. "Toxicology will confirm that. And he was distraught over his sister's death." He looked at Hector who realized what they were thinking, and Hector hesitated, deciding whether to play along or not.

"Keither *did* tell him to stop," Hector said, "but he was at the precipice before any of us could reach him." Then they all looked at me. I looked down at my shirt, at the food I'd spilled when Keither had pulled the gun.

"He ran past me," I said. I hesitated, waiting for approval. Lester nodded slightly and his eyes told me to go on. I felt slightly more confident when I said, "Knocking the tray right out of my hands."

We all looked at each other, a look of understanding, conspiracy. Keither hadn't deserved Evangeline's death, and he didn't deserve to be blamed for Erbie's.

It was about a month later when he called me to come to the house. But he didn't want any food. Just me.

I walked up the cobblestone drive, and stepped around to the back side of the house. Scaffolding climbed to the doorway where Erbie had exited this world, and I could see an elaborate balcony under construction. I turned and saw two headstones under a black cherry tree, and I walked toward them. One said merely, *Evangeline*. The other had no name, only a prayer:

Confiteor Deo omnipotenti,
mea culpa,
mea culpa,
mea maxima culpa.

I turned back toward the mansion, walked around front, and entered the foyer. I saw men working. Keither had installed utilities. I walked into the studio, and was relieved the wall hadn't been completed yet. The breeze felt good on my face. I looked down and saw that tile flooring covered the entire room. He had his canvas ready, brushes and paints. All he needed, he said, was a model.

He watched as I shed my clothes. I stood near the opening in the wall as he got the angle and lighting just right. I wondered about the stains buried under the tile, and wondered if Evangeline was at peace. A mourning dove flitted in and landed briefly on a support beam, cooing, almost purring, before departing.

Keither approached me, putting his hands on my waist and arm to position me. He moved one hand to my face to tilt it. One moment he was the artist, and I was the model. No different to him than his brushes, the canvas, the paint. A means to an end. His eyes studied my skin tone. He remarked that I was a shade darker than her. His fingers moved up my ribs. Then spontaneously his lips brushed mine. His hand wrapped behind my neck and he kissed me. I relented and our tongues teased each other, hungry and searching. But when he pulled back, I knew he'd kissed someone else.

"I can't love you," he grumbled, as though I had asked something of him. He became somber and retreated back to his canvas. I felt even more naked than before.

I looked out across the exposed vista. Past the gravestones, the lazy field of tilting windflowers, and beyond the lavender ridges in the distance. Keither's words ran through my head, and I realized I didn't need him to love me. For today, I just needed him to paint me.

Mary Beth Edelson (1933-)
Stephen Terrell

East Chicago native **Mary Beth Edelson** has been one of the strongest voices of the feminist art movement in the United States for more than forty years.

Educated at DePauw University in Greencastle and trained at the Chicago Art Institute, Edelson sent an early signal of what would become the theme of her life's work. In 1955, one of the paintings in her senior art exhibition was removed from display because it was "an affront to ministers and small children."

Edelson's artwork includes paintings, drawings, collages, sculptures, photography, books, story boxes, sketches and performance art. The common thread is her passionate view on feminism. Her *Last Supper* shows the faces of prominent women artists superimposed over the traditional figures in DaVinci's famous painting. Among her most noted performance art pieces was 1977's evocative *Memorials to the 9,000,000 Women Burned as Witches in the Christian Era*.

Active from the inception of the feminist movement, Edelson established the National Conference for Women in the Visual Arts and was a founding member of the feminist publications *Heresies Collective* and *Chrysalis*. Her activism led to her selection as a member of the Title IX Task Force with the object of increasing the work of women artists displayed in museums.

In 2002, *The Art of Mary Beth Edelson* (Seven Cycles) was published, and in 2009, she was one of the women featured in the documentary, *The Heretics*. Her work is included in the collections of The Guggenheim, MOMA, the Corcoran Gallery of Art, and the Walker Art Center, among others. In 1993, she received an honorary Doctorate of Arts Degree from DePauw University.

Ceilings

N. W. Campbell

People never paint their ceilings. I'm amazed at this. In my line of work, I get into a lot of homes and businesses and the story is the same in just about every one of them. People will paint their walls, but ignore their ceilings. It's as if they believe nobody bothers to look up, so why go to the trouble and the expense of painting something no one ever notices? But I notice, trust me. Painting has taken up half of my life. I paint for a living and I paint as a hobby, to relax. My favorite is illusionistic murals, like Michelangelo painted on ceilings. Y'know, like the Sistine Chapel? Now, I'm no Michelangelo, but I've got a project of my own I'm very involved with, so when somebody skips a ceiling, I notice.

Tonight, I'm working on the center of my project, a mural on my bedroom ceiling. First I sketch, then I paint. Sketch, paint, sketch, paint, adding detail and color a section at a time, until the mural comes alive, a mural that features April and me and shows the endurance of our love.

April, she's the other half of my life.

Painting matters to me. I've got a day job with a company that cleans and restores properties after catastrophic events, like fires, floods, earthquakes, and even crimes. First the cleaning crew goes in to scrub and clean and carry off the debris, sometimes even stripping things down to the bare studs and floorboards, just to get rid of the mold and the contamination. Then the drywall team goes in to rehang fresh drywall and to tape and plaster all the joints. Then my crew goes in. We prime and paint everything back to the customer's specifications, including the ceilings. Some of the guys will say, "Hell, this was a breaking-and-entering, the ceilings never got touched. Let's just give them a good wipe down, paint the walls, and call it a day."

No dice, not on a crew I'm running. We paint, ceiling to floor, period. Any painter who doesn't like it, leaves. After all, I live on my reputation.

It was a tough job, that last one, and April was part of it. She's a big woman, thick and luscious. In school she was always bright as hell, like I never was. We grew up together, over on Southeastern Avenue near Clinton. April left there after high school, looking for bigger and better things.

Unlike some big girls who got self-conscious, April knew that men liked curves, and she had 'em. Man, she could show 'em, too! Tight jeans, three-inch heels, scoop-necked blouses, bling hanging from her ears and around her neck and wrists, her dark brown hair pulled back with a bright bow, and the reddest lips allowed by law. All the male teachers at Clinton would glance over their shoulder at her as she walked by. The women teachers were always on her about her size, telling her she needed to slim down, but like she told me once, she knew what that was about.

"They," she told me, "wish they had it like I've got it. So I don't pay 'em any attention."

I took her to the prom and tried to make out with her under the bleachers. She was cool about it, and we were always good friends, but she let me down easy, with a friendly squeeze and a sisterly peck on the cheek.

"I like you, Matt, but like a brother, y'know? Let's keep it that way."

That hurt me bad and it must have showed on my face, because I could see the fear in her eyes when she realized how much she hurt me.

It wasn't long before I lost her. But I found her again, and began keeping tabs on her, where she lived, where she worked, who she was with, what she was doing. I've kind of backed off on that, though. I didn't want to blow my chances by giving her the idea I was stalking her, but I'm not giving up hope. She'll come back. She has to.

It really hurt me, the day I caught her and that bastard boss of hers together. I was on a job up in Castleton, at the Penny-Pincher Inn, after some guy from Ohio checked in and shot himself. That place had a reputation as a suicide retreat, right there on the northeast side of Indy, right off the interstate. Some guy gets laid off, or gets word from his broker that his portfolio tanked, or he gets served divorce papers, so he jumps in his car and heads west until he can't take it anymore, then he pulls off, checks into a room, and—*bang!* Right through the roof of the mouth. The place ought to be renamed *Can't Take It Anymore? $26 by the hour.*

Around Indy, it had another reputation. It became a handy place for short-timers looking for some afternoon delight. Don't know if I'd choose the place for that myself. Imagine banging away with some honey in room 202 and overhearing a gun going bang when some guy blows himself away in room 204. That would sorta kill the moment, I suppose.

Anyway, this guy from Ohio headed west and stopped at Castleton. According to the evening news, he was in the middle of a bad divorce, his girlfriend was pregnant, and the law was after him for embezzling a quarter of a million bucks, apparently to keep his girlfriend set up in the manner to which she was accustomed. After the scene decontamination crew was done gutting and scrubbing, even to the studs in some places, I could still see flecks of blood and brain matter on the ceiling. Apparently the guys on clean-up that day didn't bother to look up, either.

When they heard we got the job to paint it, one or two of the guys on my crew mumbled about the possibility of working on some other project. I got it. Some people were squeamish, even people who did what we did. Flood and fire damage didn't bother them, but blood and brain matter?

Since it was just the one room, I told my boss I'd take care of it myself, an easy, one-day job in room 204, on the south end of the floor, right next to room 202. Do the dry-walling in the morning, and then scrub and paint the ceiling. Stop for a bite of lunch, then come back and paint the entire room, top to floor, in that flat white all these cheap motels used.

I liked working alone. It gave me time to think. And what I thought about that day was that mural I'm painting on my bedroom ceiling. I've been at it for years, sketching and painting and perfecting the anamorphic perspective of each and every scene.

The idea came to me one evening when I was sitting alone in my place, drinking beer and listening to an opera by Wagner on NPR. It was all about this woman warrior named Brunhilde who fell for a guy named Siegfried after he jumped through a burning ring of fire to rescue her. They fell in love and had passionate sex, then Siegfried left and was drugged with a love potion by some other woman who wanted him to marry her daughter. Siegfried fell for it, Brunhilde found out and had him killed, then she stabbed herself and jumped on his funeral pyre to join him in Hell.

I'm not much for opera, but this one really grabbed me. As I listened, I could see the whole thing taking place, with April as Brunhilde and me as Siegfried. That very night, I stood up on my bed and started sketching the whole opera across that white ceiling, dragging the bed around the floor and moving furniture one way and then the other to get at the ceiling. I had to wipe out parts of my sketches and start over, time and again, but night after night I kept at it until I was sure I got everything sketched just like I heard it on the radio. Since then, I bought the CD so I could play the *Ring Cycle* over and over while I painted my sketches to life.

I spent all morning there in room 204, dry-walling and then painting that dirty ceiling, reliving the rescue from the ring of fire, with April in my arms, and daydreaming of making love. I swirled the paint on with brush and roller, with the music playing over and over in my head.

When I finished, I stepped back and looked it all over carefully. The drywall patches were smooth and ready to paint. The ceiling gleamed a stark, clean white. I washed my hands in the room sink and stepped through the door to head down to my paint van and my lunch pail. Then I heard something that made me stop cold. Laughter was coming from 202—a deep, throaty laugh—the laugh April made when I caressed her under the bleachers. Only this one sounded a bit muffled. A guy said, "Lean forward a little, will ya, so I can. . . ."

I kicked the door open.

April was naked from the waist up, lying across the bed. Her boss was standing over her with his pants down. I flushed with anger. The next thing I knew, my painter's prep tool was out of my pocket and I was cutting an ugly gash across his throat with the crack opener blade. He fell backward and I punched him in the face, hard. He went down and didn't move. Blood gushed from his throat.

April screamed, "Get out of here, you freak!"

I looked at her, stunned. He was raping her . . . wasn't he?

Her eyes brimmed with hate. "Get away from me. You've been stalking me! I'm gonna see you die in prison for this!"

I turned slowly to look at her. My face trembled and my heart pounded in my ears as the awful recognition rushed over me. She wanted this, and she didn't want me. Ever. I dove at her and my hands clutched her throat. Startled, she tried to fight back, but I clung to her firmly, my grip tightening around her throat. We struggled on the bed, my chest heaving violently from the exertion of squeezing the life out of her.

In time, it was over. She went limp, her cheeks and lips blue. I cringed, realizing that her red lipstick was gone, probably wiped off somewhere on that bastard on the floor. I didn't cry. I just went numb looking at the two bodies lying there, perfect strangers.

I felt sure my April was still out there somewhere, taking her time to come back to me.

One thing about the Penny-Pincher was that the staff was never more than one guy who sat up front to take payment and hand out room keys. All along the back of the place, where I was, anything could happen and he'd never bother to notice. The cleaning staff, usually one person, came in and gave the place a lick and a promise, then headed off to the next room. Hell, that guy from Ohio lay dead in 204 for three days before anyone knew it. His sister filed a missing person report on him and the Ohio State Patrol had the credit card company trace his charges. That's how they found him in Indiana. All this lax security was good for me, because once I'd gotten past the shock of the moment, I knew I had to do something before anyone started looking for either of these two.

I went back over to 204 and gathered up some drop cloths, which I took across to 202. Within a quarter of an hour or so, I had both bodies rolled up neatly, fully encased in plastic so there wouldn't be any dripping in the hallway. One at a time, I carried the bodies down to my paint van and loaded them in. The woman's body was the heaviest and I struggled and panted as I fought her down the stairs. Then I went back up, because now I had two rooms to clean and paint so there'd be no trace of blood or brain matter, just fresh, clean white paint.

I worked, time passed, but nobody came because nobody cared. I finished the work on both rooms, cleaned my brushes and rollers in the sink, and stopped to inspect. If anything showed, any fleck, any splatter, I would do the whole thing over. I've got my reputation to think of.

I headed across town to Tibbs Avenue where there was a junk-yard I knew of, one with easy access after business hours. It had a hole in the barrier fence they covered with the hood of an old Pontiac, and no cameras or dogs around. Everybody who worked at the place was gone. I drove as close as I could to the access and walked the few steps to where the Pontiac hood covered the hole. I pushed it aside, went back to the van, and started carrying one of the bodies into the yard. I looked around and soon spotted a Mercury Montego with a jimmied trunk lid, open just enough for me to stick the flat end of my prep tool under the lip and pry the lid open. I dumped the body and slammed the lid down, hard. Then I got the woman's body and carried it through the access. This time, I found a wrecked Caddy, pink, a real longboat. I lay the woman across the back seat, pushed the door closed, and left, doing my best to put everything back the way it was.

On my way back home, I decided to listen to the radio. NPR had a talk show with a woman describing how she finally es-caped from a guy who had stalked her and threatened to kill her.

Sick freak, I thought to myself.

I pulled into my driveway, got out, and headed straight back to the bedroom. I lay across the bed, reached for the CD play-er, and dropped in the *Ring Cycle*. My eyes scanned the ceiling above. There were several scenes left to paint, but my mural was looking better all the time. I was really pleased with the way the central scene was turning out. My April—Brunhilde—was par-tially nude, lying on a bed of sheaves. All around her, a ring of fire burned. Just outside the ring, I—Seigfried—was in midleap, passing through the flames to get to her. I stood up on the bed and began sketching.

But something was wrong. I needed more detail to finish the center of the mural, but I realized that I must see April again before I could continue. We'd lost touch, but not for long. I knew she was near, even now.

I thought I had her under those bleachers, but I let her get away. That body the cops found back then, it wasn't her. Just like the body they found face down in a dumpster two years ago wasn't her, either. Just like that body in the pink Caddy over on Tibbs. She gets away from me, but I find her, and we're back together until she leaves, like today at the motel.

I'll find her again, I will. Just like all those times before. Only this time, it will be for good.

John Chamberlain (1927–2011)
N. W. Campbell

John Chamberlain, a post-war abstract expressionist, worked in a genre described as "found" art—works made from discarded materials. But Chamberlain didn't care for the term "found." Biographer Helen Hsu, in *Fitting in Time: A Chronology*, quotes Chamberlain: "Some seem to think I work with found pieces, but I don't. They're chosen, you see. The idea is that there has been a lot of magic implied in the choice."

He made sculptures of automobile body parts, discarded foam, cast-off tinfoil, steel boxes, wire rods, brown paper bags, and Plexiglas. His choices served his concept of art as being "the right thing at the right moment." His sculptures have sold for four and a half million dollars at auction. He drew, painted, and made films. He chose fanciful names for his works, like *Cone Yak* (1990), and *Whirled Peas* (1991).

Chamberlain was born on April 16, 1927, in Rochester, Indiana. His great-great uncle, Alexander Chamberlain, plotted Rochester in 1835. His first major retrospective was at New York's Guggenheim Museum in 1971. His work is on permanent display at the Garosian Gallery in New York, the Chinati Foundation in Texas, and the Das Maximum Gallery in Germany. The Indianapolis Museum of Art has two Chamberlains: *Madame Moon (1964)*, a sculpture of auto body parts, and a color lithograph, *Flashback #2 (1977)*. A sample of his art went to the Moon on a ceramic panel alongside works by Andy Warhol, Forrest Myers, and other pop artists, in the Apollo 12 lunar lander.

Chamberlain received many awards: The John Simon Guggenheim Memorial Foundation Fellowship (1966, 1977) and the Skowhegan Medal for Sculpture (1993). In 2006, he was elected into the National Academy of Design. He died on December 20, 2011, at age eighty-four.

The Picasso Caper

S. Ashley Couts

King's Cross Rail Station, London:

The American teens at the entry, wearing T-shirts and shorts, posed for selfies. In their youthful excitement, they totally missed the two criminals heading for the entrance.

Doggedly trudging toward the entrance were the honeymooners, Mavis and Alex Greenwalt. He pulled a battered, lime green suitcase tied 'round with a bungee cord. Her cross-body shoulder bag contained cosmetics, sundries, and her medical needs. Among other ailments, she was diabetic. Both ached from the trip, her corn throbbed and his arthritic knee caused a bit of a limp, but they were dressed for travel in matching white windbreakers and thick rubber-soled shoes. Grandma and grandpa on vacation heading to catch the train out of King's Cross.

The suitcase wobbled as the wheel caught. Alex let out an exasperated sigh. It was heavy, but they'd soon remedy that. In fact, they would not take a train to Bath or Glastonbury nor would they watch the sunrise over Stonehenge. They were not at all what they seemed to be as they walked through the station and headed toward the public restrooms.

He had plotted out this course in detail, figuring schedules to the minute. *Their thrilling vacation plan,* he called it. They only met a few months ago and now, looking upward, Mavis could see the architecture that he described to her—the contrast of old brick against the towering white fluted pillars. She vaguely recalled being here many years before, but it was different than she remembered. She was still familiar enough to assist with the plan though.

He gave her hand a small squeeze to encourage forward movement. She was smitten at first sight, one of those successful date match stories. His online profile touted his experience as an art dealer, world traveler, and investment banker who was up for adventure. Of course, her Euchre club looked at the handsome photo, clucked their teeth, and then barraged her with horror stories from Dr. Phil. They urged her to run a background check. Not one of them attended the wedding held in the City-County Building back home in Indiana.

"Isn't this amazing," Mavis said with a gasp, scurrying to keep pace.

The wheel on the suitcase twisted, then tipped as they rounded the corner near the big clock. "Damn it," Alex said as he struggled to wrangle it forward again. If they got caught with what was inside, it wouldn't matter that he was seventy-seven years old or that she had a really good reason for stealing it. What would matter was this was not his first go-round at this kind of thing.

Under the barrel roof of the huge station, everything echoed. The cavernous space was alive with movement—uniformed conductors in snappy red, black, and gold; tourists in all shapes, sizes, and manner of dress pushed, pulled, and toted luggage, bags and knapsacks.

"Just imagine where all these people are heading off to," Mavis said. "Following their dreams to some exotic location. What an amazing place to be." She caught his eye. "Don't you think so?"

She never thought she'd return to this place. For a moment, she was transfixed by the mix of sounds, the click of heels against brick, flashing lights, the swish of the train moving on the track. A thundering voice announced departures and arrivals. Cornwall. Leeds. Alex nudged Mavis, who stopped to read the changing schedule board. "I've always wanted to see Paris," she told him, knowing that would not happen, not now anyway, but they were so close. It was too bad they couldn't just take that train. They'd been in London two days and had barely seen the city.

"Are we in the clear, sweetheart?" she asked, glancing around, wondering if she should have paid more attention to their surroundings.

"Uh-huh," he said, glancing toward the Starbucks. He wanted coffee. *Damned doctor.* His prostate was good but his kidneys weren't and caffeine exacerbated the tremors. People expected an old man to tremble a bit but he'd need steady hands for the coming task.

Mavis patted her shoulder bag. "I should really eat soon."

"You'll be fine," he said. "That would throw us off schedule. I saw you stuffing your face at breakfast. That should hold you over for a while." He smiled then, that winning smile as if he meant this as a joke. Then he placed his hand on the flat of her back and steered her toward the door to the loo and gave her a little shove.

"Okay now," he said. "Go in and do your business and do not forget any of the steps. Follow each one to the letter or this won't work. We can't afford a misstep at this point of the game."

"What if someone is in there?"

"You have a brain, woman. Use it. Don't let anyone see you."

His face in the speckled washroom mirror was flushed. He theorized that most older people looked alike. He had explained this theory to his wife, saying that old folks were often overlooked and ignored, slighted. But even those chirpy teens outside—blond hair, cell phones, blue eyes, and summer tans—all dressed alike in shorts and T-shirts with sweatshirts wrapped around their butts and shoulders—couldn't be picked out one from the other in a crunch.

Mavis, for instance, was pretty in her online profile photo, but in real life fairly ordinary and not someone easily picked out of a crowd. This, he assured her, was not a handicap, but a good thing—especially at their age.

Besides, he told her, he had an ordinary face, too. Kind, with blue eyes, one distinguishing spot in the right iris too small to make a difference. He removed a comb from his breast pocket and slicked down the mess of white hair, thankful, as always, to have it. It took less than four minutes to complete his own personal business and turn his jacket inside out so that now it was black.

Mavis, however, was not so quick, leaving him to worry. He paced in front of the door for ten minutes, then slouched on a bench, and wondered if he should barge in and drag her out. He could get up and walk away, but then what would be the point of all of this?

"Good God," he said when she finally appeared, pulling the smaller, gray suitcase, her hair tucked under a matching gray scarf with tiny printed flowers. "Did you fall in?"

"There were ladies in there. I had to be careful, you know, so no one saw me."

"I guess you did it then." He glanced at the carry-on case, her black tote, and large purse.

"Yes. It's done."

"Your dilly-dallying around has totally put us behind schedule. I can't imagine why on earth you took so long."

She smiled and patted his arm. "Relax. My hair was a mess. I haven't washed it in two days," she said, picking lint from her dark jacket sleeve. "These reversible jackets were a good buy, but this side shows every bit of dust and lint. See?" She pinched up the front placket. "On the other hand, they are perfect for any weather, and look, no wrinkles."

Alex frowned. "Good God, woman. Do you think we are tiptoeing through the tulips here? Have you forgotten what's at stake? I send you on a simple task with a crucial time table and you come back an hour later."

"It was not an hour and you told me to make changes, step-by-step. I was following your orders the way you told me to." Her lower lip quivered, and the catch in her voice meant she was holding back tears.

"Okay, okay. Where did you stash it?"

Mavis flashed him a puzzled look. Her toe was killing her.

"The suitcase? Where did you leave it?"

"Oh, that. I left it in a stall and good riddance. That thing is so ugly. If it were up to me, I'd have blown it up years ago. My gosh, I've had that thing for what seems like a hundred years and have always hated that all-over apple pattern."

He was already moving toward the exit.

"It just took me some time to repack everything. I had to leave stuff behind."

Alex stopped and glared. "What? What did you leave behind?"

"Oh nothing that can be traced to us. Stuff we bought yesterday, souvenirs, those bulky sweatshirts with the Union Jack splattered across the chest. My gosh, they made us look huge. I left them in the suitcase."

"Did you hide it?"

"No. I left it in the stall, sitting by the toilet."

"Okay. But you did the rest? Like you were supposed to?"

"Oh, yes," she said. "The way we planned it. Is anyone following us?"

He glanced around and nodded for her to follow. So far they seemed to be in the clear, and she thought Alex was right in doing it this way.

Outside, the couple scurried into the flurry of people, quickly blending into the moving crowd of tourists waiting for cabs, buses and lights to change. Alex hailed a black cab at the corner. In a few hours they'd be on a plane, headed home and, if all went well, they would have pulled it off. That nice little Picasso etching, worth nearly one hundred thousand dollars, would belong to her and no one would be the wiser.

So far no one had followed them from the gallery to the hotel or from the hotel to the rail station where they'd switched their appearance. Now, they were off to the next destination. It was what Alex called 'a wild goose chase for the police or London's Bobbies' and he assured her it would work because he'd pulled it off countless times in the past.

The stolen Picasso was small enough to fit into her large, black tote. She'd fallen for it years before while working at the Avignon Gallery. It was her first job in the city but her employer, Henry Livengood, a tyrant, had cheated her time and again out of money she'd legitimately earned on commission. Firing her was the last straw, because that left her nearly penniless and alone in a foreign country.

All this, her sad story, she'd confided to Alex early on. He'd convinced her of a way to not only obtain the treasured print but also give old Mr. Livengood a bitter taste of comeuppance.

"But just go in and steal it? I couldn't do that."

"Sure you could. It's easy," he'd said, with one hand on her knee and the other stroking her neck. "I can show you how and I promise you'll never get caught."

"But what do I do with it once I have it?" she asked, thinking of the priceless etching and wondering how to display it without raising questions.

Alex had an answer for that one as well, and before long, they had cashed in her airline mileage and were off to London. She felt very much alive, all of her nerve endings zinging and her heart bubbling over when she looked at him. Of course, she remembered she had not eaten for a while and that might account for some of it.

* * *

The cabbie was Middle Eastern with a thick accent and a mole on the side of his face. Dark hair drifted over his collar. Mavis suspiciously eyed his skin, the color of old, tarnished leather. Still, he was polite, efficiently opening and closing doors for the two of them. Alex gave him their destination. Soon, they zipped in and out of traffic, their suitcases safe in the boot of the automobile.

Of course, there had been a fuss. Alex wanted to keep the suitcase with them and argued there was plenty of room—and there was. But the driver, in his broken English, pointed to his license and said something about regulations.

"Just sit back and enjoy the ride," Mavis said, patting the inside crook of Alex's arm. In her mind, she was counting. He had six cloth T-shirts tightly rolled the way the YouTube video showed. His oxford shirts were carefully folded. Four of them. Her black wool dress—good for all occasions—three blouses and matching polyester slacks, two sets of flannel pajamas and her nylon nighties, three pairs of panty hose, seven pairs of dress socks and white anklets, an afghan wrapped around the stolen Lino-cut etching, inside a layer of trash bags wrapped in tin foil.

They'd walked right into the gallery that night. The place was packed with people for the open house—some German artist she'd never heard of. Winding through the crowd, she inhaled the mix of colognes and perspiration.

The wine was top-shelf, the appetizers cut into tasty little morsels. In the corner, her former boss's eyes met hers with maybe a flicker of something and her heart stopped a moment. But then, dismissing her, he'd looked away.

Seizing the moment, Alex moved in to inquire about the huge Rothko, then the Basquiat, chatting the guy up about prices, techniques, methods, and art history. Meanwhile, unnoticed, Mavis headed to the back room. She slipped into the familiar space and found the desired etching leaning against the wall near the base board, partially enclosed in bubble wrap. She slipped it into her large purse and escaped without being seen.

Mavis stared out at the buildings of London as they headed toward Heathrow with a stolen etching hidden inside their taxi. In the past few hours, the odd, musical sound of sirens cutting through the air had set her on edge every time.

"They won't miss it for a while," she whispered, crossing her fingers.

"Relax. This is better than sitting at home watching *The Young and Restless* for thrills."

"You best get me out some crackers or something." She waved toward her shoulder bag. "I feel a bit off."

Digging through her purse, he found a packet of graham crackers and a bottle of juice. "Don't you be going into some diabetic attack on me, sister," he said. "I can't afford drama right now."

Through the window, the arched glass of the terminal loomed. Mavis silently mouthed the words on the sign—WELCOME TO HEATHROW—as the cab pulled to a stop at the curb. Her stomach was tied in knots and Alex's hand in hers felt lifeless, clammy.

"Maybe we should just check the bag?" she suggested.

"Um, no," Alex said. "Too much of a risk."

Inside the terminal, Alex held the suitcase in one hand and propelled her forward with the other. Her heart raced as they threaded their way into line. She glanced at Alex—his mouth was set in a determined scowl.

Alex, on the other hand, chuckled to himself. The thought of the Picasso hanging on her living room wall between those fakes, *Blue Boy* and *Pinky*, was a real hoot.

"It was easy back in the day," he had confided. "Before the Internet, before everyone could get on a cell phone or send out a tweet. Back in the day, you could steal a work of art and go underground. You had networks, a backup system." She was so gullible. An easy mark. The passports were legit, although he'd borrowed someone's social security and identity, which was not so hard to do anymore. His was courtesy of a friend from the pool hall who'd recently had the good graces to go on to a better life in the sky.

As they wedged their way into the crowded line, she said, "I wish we'd had time to sightsee. I would have loved to have taken a tour on one of those double-decker buses, but the cab was cute. I love London cabs. So old-fashioned looking, don't you think?"

"Why are things always cute with you? An automobile is an automobile. It isn't cute. It's simply a vehicle with a purpose." He clasped his fingers together to still the tremors that put him out of commission. This was his big come-back. He'd ditch her and head for Vegas maybe, double the take or just fence the thing and live a lush life until the next lonely sucker fell into his lap. Lonely ladies were all over the Internet.

As they neared the X-ray machines, he began to worry. They might question him about the tremors. He would have to hold his temper and explain it was hereditary—essential tremors—passed to him from his lovely mother. Lucky him, he would tell them.

He placed the case on the roller and watched it move through without raising any red flags.

He jumped as Mavis nudged him. "You have all the paper-work in order? The passport? My medical papers?" Her husband reached into his inside pocket and produced the papers.

"I've got the carry-on," he said with relief as they examined her medical bag. The clerk, an unsmiling, heavyset woman, towered over Mavis, who perched on tiptoes in front of the booth. Her fingers trembled, too, as she handed the woman her open passport.

"What is your business in New York?"

Mavis's eyes strayed to her husband at the next agent, who had opened his passport.

"What is your business in New York," the woman demanded.

"Oh, sorry," she said, her eyes now on the open passport laying before her, on the woman's long, black fingers and her dark polished nails.

Mavis remembered Alex's instruction to smile and answer in a pleasant tone. "I am returning home. My husband and I have… well, his sister, Edith, passed and we have been here for that. It was very sad, a very sad trip for my husband, who is also ill. This trip has been very hard on him."

She motioned back toward Alex with a sad look. She explained that she was diabetic, and once again, allowed for an exam of the leather satchel containing her insulin and medical supplies.

"It is all okay, isn't it?' she asked. "We checked with the airline. I have the necessary paperwork right here." Alex had suggested this chatter but it seemed to only annoy the clerk.

"Do you have anything to declare? Did you purchase anything while here?"

"Oh, no. Nothing at all. Well, I did buy a couple of sweatshirts with the Union Jack on them but I gave them to the nephews where we were staying. That doesn't count, does it? I mean you want to know if I am taking anything back home, right?"

Finally, Mavis heard the rubber stamp thunk, thunk, thunk against her open booklet, then, "Move on. Next."

The plane had three sets of seats across and smelled of stale air. They picked their way along the right side, counting seats and reading numbers until finding theirs side by side near the back of the plane and not too far from the restroom, which made Mavis happy.

She stashed her things under the seat and slid to the inside so she could see out of the window while Alex gazed upward at the open bin. He didn't want to let go of their carry-on.

"Here, let me help with that," said a rumpled soldier, leaning down to enclose his hands over Alex's on the handle. Alex relinquished the bag.

Mavis's throat began to close as the plane filled with people and quiet shuffling, the soft banging of closing bins, and a crying baby somewhere up front.

"I hope that won't go on the whole way home," Alex said, settling into the seat. "I think you should eat and take care of your sugar as soon as we're airborne."

Mavis nodded and waited while the passengers filed to their seats and the flight attendants went through the pre-takeoff rituals. Soon the plane was racing forward, and then it lifted skyward. Mavis tensed when she felt the slight bump of the wheels folding into place.

Alex squinted his eyes shut against the wail of baby screams. When they were thirty thousand feet in the air, and the earth below had disappeared into a mist, Mavis opened her big, black bag, and handed him a bottle of water. They'd had time before boarding to pick up sandwiches from a kiosk just outside the boarding area. The cellophane crinkled while Mavis unwrapped the turkey sandwich and began to loudly chomp. Alex struggled with his packet of mustard, which squirted suddenly across the aisle, landing squarely on the tattooed arm of a scary-looking passenger.

The man's fists curled as if to hit Alex. Right away, though, someone from behind offered a moist towelette. Alex opened his mouth to say something but shut it again.

Mavis leaned forward and smiled apologetically. "I like your skin art." From what she could see, it looked like Hebrew or Islamic script on his neck and arms and numbers across his forehead. "Very interesting. Does it have meaning?"

"Mind your own business lady," he said. He was bald, maybe one of those London Skinheads she'd read about. She couldn't stop looking at him.

"I didn't mean to pry," she said. "I studied art and find all that fascinating. Is that Arabic? On your neck and face? Honestly, I don't mean to offend. I've never seen anything like that before."

Alex pinched her arm and whispered, "Stop talking to him. Those are prison tattoos. Shut your fool mouth before you get us killed or something."

Trying not to be obvious, Mavis leaned forward a bit to see the prison tattoos. "I think he's a terrorist," she whispered.

"Shh. He'll hear you." Alex moved Mavis's insulin bag closer and reached inside. He removed the syringe and, despite his tremors, tried to surreptitiously take off the protective cap. "Your insulin is ready."

"Not here," she said.

"Mavis, don't be so squeamish. No one will see."

"I'll step into the little restroom and you can inject me from the doorway. It worked out okay on the way over."

Alex sighed and checked the aisle. Ahead of them, the aisle was blocked by the food service cart, but, behind them, there was only a short way to the restroom. He stood, making a move in that direction, but the tattooed man put his foot out and tripped him.

"You got a problem or what?" Alex asked, maintaining his balance.

"I don't like the way she's staring at me." He stood and grabbed

Alex by his collar and said, "She makes me nervous."

From the cockpit, there was an announcement. "This is your captain. I have turned the seatbelt sign back on. We're heading into some turbulence. All passengers must return to their seats immediately and fasten your seatbelts."

Then, the plane pitched sharply forward, causing the two men to fall into one another with great force. Alex accidently jabbed the man's tattooed arm.

The man yelled. "What the hell? Mother-fucker stuck me with a needle!" He slugged Alex in the nose and Alex fell, hitting his head on the floor. The syringe rolled out of view. People in adjacent seats gasped and screamed. Two men jumped up from their aisle seats and grabbed the tattooed man's arms.

"Hey, there, buddy," one said. "Calm down."

"Calm down, my ass. He stuck me with a needle. Who knows what the hell's in that. HIV, HepC. I need a doctor, right the fuck now."

"Sir...sir, please," the flight attendant interrupted. "Please we'll get you medical attention, I promise. Can you take your seat and belt in?" She raised her voice. "Do we have a doctor or nurse on board?" She knelt down and helped Alex to his feet. He was bleeding from a cut above his temple.

"Mommy, look what I found." The child two rows in front of Alex held the syringe in the air. Her mother screamed, "Emily, drop that. Oh, God, did it stick you? Doctor? Where's the doctor? My child was pricked by that needle."

As the plane hit the next air pocket, the pilot announced an emergency return to London. Mavis stared at the angry guy's colorfully inked neck, the panicky mother, and the syringe filled with enough insulin to kill a horse. She wished she were anywhere in the world but in seat number twenty-six on flight 456.

As soon as the plane landed, airport security boarded, confiscated the syringe, and took Alex out in handcuffs. Alex told Mavis to wait for him while he explained the situation to security.

Mavis calmly gave herself an injection, put her medical bag in her purse and removed the carry-on from the upper compartment. She followed the other passengers out of the plane. As she rolled the suitcase to the gate to await the airline's instructions for boarding another flight, she grinned and thought she knew the perfect place to hang her Picasso.

Olive Rush (1873–1966)
N. W. Campbell

In Fairmount, Indiana, native **Olive Rush** discovered her calling at age three while sitting in her parents' farmhouse kitchen. "I was drawing. For a long time I tried to make a horse. And suddenly I made a horse. It was the most ecstatic moment of my life. I suppose it was sure then that I would be an artist," she said. She was one of the earliest American women to devote herself to a full-time career in art and became known for her murals and her paintings of native peoples of New Mexico.

Rush studied at Fairmount Academy, the Quaker school her parents established, and then moved on to Earlham College to study with John Elwood Bundy, founder of the Richmond Artists Group. She entered the Art Students League of New York, vowing never to see any young man more than once, to discourage would-be suitors from diverting her from a successful art career. She was a staff artist at the New York Tribune and an illustrator for Harper and Brothers. In Delaware, she studied under illustrator Howard Pyle.

Rush accepted a commission to design a mural for St. Andrew's Episcopal Church in Wilmington. She designed murals for the La Fonda Hotel in Santa Fe, libraries, post offices, and other public buildings. Her arts education programs with the Pueblo, Navajo, Kiowa, Hopi, and Zuni began at the Santa Fe Indian School, where she taught the children to create murals featuring native cultural lore. In 1914, she befriended Georgia O'Keefe, with whom she collaborated on several projects.

In 1963, Rush underwent a serious illness that eventually claimed her life. She turned to the local Quakers for help with her medical bills and gave them her Santa Fe home for a meeting house. She died in 1966.

Expose Yourself to Art
Stephen Terrell

It was planned to be a lazy Labor Day for me. The Indianapolis Indians were playing their last home game of the season, and I had my usual seat in the front row of the upper deck along the first base line. I loved baseball and tried to catch a dozen or so Indians games each season, plus a few major league games in Cincinnati or St. Louis. Even though I was the detective on call, I hoped to get through this in peace. I knew it was unlikely.

It was the middle of the third inning when my cell phone vibrated. Marda Johnson's name showed on the screen. She was a decent field detective but an even better politician, so she was my boss.

"Vandever," I answered.

"Art, it's Marda," Her voice was sharp, her words clipped, as always. "Morgan County's got a body. Somebody's dog found it. They want us to take the lead."

"And by us, you mean me?"

"I don't know much," Marda continued, ignoring my comment. "Body apparently is wrapped up. Could be that missing co-ed. I already sent crime scene forensics. Cheryl Etherton will meet you down at the site."

Behind me, I heard the crack of a bat. The distinctive sound meant only one thing. I turned my head to see the ball sailing over the left field lawn seating and onto Washington Street. "Where is it?" I asked, already annoyed at having to miss the rest of the game.

"Morgan-Monroe State Forest on the Morgan County side. I'll text you the GPS coordinates. How long will it take you to get there?"

I did some quick calculations. "Forty minutes or so."

* * *

Driving with flashing lights through sparse Labor Day afternoon traffic, I made it to the State Forest in just under forty minutes. I really didn't need the GPS coordinates; the array of flashing lights on the main forest road signaled the scene. I pulled my car to the end of the line and walked to where several county deputies were huddled in their brown uniforms. I showed my badge and signed the crime scene log. The most senior officer directed me down a narrow path through the woods.

"Down there about a third of a mile," he said.

The path wound upward at a gentle slope, twisting around thorny bushes and saplings under a canopy of larger sugar maples, shagbark hickories, and black walnut trees, their leaves showing the first turn of color. I could hear the scene before I reached it, hushed voices and the muffled crunch of feet shuffling among the dried leaves. Just past the top of the ridge, there was a cordon of yellow crime-scene tape. About fifty feet to my left, six people moved carefully around a depression in a small clearing.

"Art!" I recognized Cheryl Etherton's voice. Cheryl was a familiar sight at crime scenes. I had known her for nearly a dozen years. In her late thirties, she stood only a little over five feet tall, with full breasts that pulled her navy cotton shirt tight against its buttons. A blue ISP baseball cap covered her short, reddish-blonde hair. I often thought that if I had the courage of a few stiff shots of bourbon, I might admit to being attracted to her and ask her to dinner. But I carried an extra fifteen years and thirty pounds that I thought put her out of my reach.

I made my way over to Cheryl. "What have we got?"

"Couple out this morning running their black Lab. Dog came down to this clearing and was pawing at something. Wouldn't come when called. They went down to retrieve him, and saw him gnawing on what was left of a hand."

"That'll screw with a morning walk," I said.

"They called Morgan County, and County called us. I've been here about an hour."

"What have you done so far?"

"We've taken photos of the entire scene. I set up a grid and walked through it for any obvious evidence, but there wasn't any. Wanted to wait until you got here before we started disturbing things."

I nodded. We spent the next thirty minutes walking the

perimeter of the scene, but it was as fruitless as Cheryl's first effort. I took one last look around to make sure I wasn't missing anything, then said, "Let's start digging and see what we find."

I left the scene to Cheryl and her team of crime scene techs and walked back to the road. A deputy directed me to the couple that found the body. They were oddly excited, almost giddy. I interviewed them, going through each of their actions in meticulous detail. It only took twenty minutes. When I folded my notebook closed, they seemed deflated.

"Is that all?" the young woman asked.

"If we need anything more, we'll get in touch."

"That's it?" she said again. "Aren't the television people going to show up to interview us?"

I scanned the roadway in both directions. Nothing moved. It was silent except for sounds from unseen birds and insects. I shrugged. "Guess not." I walked to my car, leaving them standing in the road with their mouths open, visions of stardom vanishing with the suddenness of a crumpled Powerball ticket.

* * *

An hour later I was back at the depression in the meadow looking down at an unearthed, deteriorated body partially covered by a discolored white cloth. The exposed clothing, a dark blue sport coat over a gray sweater and gray pants, indicated a male. The face was partially covered by the cloth, but I could see that more than just a skeleton remained.

"Anything preliminary?" I asked Cheryl.

"How about a name. Tobias Salyers, age forty-eight. Lives in Carmel. He's President of Salyers Gallery with locations in Carmel and Fountain Square in Indianapolis. 'Fine Art for Fine People.'"

My surprise must have shown even though I didn't say a word.

"His business card," Cheryl said, a wise-ass grin spreading across her face. "Found his wallet in the inside jacket pocket. He was carrying close to twelve hundred dollars, an AmEx black card, and membership cards for Columbia Club and Meridian Hills Country Club."

"Looks like he's been in the ground for a while."

Cheryl nodded. "Six months, maybe a year. We had a dry spring, and he's up on a high spot. Decomposition isn't as bad as it could be."

"Think you can determine cause of death?"

"Maybe, but don't count on it."

I nodded, speaking more to myself than to Cheryl. "Don't often find someone like that dumped. Wasn't there some publicity about an Indy businessman disappearing a few months ago?"

"Yeah, I remember that," Cheryl said. "Think it's him?"

"Maybe. Laptop's in my car. I'll see what I can find."

* * *

Back in my car, it took me less than ten minutes to find the missing person's report on Tobias Salyers. It was filed December 17th with Carmel police by his wife, Robynn Dresel. They were separated and she hadn't seen or talked to him since late November. When people began calling about her husband missing meetings and parties, she became concerned. A supplemental report noted that Salyers was last seen on November 30th having lunch with Jamison Pippin, the owner of *Indy Scene*, a local art magazine. They discussed an article Salyers was writing, then he headed back to his Fountain Square gallery. No one had seen him since.

I made a few notes then called Marda. As we talked, I could hear the sounds of a Labor Day cookout in the background.

"Got an ID on the body," I said.

"You sure?" Her voice carried a wary disbelief.

"Sure as we can be without DNA or dental. He had his wallet on him."

"He?"

"Yeah. Indy businessman named Tobias Salyers. Been missing since the end of November. Looks like he's probably been in the ground since about then."

"We got enough to make notification?"

"I think so."

"You want to do it?"

"No. I'd like to look into some things before I talk to the missus. If she did it, she's had months to get her ducks lined up. A couple more days won't make a difference. Can you have one of the chaplains make notification?"

"Your call," she said. "But if she lawyers up right away, that's going to be on you."

I hung up, certain Marda would note her comment in the file, just to make sure she covered her ass if things went south.

* * *

I spent Tuesday and Wednesday sitting on an uncomfortable, wooden, straight-back chair in a small, southern Indiana courtroom. I was assisting a sharp, young county prosecutor in the trial of two meth dealers. I arrested the pair after a multi-county investigation into a meth epidemic sweeping through rural parts of the state. On the first day of the trial, I watched the jury of hard-working, Old Testament-believing churchgoers as they stared at the sunken-cheeked, tattooed defendants. Before the first witness was sworn, there was no doubt about the verdict. They would end up doing fourteen years—four years for meth and a decade for refusing to take the deal offered by the prosecution. Can I have an amen?

Wednesday night shortly after the jury came back with its verdict, Cheryl called and informed me that dental records were a positive match. The body was Tobias Salyers.

The next morning I finished some paperwork, then turned to the Salyers matter. I read the initial missing persons interviews and related news stories several times. They were cursory at best. They always were. A couple of million people go missing each year. Most just walk away from a situation they can no longer tolerate, but from which they cannot extricate themselves. Sometimes it's unpaid bills. Other times it's a relationship that's no longer tolerable. Sometimes it's just a life someone no longer can stand. But once a body was found, the dynamic changed. So I headed off to interview the last person known to see Tobias Salyers alive.

* * *

Indy Scene was located on the fourth floor of a renovated nineteenth-century building on Massachusetts Avenue in

Indianapolis. Living on Lemon Lake between Bloomington and Nashville, I knew little about Indianapolis and nothing about art. Some evening internet research revealed that Mass Ave, as it was called, was home to several art galleries and an eclectic assortment of shops, bars and restaurants. There was a neon-light sculpture of a woman waggling her hips—Annie, they called her—and a building with a six-story painting of author Kurt Vonnegut on its side.

The *Indy Scene* office was spartan, with exposed, polished wood beams, a minimalist glass-top desk, and two simple chrome and black leather chairs. The woman behind the desk was in her early twenties, with buzz cut black hair, her neck and arms adorned with heavy jewelry and bright, ornate tattoos of flowers in shades of blue, orange, purple and green. She provided me with a cup of extremely strong coffee and then disappeared through a frosted glass door.

A few minutes later, the young woman returned, followed by a bald man in his mid-forties. He was about five-nine, fit but not muscular, dressed in a stylish, cream-colored, summer-weight suit and pale lemon silk shirt open at the collar. His grip as we shook hands was firm and his smile perfect. He introduced himself as Jamison Pippin and led me back to his spacious office with floor-to-ceiling windows looking out on Mass Ave.

I didn't bother with perfunctory chit-chat. "When did you last see Tobias Salyers?"

"I don't know," Pippin said. "I had lunch with him back, oh, sometime after Thanksgiving, I think."

"What did you talk about?"

"A critique he was doing. A week later, he missed the deadline. I was pretty upset. I couldn't reach him. I even called his wife, but she didn't know where he was. A couple of weeks after that, some policeman came around and told me he was missing. I haven't seen him since."

"I wouldn't count on any more critiques from him. We found his body Monday."

Pippin's mouth curled into a grimace. He turned and stared out the windows. Without turning back, he said, "I was afraid of that. Tobias just loved to make all the holiday parties. When he didn't make them last year, I was afraid something happened. Was it a heart attack?"

"We don't think so," I said, still studying his reaction. "Did he have health problems?"

"Nothing I knew about. It's just, well, he was high strung and getting to that age where a lot of people have problems. But I wasn't aware of anything specific."

"He was murdered," I said.

"Oh, good Lord. Really?" Pippin turned back toward me. "Was it a robbery? He always carried way too much cash, and wore that diamond Rolex. I warned him about that."

"We don't know," I said. If Pippin was acting, he was good at it. "What else can you tell me about him?"

"Tobias? Well, he was probably the city's most influential art dealer and critic. He was nationally recognized. He had a top-drawer gallery in Carmel and also a little place down in Fountain Square."

I made a couple of notes. "Pretty well off?"

"Quite," Pippin said. "Lot of old family money. He owned a substantial interest in some of the most expensive office buildings and commercial real estate in the city. A few years ago he bought up a lot of Fountain Square real estate. That was before it took off. That's why he had his second gallery down there."

"Were you good friends?"

"Professional friends," Pippin said. "I don't know if he had any real friends. You have to understand, Tobias was a prick. I don't mean to speak ill of the dead, but he used his money and arrogance to run over people. People hated him. But they feared him more. He had so much money, so many connections. He didn't hesitate to use both if you got on his bad side."

"And who was on his bad side?"

"Well, if you mean who might want to see him dead, I'd start with his wife, Robynn Dresel."

"What can you tell me about her?"

"She's his second wife," Pippin said. "They were both married when they had this torrid affair. Quite the social scandal for a while. Tobias divorced his first wife and traded up for a newer model. Robynn traded up for money. She runs Robynn's Nest

Bistro & Catering, which I think Tobias financed. She's done well with it. Caters most of the city's top social events."

"Why do you put her on the list?"

"Everyone knew Tobias was looking to trade in for a newer model again. He was sleeping at his downtown condo rather than their house up in Carmel. I suspect that's one reason he opened the Fountain Square gallery. I don't know if Robynn could actually. . . ." There was a catch in Pippin's voice. "Uh, murder him. But she won't shed many tears."

"Anyone else that might have it out for Tobias?"

"Sure. Do you have the phone book handy?" When I didn't laugh, Pippin continued. "William Stanley would be on top of my list. Bill is a bit of a rough customer. Not the normal person you find in art circles. Made his money manufacturing and selling those pills you see in truck stops and convenience stores, not that I would ever go into one of those places. There are even stories around that he's connected to the mob. He keeps trying to buy his way into social circles. Big contributions to several museums, the symphony, that type of thing."

"So why would he want to kill Salyers?" I asked.

"Bill hired Tobias a few years ago to procure some art for him. You know, the type of stuff he could show off at parties. They made some trips to New York, London, Italy, all on Bill's tab. He bought a lot of art and paid a great deal. Later, he found out most of it was pretty low-rent stuff. It was a major embarrassment. He sued Tobias to get his money back, but lost. Bill isn't the type of guy who forgives and forgets, particularly when it comes to money."

I nodded. "Anyone else?"

"Mathieu Clemens. He's a local artist. Had a big blow up last year when Tobias kept him out of the Penrod Art Fair. You know anything about local art?"

"Nothing past an eight-pack of Crayolas when I was in first grade."

"Penrod is the biggest event of year. It's on the grounds of the Indianapolis Museum of Art. Every regional artist wants to be there. Particularly for young artists, it can be the difference in being able to make a living with your art and having to wait tables. You submit your work and a panel selects who can participate. The selection committee wanted to pick Clemens, but Tobias called his work hackneyed and amateurish. He threatened to resign from the committee if it selected Clemens. So they didn't. But there are no secrets in the art world, and Clemens found out. He came in here looking for Tobias. I've never seen someone so angry. He said if Tobias thought he could destroy someone's life without paying for it, he was wrong."

"Anyone else?"

Pippin thought in silence, then continued. "Kendall Korsgaard might be someone you want to talk to. He owns another gallery. Matter of fact it's just up the street a bit, although you won't likely find him there today. His day job is restoring artwork at the museum. Salyers was very critical of his work over the past couple of years. Wrote some scathing reviews. Said he was nothing better than a color by numbers technician. He's a bit of an egotistical prick, too, but nothing like Tobias."

I finished making some notes. "Looks like I've got some legwork ahead of me. You know where I can find these people?"

"They'll all be at Penrod this Saturday. Korsgaard took Tobias's place on the selection committee. Clemens was actually selected as an artist this year. Robynn has a catering tent at Penrod. And Bill Stanley is always there, I think more to be seen than anything else. I think you could talk to all of them there."

* * *

Later that night I was at home watching a rare, meaningful, late-season game between the Cubs and Cardinals when my cell phone buzzed. It was Cheryl Etherton.

"Got some results for you on that Salyers matter. Thought you'd want to hear immediately."

"Go ahead," I said.

"Looks like death was likely due to strangulation, probably with some type of ligature. The hyoid bone was crushed."

"You sure it wasn't just decomposition?"

"No, not this. Dr. Schopmeier did the autopsy. He was certain. The damage was just too extensive. Date of death is difficult to determine, but it was in the range of eight or nine months, give or take."

"That fits with when our guy disappeared," I said. "Anything else?"

"One thing that's a bit odd. With that hyoid bone crushed, there's not much doubt about cause of death. But the skin and tissue were pretty well-preserved. There's evidence of some big slashes, one across the neck, one on each leg. They bear all the indicia of being post mortem, although there is a bit of speculation on that."

"Strange," I said, trying to fit the information together.

"One other thing," Cheryl continued. "We identified the cloth the body was wrapped in. It's canvas."

"Like a tarp?"

"No. He was an art dealer. It's canvas like an artist uses, like painters or I guess some photographers."

I thought for a second. "Can we track down where it came from?"

"Not really. Certainly it came from an art supply store. But there are thousands of artists, art students, and art instructors in Indiana. And there's no markings to show where it came from. If we have a sample from some other piece, like from a suspect, we might be able to make some micro-inspection comparisons, but I'm not even sure about that. I'll have a report tomorrow, but I thought you'd like to hear tonight."

"Thanks," I said. Then a thought occurred to me. "Hey, your ex was an artist, wasn't he?"

"My first ex," she said.

"You know anything about this Penrod Art Fair thing?"

"Sure," Cheryl said. "Love it. Lots of fun. Most years I still go. It's coming up this weekend, but I hadn't made any plans."

"Would you like to go this year?"

There was a short pause. "Why Art, are you asking me on a date?" she said with a lilt in her voice.

I thought maybe there was a hint of flirting in Cheryl's tone, but quickly dismissed it as my imagination. I was thankful that we weren't on a video conference call. I could feel the color rising in my face and was sure it was turning a bright crimson. "No," I stuttered. "I mean on the clock."

"What do you mean on the clock?"

"There are several people connected to the victim that I need to talk to. They're all going to be at this Penrod thing. Thought maybe you could come along and help out. You know these people better than me. You can let me know what impressions you have. Make sure I don't miss something."

"Count me in," she said. "But we have to look around some while we're there. Business and pleasure. Deal?"

"Deal," I said.

* * *

Cheryl met me at Acapulco Joe's in downtown Indianapolis for a breakfast of huevos rancheros and the city's best biscuits and gravy. We avoided shoptalk. Neither of us had children, and failed personal relationships didn't go with eggs and gravy. Instead we talked about baseball, classic rock and roll, and old movies, interests I was surprised to find we both shared. It was the best start to my day for a long time.

We took my car and arrived at the art museum before nine o'clock. It was still more than an hour before the public would be admitted. I used my credentials to get a parking spot inside the grounds.

The museum surroundings looked like a civil war encampment. More than a hundred uniform white tents were spread in long rows against a backdrop of rich, green, manicured grass and bright blue late summer sky. We picked up a flyer that included a map, and after a few minutes of study, I found the location for Robynn's Nest Catering.

After getting our bearings, we made our way to an oversized, glistening, white tent removed from the array of artists' tents. Folding chairs and tables were set up on the grass for an anticipated hungry throng. A small army of white-aproned young men and women were carrying containers of food, while others were setting up serving tables. In the center of the tent, an attractive blonde woman in her late thirties barked orders in a manner that left no doubt who was in charge.

Cheryl and I approached her. "Robynn Dresel?" I asked.

She turned sharply. "Sorry, but I'm busy now." She barked out several more orders. As I watched, I noticed several sheathed chef's knives hanging from a belt around her waist.

"I'm Art Vandever," I said, making my voice as authoritative as I could. "I'm a detective with the state police looking into your husband's murder. This is Sergeant Cheryl Etherton. We need to talk with you. Now."

Robynn turned to face me, her green eyes flashing irritation. "Look, I don't have time. This is my biggest day of the year." She was nearly spitting the words at me. "You want to know if I killed him? I didn't. God knows I had plenty of reasons. He was sleeping around. He was trying to screw me out of money, including grabbing an interest in my business. I'm not shedding tears over him. He deserved killing. But I didn't do it."

"Some people seem to think you might be involved," I said.

Her face turned sour. "So who told you I did it? Was it that asshole Jamison Pippin? You want a suspect, you should talk with him."

"Pippin? Why him?"

Robynn's face broke into a sardonic smile. "Tobias told him he wanted to buy *Indy Scene*. If Pippin didn't sell, Tobias was going to start a competing publication. And with his contacts, Tobias could steal away his writers, his photographers, even his advertisers without a problem."

"Was that what they were meeting about just before your husband disappeared?"

"Don't call him that," she snapped. "He didn't deserve the honor. I don't know for sure, but that's my guess. Jamison doesn't need the money, but that publication is the one thing that makes him important, at least in his own mind. One way or another, Tobias was going to take it from him. If I were you, that's where I'd be looking. We'll have customers in forty minutes. I've got to go."

"She's a gem," Cheryl said, as we walked away from the food tent. "Did you catch those knives she was wearing? Those could make the wounds I saw on the body."

I nodded. "She certainly feels she is a woman wronged. But I don't think she fits this one. She's too open about not being sorry he's dead. I'm intrigued by Pippin, though. It seems he didn't come clean when I talked to him."

"Where are we going now?"

"Let's check out that artist, Mathieu Clemens. I think his tent is just down here."

* * *

Clemens's tent was located at the end of a center row. Twenty or more paintings were set out in full display, disturbing images of abstract figures and anguished faces in deep reds, oranges, purples and blacks.

As we walked into the tent, Cheryl gently placed her hand on my shoulder. "I like his stuff," she whispered. The artist was on the far side of the tent, setting up a blank canvas and arranging his paints. He was tall, perhaps six-four. His arms showed the well-developed muscles of someone accustomed to working out. In his late twenties, his black hair was gathered in a ponytail that stretched to the middle of his back.

"I'm not open yet," Clemens said in a harsh voice, not bothering to turn around. "Come back later."

"We're not buying," I said. "Police. We need to talk with you."

Clemens turned around, stirring a small paint can in his hand. "Sorry, but as you can see, I'm mixing paints. Always draws more attention if you actually work on something at one of these shows."

"We need to ask you about your relationship with Tobias Salyers."

Clemens put the can down and walked to us. "I heard about Salyers on the news," he said. "Awful."

"We understand you had a run in with him. Made some threats."

Clemens shook his head and gave a half laugh. "Well, yes. I guess I did. But that was ages ago. I actually owe a lot to Salyers."

"How so?" I asked.

"After our little row where he kept me out of this show last year, I rethought my work. Salyers was right. It was formulaic. It said nothing about the human condition." Clemens swung an open hand indicating his displayed paintings. "But I've evolved.

My recent work captures the frustration and isolation of human life in an age of technology. It's become my message. A year ago I was struggling to get five hundred dollars for a painting. Now, I am getting noticed in galleries in Chicago and even one in New York. I have Salyers to thank for that. You might say he's a part of every painting I do."

I got some particulars on when Clemens had last seen Salyers, but nothing seemed significant. As we were leaving, I stopped to look more closely at one of the paintings, holding the corner in my hand.

"Stop that!" It was a sharp rebuke from Clemens. I turned to see the artist, his eyes filled with anger, marching toward me. "Don't touch my work. I don't care who you are."

I let the painting slip back into place, feeling the tackiness of a trace of paint left on my fingers. "Sorry," I said.

As we left the tent in search of Kendall Korsgaard, Cheryl leaned close. "He may be a jerk, but his work really is quite amazing. Very powerful. If I had some extra money laying around, I would seriously consider buying one of his paintings."

"If it's not on black velvet, I don't have much interest," I said with a wink.

* * *

We found Kendall Korsgaard standing in front of the Lilly Mansion, an enormous ornate building that dominated the grounds. It seemed too large, a private home more suited for a French nobleman than an Indiana businessman. Korsgaard stood, hands on hips, surveying the grounds with only minutes to go before the gates opened. He was dressed in soft yellow slacks, a rose polo shirt, and a light tan sport coat with an IMA chevron on the breast pocket.

We talked in general about Salyers, but Korsgaard kept scanning the grounds watching for the crowds to appear as the gates opened. After a few minutes of getting nowhere, I said, "Salyers attacked you pretty viciously about your restoration work. Might give you a reason you would like to see him harmed."

"Oh that," Korsgaard said off-handedly. "That was just Tobias being Tobias."

"You weren't upset?"

"Oh, a little peeved, but not really upset. Everyone knows Tobias. They know he spouts off and likes to make a commotion. Well, he used to. Don't get me wrong. His art critiques were incredibly insightful. But sometimes he just liked to stir the pot."

"You didn't have any repercussions with your restoration job at the museum?"

"Oh, not at all. The Director knows me and my work." Korsgaard looked around to make sure no one was eavesdropping, then spoke in a voice just above a whisper. "It's not been announced yet, but I'm being elevated to the head of the restoration department."

I obtained contact information for the director to confirm Korsgaard's story, but it was so easily checked that I had little doubt about its veracity. "Any idea where I could find William Stanley?"

"Bill?" Korsgaard rubbed at his chin. "I saw him just a bit ago. As a museum patron, he has some special privileges, like early admission. He was wandering around getting a head start on the crowd, making sure he gets first pick of the art he likes. He's a huge man, maybe six-five. He's wearing a big white cowboy hat and a god-awful multicolor Hawaiian shirt." Korsgaard pointed out to the sea of tents. "But the crowd is coming in now. It might be hard to find him."

* * *

Korsgaard was right about the crowd. It swept through the grounds like an all-encompassing wave. Trying to find someone, even a person who apparently stood out as much as Bill Stanley, was a challenge. As we wandered, we kept one eye out for Stanley and the other on the artwork on display. Cheryl gave me an impromptu art lesson. She took my arm and directed me to pieces she particularly liked, commenting on various styles of painting, sculpture and even crafted jewelry.

At the entrance to a tent featuring large rural landscapes, we spotted William Stanley. He was as big as advertised, maybe bigger. He was accompanied by a tall, buxom blonde woman, her natural height elevated by four-inch red pumps. She was in her mid-forties but trying to look like she was still in her twenties, and largely succeeding. She wore skin-tight designer jeans and a crisp white cotton shirt unbuttoned enough to show a glimpse of a bejeweled bra. On her left hand was a wedding set with a diamond so large that I wondered if her hand got tired toting it around for public view.

I introduced myself to Stanley and directed him to a corner of the tent. Cheryl subtly kept his wife a few feet away. "I'm investigating the death of Tobias Salyers. Several people have told me that you were quite angry with him, that you had made threats."

Stanley's face expanded into a broad friendly smile. "Shit, at one point I'd have liked to have killed that sumbitch," he said, speaking with more than a trace of a southern Indiana accent.

"Did you?"

Stanley's brows furrowed for a moment, then he laughed. "Hell, no. I didn't kill that peckerwood." The smile disappeared and he lowered his voice. "He stole money from me, just as sure as if he had a gun and took my wallet. I paid for two trips to Europe. Paid him a commission on everything he used my money to buy. Eighteen pieces. Spent close to a million dollars. Then when I got back here and got it appraised for insurance, I found out it wasn't worth half that. Oh, there were a couple of decent paintings, but most were by these young artists that Tobias had a thing for. But apparently no one else does."

"That's half a million reasons to want him dead," I said coolly.

"Don't get me wrong. I was plenty upset," Stanley said, his eyes boring into me. "Just between us boys, I know people that could have made him disappear. Would have done it just as a favor to me. But I didn't. Half a million isn't chump change, but it ain't going to break me. I took him to court. I lost. Cost me even more money 'cause I had to pay my peckerwood lawyers." Stanley gave a shrug of his massive shoulders. "So now I'll just hold onto that crap and hope it appreciates. I ain't all broke up over Tobias being dead. But I worked too hard, and I got too good a life to risk it all over some piss ant."

I nodded. Stanley seemed too candid to be hiding something. "Who would you look at if you were trying to find who killed Salyers?"

The grin slid back on Stanley's face. "Well shit, that little gal of his would be on top of my list. Everybody knew he was getting ready to dump her, and she was plenty pissed. And I think ol' Jamison Pippin was pretty upset with him over some business deal."

"Anybody else?"

Stanley slid a giant hand across his chin and down his neck. "Hadn't really thought of it until just now, but that artist guy, Mathieu Clemens. His head just seems screwed on a little different. Hell, he even changed how he spells his name so it looks French. But he ain't no more French than me. I know for a fact Clemens grew up in Connersville. Of course, most artists are about five degrees off plumb, if you ask me."

"So why did you mention Clemens? Anything particular other than just being odd?"

"When I was walking around this morning before the gates opened, he actually came out and grabbed me by the arm. He was insistent that I look at his paintings."

"That's what he's here to do, isn't it? Sell you something?"

"Yeah, but this was different. He kept talking about how he knew I hated Tobias for what he did to me. He said that if I really wanted to get back at Tobias, I needed to buy a couple of his paintings. I guess he thought that looking at a painting by someone Tobias couldn't stand was some type of revenge. It just seemed, well, weird."

I nodded and thanked him for his time. I walked back to Cheryl. She was watching the artist in the tent mix paints. Behind the artist, an assistant worked stretching a white canvas across a wooden frame. I looked down at my fingers, still carrying the tacky residue from holding a painting.

The pieces clicked into place.

"Let's go," I said, taking Cheryl by her arm. "I know who killed Salyers."

* * *

With Cheryl following close behind, I maneuvered past several people and walked into the tent. Mathieu Clemens was sitting in front of a canvas now splashed with streaks of red, yellow and orange. He turned on the stool to face me.

"So did you plan on killing Salyers, or did it just happen?" I said in a matter-of-fact tone.

"Me? Why would you think it was me?" Clemens's voice was flat.

"You're an angry man, Mathieu. After talking with Cheryl here, I can see it in your work. And the way you blew up at me when I touched one of your paintings, that was much more than just normal anger."

"A lot of people get angry," he said. His voice was still calm, but his face was beginning to glow pink.

"As I walked around here today and saw how big this event is, I can't imagine what that did to you when Salyers kept you out last year."

Clemens jaw tightened and his face was now crimson, but he said nothing.

"Bill Stanley told me how you were insistent about him buying one of your paintings. How it would somehow be his revenge against Salyers. Then a few minutes ago I saw an artist in another tent mixing up her paints while someone else was pulling this white canvas over a board frame. And it just clicked. What you said about Salyers being a part of every painting you do. When I saw you this morning mixing up the paint, you were mixing in some of his dried blood, weren't you? That's why his body had slash marks. You drained out his blood and began mixing it in your paints."

There was a gasp behind me. I had not realized that everyone looking at the paintings was now listening to my exchange with Clemens.

"You're just guessing," Clemens said.

"What do you want to bet that when we execute a warrant and match microscopic fibers, that the canvas you've been using for your paintings matches exactly with the canvas that was wrapped around Salyers. And you remember me touching your painting, the one you yelled at me about? I'm having Sergeant Etherton here run a DNA test on the paint residue on my fingers, and on these paintings." I glanced around at the artwork hanging in the tent. "I'm pretty sure we're going to come up with DNA that's going to match old Tobias."

Clemens glared at me in a long silence. Finally he spoke through clenched teeth. "He wanted to ruin me. I went to his gallery to see what his issue was with me, and he just laughed. Told me I had no talent and he'd see to it that I never sold another painting. He was hanging paintings in that rat trap in Fountain Square that he called a gallery. There was some wire there. I grabbed a piece and before I knew it, he was dead. Then when I was thinking about what to do with the body, I decided to collect his blood and make that bastard a part of every painting I did. Can you imagine? He so hated my work, and now he's part of it."

With a sudden motion, Clemens flung his easel at me and took off for the open side of the tent. I lunged at him, but he was past me before I could get to him. He ran toward the tent entrance where Cheryl was standing. In an instant, Cheryl grabbed a hanging framed picture and swung it sharply, edge first. The frame edge caught Clemens square in the chest, then like an uppercut, smashed into his chin, where it shattered. He went down in a heap. Cheryl was immediately on top of him, flipping him onto his stomach, pulling his arms back and handcuffing him. It was over before I could even reach her.

"Nice work," I said admiringly.

She looked up with a smile. "Performance art," she said.

* * *

Within ten minutes, uniformed Indianapolis Police officers were on the scene. They took Clemens into custody and led him off to a nearby cruiser. Other officers sealed off Clemens's tent with crime scene tape.

I called Marda to update her and get someone working on a search warrant for Clemens's home and business. Cheryl worked on getting her techs out to the scene to take control of the paintings, canvas, and paint.

As we stood catching our breath, Kendall Korsgaard walked up. "Is it true that Clemens was mixing Tobias's blood in his paints?"

"Looks that way," I said.

"Brilliant," Korsgaard said, a huge smile beaming across his face. "How utterly brilliant. Can you imagine how much people will pay for his paintings now?"

Cheryl turned with a look of appalling disbelief. "You've got to be kidding."

"Not at all," Korsgaard said. "Everyone will want one. You obviously don't know much about the art world, my dear. You simply must expose yourself to art."

Cheryl slid her arm inside of mine and leaned close against me. She gave me a small wink. "Well, Art, I think that's exactly what I'm going to do."

Penrod Art Fair
Stephen Terrell

Penrod Art Fair, perhaps Indiana's most prestigious art festival, celebrates its fiftieth anniversary in 2016. It is promoted as 'Indiana's Nicest Day.' The event is named for Penrod Schofield, the precocious 11-year-old boy that is the subject of Indiana author Booth Tarkington's book, *Penrod.*

The one-day fair is one of the highlights of summer in Indianapolis. It is held on the Saturday after Labor Day, rain or shine, and draws over twenty-five thousand people. It features over three hundred artists with works that include painting (oil, acrylic, and watercolor), sculpture, jewelry, textiles, ceramics, woodworking, photography, and mixed media. Penrod also features live entertainment on multiple stages, a variety of food and beverage vendors, many local arts-related organizations, and a children's area.

Penrod is a showcase for the grounds of the Indianapolis Museum of Art, which is the uncredited star of the event. Robert Indiana's iconic LOVE statue, the Lilly Mansion, the Hundred Acre Woods, and the immaculate grounds along the banks of the White River are the perfect setting for the sea of white tents that house the artists and vendors.

The art fair is planned and hosted by the Penrod Society. Proceeds benefit a wide variety of central Indiana arts organizations.

Framed

Diana Catt

"Bertie," my mother said in a lilting voice which echoed up the stairway. "Find Jenny and come down to the parlor. Monsieur Lemmen has arrived."

I sighed. I'd hoped Mama would change her mind. I didn't want to sit for a portrait, motionless for hours, only to end up framed for eternity. And getting Jenny to sit still for anything other than a book was impossible. The whole project spelled disaster. Maybe the artist would take one look at us and turn down the job. I mussed up my hair and sauntered down the hallway.

"He's here," I announced upon entering Jenny's room.

She put down *The Experiences of Loveday Brooke: Lady Detective* and looked up. "Do we have to do this?"

"Maybe if you beg and throw a tantrum," I said, "we might get out of it."

Jenny marked her place in the book and looked thoughtfully at me. "You're right. That usually works for me. I'll see what I can do."

I put my hands on my hips and growled at her sarcasm. "Just come on. Mama wants us downstairs." I led the way out of Jenny's bedroom and downstairs to the parlor.

I'd had a glimpse of Monsieur Lemmen last month at our parent's dinner party to ring in the New Year, 1894. He'd perched on the edge of the dining room chair, thin and hawkish around the nose and eyes, as he engaged my father in passionate conversation. My older sister, Yvonne, was an artist-in-training with Monsieur Lemmen and, as a result, he and my father had become fast friends. I believe that was when Mama began the campaign to have our portrait painted by the famous artist. I wished Yvonne would do it instead. I always liked sitting for my sister when she was practicing her talent.

"Lovely," M. Lemmen said as he tilted Jenny's face toward the light. She stuck out her tongue and squinted her eyes.

"Jenny Serruys, behave yourself," Mother said. "I'm so sorry,

Georges. She's only eight. I hope you have patience."

"Patience, yes, my dear Marie, but only in limited amounts. After a point, the price. . . it goes up."

My mother gave a little laugh, but I could tell she thought he might be serious. "I'll speak to her." She gestured toward the cloth-covered table in the corner of the room. "I was thinking about this spot, no?"

The artist studied the corner and positioned Jenny and myself near the edge of the table. "We need something. . . ." He looked around the room and spotted the gold vase containing a dried arrangement of Lunaria. He moved it to the corner of the table. "There, perfect. We will start at once."

I raised my eyebrows at the back of Jenny's head. She couldn't see me, of course, and remained silent. No tantrum on the horizon. Just then, the front door opened and Papa's voice boomed into the house. "Marie? I'm home."

Jenny was faster off the mark than I and beat me to the doorway where she threw herself into Papa's arms. But I was a quick second. Papa hugged us both warmly, then he kissed Mama and shook M. Lemmen's hand. He hadn't even released the artist's hand before there was a knock on the front door.

"Are you expecting someone else?" he asked Mama.

She shook her head and peered through the curtain. "I don't recognize him."

M. Lemmen lost Papa's attention as Claudia, our maid, answered the door.

I could hear the stranger introduce himself as Reverend Vermeulen and request an audience with my father. I peeked around the doorway and saw Claudia escort the visitor into the library. All I witnessed of him was the back of his gray overcoat, tattered at the hem, and long, black hair atop his uncovered head. I whispered his name to myself, spilling it over Jenny's head and toward M. Lemmen's ears. I thought I caught a spark of recognition in the artist's eyes.

"I know of this Reverend Vermeulen, my friend," M. Lemmen said, also in a whisper, to Papa. "He is a missionary to CFS. Probably wants money. I wonder if he knows about the rumors?"

I knew CFS stood for Congo Free State, which, according to

Papa, was one of our King's most prosperous holdings. I didn't know anything about rumors. Later, I wished I had noticed more about the missionary because our house turned out to be the last place he was seen alive.

The front door burst open again and Yvonne bustled in, all arms and sketch pads and easel boards. "Sorry I'm late, Georges," she said, unloading her burden in the living room. "Mama, you look divine as always." She kissed our mother on each cheek. "Papa." She kissed him likewise. She unwrapped her scarf, tossed her coat onto the sofa, and then opened her arms. "Jenny, Bertie, a hug first, then to work."

We embraced our sister, and then returned dutifully to our positions next to the little table. Yvonne took out a sketch pad. "I'm going to do a few sketches for M. Lemmen, then he will choose the final pose."

"Vonnie, can we talk or do we just have to stand here?" Jenny asked.

Yvonne shot a glance at M. Lemmen before she answered. "You know how fast I can sketch. Just try and hold still for a little bit. But if you must speak, please try not to move your head, my darling."

Jenny giggled and her head definitely moved.

"Stop it," I said, gripping the edge of the table. "We'll be here forever and you won't get back to your precious book."

I wished I'd spoken sooner. Jenny whipped around to face me and sent me a glare, but her laughter stopped. Now, maybe she'd turn on the whine.

Papa intervened. "Hey, you two villains in disguise, settle down, please. You know my dream is to hang both of you in the library." He laughed at his own joke. Jenny turned back to face the front with a muffled huff only I could hear. I straightened out the tablecloth and relaxed my hand again. We both knew better than to try any more delay tactics after Papa's intervention.

"Georges," Papa said with a click of his heels and a slight bow, "I entrust my beautiful Serruys women to your artistic influence. Good luck, *mon ami*."

M. Lemmen returned the gesture and Papa headed toward the library, handing off his coat to Claudia. I noticed he left the door open a crack and wished I could eavesdrop on the Reverend's strategy to see if it worked on Papa. Not that I had any intention of becoming a missionary. I wanted to become an artist like Yvonne and for that I'd need the patronage of someone maybe even wealthier than my father.

* * *

Georges Lemmen stationed himself near the living room doorway, ostensibly overseeing his lovely apprentice, Yvonne, sketch her younger sisters. In reality, Lemmen intended for his departure from the Serruys residence to coincide with the missionary's. The evangelist was fresh from the Congo and should have some answers to the ugly rumors circulating among Lemmen's dissident artistic community.

Yvonne picked up on her mentor's agitation. "Have you told my father what you've heard?" she asked.

"What?" Jenny asked. "What have you heard?"

The child's round cheeks took on a pink flush. It was so striking Lemmen momentarily debated whether or not to capture that exact color in his finished portrait. He returned his thoughts to what elicited that lovely response in the child, then made a face at Yvonne and tilted his head toward her younger sisters.

"This is not the place." But he knew Yvonne was correct. And though he'd spoken with Edmond about the political unrest, he wanted to have eye-witness testimony, not rumor.

"Would you do a few sketches of the girls in those red dresses they wore at the New Year's dinner?" Lemmen asked Yvonne, knowing the garment color would help him decide on the skin tone for the portrait.

The buzz of conversation from the library took on the air of finality and the master artist whispered his farewell to Yvonne. He took up his coat and reached the front entry as Edmond and Reverend Vermeulen emerged from the library. Vermeulen stood ram-rod straight, shoulders back, and slipped a thick stack of bills into his shabby coat. Lemmen realized that Edmond not only supported the arts, but his faith and charity as well. Lemmen approved of his patron and dared not endanger him with subversive conversation of rumor discussed openly in his own foyer.

Lemmen waved his farewell and exited the house only seconds before the missionary. His last glance into the living room caught the taller daughter, Berthe, watching the money exchange with the same intensity he felt.

Lemmen walked slowly and soon Vermeulen caught up to him. "Good evening, Reverend," he greeted the minister and provided his name. "I pray your quest with M. Serruys was a success."

The innocent man's face lit into a ready smile. "Indeed, the gentleman was most generous."

"May I offer you a drink and a warm meal, sir, and give you a chance to tell me of your mission? I've heard . . . staggering reports."

Vermeulen's smile faltered and he paled beneath his mass of dark hair. "What have you heard?"

"Come, let's speak freely and honestly, in the warmth of the tavern ahead."

The missionary nodded, held his coat together against the cold, and followed the artist to the inn.

Lemmen spotted his friend and compatriot, Guillaume, sitting at an isolated table in the far corner of the room. On his way to the table, he greeted Felecia, the barmaid who was also his sometime model, and ordered meals and pints for three. Guillaume stood at their approach and Lemmen introduced his guest.

"Ah, Monsieur, we have many questions," Guillaume said with a vigorous handshake.

"First, let us eat, drink, relax," Lemmen said. "Tell us, Reverend, about your journey home from Africa. Were the seas favorable?"

Following the meal, Guillaume again broached the topic of their concern. "Reverend," he began, "Georges and I, as well as others in our community, have heard disturbing rumors that our King is profiting from the rubber production at a horrific human cost. His exorbitant income at the expense of the workers' lives is reprehensible to many honorable Belgians."

The missionary began to shake and glanced over his shoulder to survey the room. He let considerable time pass before responding. "I have witnessed horrors beyond belief," he said when he turned back to face his hosts, lowering his voice. "There are many souls in need of salvation and we can't reach them all before they are dispatched to the afterlife."

"So the rumors are true?" Lemmen asked. "People are being tortured and murdered?"

Vermeulen took a long pull on his pint of ale, but it did not steady his tremor. "Gentlemen, it is impossible for anyone sitting here in the comfort of this warm, friendly establishment to fathom the true conditions in the Congo."

"Please, sir," Guillaume said, "we want to understand—to put a stop to the abuse."

"You won't be able to stop it." The missionary frowned. "King Leopold's gunmen are stationed everywhere to prevent mass exodus from the region. Even worse, they've been ordered to account for every bullet they use by presenting a hand from each corpse to the designated 'keeper of the hands.'" He shivered. His next words were spoken as if he was holding back the urge to vomit. "The hands are smoked to preserve them, I've heard."

His reveal trumped the rumors. Lemmen felt his stomach turn. He needed something stronger than ale to get through this conversation.

He signaled Felecia and ordered whiskey for all. Lemmen watched the other patrons in the inn eat, drink, and laugh, unaware of the atrocities his tiny group in the corner contemplated The men waited in uncomfortable silence until Felecia returned with the drinks.

Guillaume and Lemmen stayed silent while Reverend Vermeulen gathered his thoughts. Lemmen studied the man's face and realized with a shock that he was considerably younger than he'd earlier assumed. Maybe even younger than his apprentice, Yvonne, who was herself barely twenty. What a toll it took on a devout man of any age to live in the midst of such horror. But someone so young and inexperienced would surely be overwhelmed, unable to deal with the situation.

Vermeulen finally spoke again in a very low voice. "I . . . I heard . . . but it was so hard to believe, you've got to understand . . . I mean, the extent of their cruelty." He met Lemmen's gaze.

"Until I saw the boy." Vermeulen couldn't go on. Tears ran down his cheeks. He pulled a crumpled kerchief from his pocket and dabbed at the tears, took another drink. After a few deep breaths he tried once more.

"The child was only six or seven. His stick-thin brown arms were bandaged at the wrists where his little hands should have been." Vermeulen's misery flowed out of his words. "I personally know the boy's family. I've been instructing them in the faith. The boy's father, Milandu, did not try to escape, but is a worker on the plantation." He twirled his glass, now nearly empty. "Milandu didn't meet the weekly quota."

"*Mon Dieu*," Guillaume whispered, stood suddenly, sliding his chair noisily across the uneven stone floor in the process, one hand on his waist and the other passing through his hair. "They did that to his child?"

Lemmen grabbed his shirt and pulled him back down to his seat.

"I'm thinking you're targeting the wrong souls for redemption," Lemmen said. "You need to tell someone here."

"I've written to my superior and I have a meeting with him in the morning. I don't think he believes it's as bad as I say."

"You should go back to M. Serruys. Tell him what you've witnessed. He's wealthy, but not in bed with the King and has connections in Great Britain. If this can get to the press outside of Belgium, there might be a chance to bring about change. We need to expose the butcher for what he is."

* * *

Jenny and I were bored. Mama took pity on us and allowed a tea-time break from our forced immobility. Mama played the piano while Jenny, Vonnie and I sang our favorite ballads and danced around the living room, narrowly avoiding many a disastrous collision with the easel. We stretched the interlude out as long as possible. However, once Vonnie deemed we'd used enough energy she ended the entertainment. "Go change into those lovely red dresses M. Lemmen requested," she said. "I'll do a couple more sketches and we'll be done for the day." Jenny and I ran upstairs to change.

The wilted missionary was back in the foyer when I returned to the living room and I watched Papa escort him into the library. Mama continued her piano playing and singing so I couldn't hear any conversation leaking from the partially open library door. Papa had given the man some money earlier today, so I couldn't imagine why he'd be back so soon. I stood erect for Vonnie but kept one eye on the front lobby, waiting for the missionary to emerge.

At the moment the library door opened wider to reveal Papa and his guest, Mama finished the piece she was playing. In the sudden vortex of quiet, I distinctly heard Papa say, "Be careful what you say, sir. Your life may depend on it."

I didn't know if that was a warning or a threat.

Then Mama started playing again.

* * *

George Lemmen had a bad feeling about the little missionary. He heard that Vermeulen missed his morning appointment with his superior and by the following day was officially considered missing. Since Lemmen had been one of the last to have spoken with Reverend Vermeulen, he suffered through an afternoon at the police station under interrogation regarding the activities of the young missionary.

Exhausted and agitated, Lemmen returned to his studio to find his friend, Guillaume, waiting and chatting with his assistant, Yvonne Serruys.

"How long did they hold you?" Guillaume asked.

"Nearly three hours, the bastards," Lemmen said.

"I was there all morning," Guillaume said.

"What did they want?" Yvonne asked as she set up the multiple sketches of her sisters for Lemmen's consideration.

"We took the missionary out for supper after he met with your father," Lemmen said, walking from sketch to sketch. "The police wanted to know what we talked about and if we knew who else he planned to proposition for funds."

"Seems like more effort from the king's men than you'd expect for just a missing missionary," Yvonne said. "Did they get wind of what he intended to tell his superior?"

"You told her?" Guillaume asked.

Lemmen laughed. "She's one of us, *mon ami*." He studied the last sketch for a minute then answered Yvonne's question. "They seemed to know something. But I certainly wasn't going to tell the king's pawns what I've heard of royal atrocities. I might go missing, too."

"They found him, I heard," Guillaume said. "His beaten body was hidden in a dogcart along the Senne way over on the other side of Brussels."

Lemmen was quiet for a moment, then he backtracked to the middle sketch which depicted Berthe Serruys's angular face turned toward the activities in the front foyer of her home. He pointed to it. "This one," he said, his expression turning serious. "I'll always remember the little missionary when I look at your sister's expression in this pose."

Guillaume walked over to look at the sketch. *"The Surreys Sisters?"*

"I think *The Two Sisters*, but we'll see. Red dresses, pale complexions, blue background. Pointillism, of course. I'm going to try something different and extend the technique to the frame as well."

Guillaume found an empty frame and held it in front of the sketch. Lemmen gently raised the frame slightly to cover the Surreys girls' hands at the bottom of the sketch and met his friend's sad eyes. The girls' stick-thin white arms became 'bandaged' by the wooden frame—where the little hands should have been—creating a memorial to the missionary and his tortured family of converts in Africa.

* * *

Jenny and I were dancing to Mama's music when Yvonne and M. Lemmen delivered the finished painting.

"Edmond," Mama called out toward the library. "The portrait is here." She didn't wait for him. She carefully clipped the binding and removed the paper wrapping. Her eyes took on that soft expression she reserved for babies and other cute things.

"Oh, it's beautiful," she said. "Thank you, Georges, thank you."

"Let me see," Jenny said, jumping up and down.

I was just as excited, but didn't jump in front of company.

Mama turned the painting around and my heart sank. It was awful. I looked like a mean old woman dressed like a little girl. Even beautiful Jenny looked pouty. I didn't know what to say without crying or hurting Vonnie's feelings. Was that really how we looked to her?

Vonnie must have noticed because she put her arm around my shoulders and squeezed. "M. Lemmen chose the pose," she said in a whisper. "He said that was how he remembered you that day."

"You were mad at me, weren't you, Bertie?" Jenny asked. "You look mad."

I growled. Well, I certainly was mad at her now.

Papa joined us just then.

"Welcome, *mon ami*," he said in greeting, shaking M. Lemmen's hand. He took the portrait from my mother and studied it. "My darling Bertie," he said. "What were you looking at so intently?"

I fought back the tears but didn't answer. Just lifted my shoulders in a shrug.

"She was focused on the little missionary that was visiting you," M. Lemmen said. "Remember?"

In my misery, I almost missed the look that passed between Papa and the artist. It jogged my memory. The police had been around asking us what we knew of the missing man.

Papa looked at the picture again. "Thank you, Georges. Now, I'll never forget that day."

"It's not so bad, Bertie," Jenny said. "And don't worry. It's going in Papa's library. No one else will ever see it."

Author's note: Little Jenny Serruys in my story was wrong—*everyone* can see the painting. *The Two Sisters*, (1894) is on display at the Indianapolis Museum of Art. The Serruys family and the Neo-Impressionist artist, Georges Lemmen, were real. Also the atrocities of King Leopold II related to the people in the Congo Free State (1888-1908) are well documented. However, the events described in my story connecting the two are products of my imagination.

Jon Magnus Jonson (1893-1947)

Janis Thornton

Frankfort, Indiana, was elated when their resident sculptor, **Jon Magnus Jonson**, was deemed Outstanding Exhibitor at the 1935 Hoosier Salon in Chicago. Critics called his *Mother and Child*, executed in pink marble, "a striking study."

By then, Jonson was already established as an innovative artist. His wood, bronze, and marble renderings were hailed from Salt Lake to New York City. The head of Lincoln, carved from African walnut, and the massive, architectural sculptures gracing the International House in Chicago are among his best-known works.

Jonson started life on his Icelandic immigrant parents' North Dakota farm in 1893. By nine, he was herding cattle and dreaming of becoming an artist. While serving with the American forces in France during World War I, he visited art museums throughout Europe. Afterward, he studied at the Chicago Art Institute, where he met Lelah Maish, a beautiful sculptor and poet from Indiana. They married Christmas Eve 1923 in New York City and soon relocated to Utah, where Jonson helped sculpt the Mormon Battalion Monument.

Lelah fell ill in 1928, and the Jonsons moved to her family farm near Frankfort. Farming was in Jonson's blood as much as art. In Frankfort, he enjoyed both. His Indiana commissions include sculptures in Purdue University's Elliott Hall of Music and its Memorial Union, George Rogers Clark Memorial at Vincennes, and fountains in Richmond and Frankfort.

Jonson died unexpectedly in 1947 in Bloomfield Hills, Michigan, where he taught at the Cranbrook Academy of Art. He was fifty-three.

No Good Deed
Brenda Robertson Stewart

I could hear loud voices in my head, but my eyelids felt like lead and I struggled to crack them open.

"Ms. Wolfe, can you hear me?"

"There's a lot of blood around that head wound."

"Looks like she was struck with that shepherd statue lying on the floor. It's covered in blood."

"EMTs are on their way."

I opened my eyes and saw a circle of people around me, some wearing uniforms. Startled to find myself lying on the floor, I tried to sit up. Blinding pain shot through my head and I fell back to the floor as I heard a siren.

"Help's here," someone said.

I must have passed out again because the next thing I knew, I was seeing bright lights in total blackness. I thought I must be in the tunnel I'd read about in articles about near-death experiences.

"Are you awake?" someone asked.

I opened my eyes and saw that I was lying in a draped cubicle. There was a woman dressed in a white coat standing by my bed.

"I'm Dr. Chambers, an emergency room physician on the staff of General Hospital here in Indianapolis. Can you tell me your name?"

"Lettie Sue Wolfe."

"Do you remember how you suffered a blow to your head?"

"No, but I heard somebody hit me on the head with a statue. I've got a violent headache."

The doctor asked me multiple questions and checked my reflexes. "You've got a mild concussion and we're going to keep you in the hospital overnight for observation."

"I need to go home to Bloomington. Pets need to be cared for." I could tell I stumbled over my words.

"You need to take care of yourself right now. I understand someone has been notified who can see to your pets. It's important for your full recovery that you rest your brain. However, there are two policemen here who would like to talk to you. Do you feel up to answering their questions?"

"Sure, but my memory might be a bit fuzzy right now. Can you give me something for this raging headache?"

"Memory problems are common with a head injury. I'll order some acetaminophen for the pain. Other pain killers can cause bleeding in the brain," she said.

Sometime later, two men walked into my cubicle. I think they were wearing suits and ties, but my vision was so blurred they looked like distorted images in a fun house mirror.

"I'm Detective Mike Spencer with IMPD and this is my partner, Detective Amos Sharp. We'd like to ask you a few questions if you feel up to it, Ms. Wolfe."

"I feel like I've been hit by a truck, but go ahead."

"Can you describe what happened before the assault and theft?"

"There was a theft? What was stolen?"

"I'll get to that in a minute. Tell me about your day. Take your time. We're in no hurry."

"My friend, Zach, owns a photo studio and small art gallery in Camby. He's on a photo shoot in California and I volunteered to man the gallery to help out for a few days to give his mother a break. She's been working there until he can hire an employee." I stopped to think. "It was a quiet morning—only one person came in. He looked at the artwork, said he might be interested in one of the paintings, but wanted to check with his wife before he spent that much money. He left and I went to the back room of the shop. When I came back to the front, I rummaged around in some files I had brought with me involving a facial reconstruction I'd been working on. I'm a forensic artist. I was bent over the table and thought I heard a noise behind me. I started to turn to look and wham—my head exploded and that's the last thing I remember." I closed my eyes and laid back to rest.

"Can you describe the customer who was in the gallery?

"He was about five-ten, one hundred sixty pounds, brown eyes, longish brown hair, mustache, and teeth stained with a tobacco tint. Spoke with a west Texas drawl. Wore a gray windbreaker and black leather gloves, which I found strange considering it was such a warm day for early March."

"Good. You were very observant. Do you think you could work with our forensic artist to get a likeness of the man?" Detective Spencer asked.

"I can do better than that. When the stabbing pain in my head quiets down, I can draw his portrait myself."

"Excellent. What can you tell me about a painting of a shepherd that was hanging in the gallery?"

"Is that what was stolen?"

"That's what the gallery owner's mother told us."

"*The Shepherd Boy* is a beautiful painting by a west Texas artist named Randy Maloney. An Indiana relative inherited it after she died. It was said many people had tried to purchase the painting while the artist was alive, but she refused to sell it. According to the relative, it was always displayed with the small terra cotta statue that apparently clouted me, but no one seemed to know the significance of the statue—except it was also a shepherd."

"Yes, you were hit by the statue. Your blood was on it," Detective Spencer said.

"Head wounds bleed a lot. Was it broken? I've been told I have a hard head."

"It looked intact," he said.

Fatigue seeped into my bones, but I continued. "The canvas is about forty-eight by thirty-six inches and depicts approximately two thirds of the shepherd's body. Earth tones dominate in the background and in the blanket that is pulled up around his shoulders and head almost like a cape. A shepherd's crook is in the boy's right hand. I was thinking of buying the painting myself. The price was five thousand dollars. It was on consignment in the gallery. The sellers said they needed the money to help with their son's college expenses."

"Did you see what the customer was driving?" Detective Spencer asked.

"I looked out the window as he was getting into a small blue SUV. I can't tell you the make. He must have come back into the gallery while I was in the rear and hid in Zach's photo studio which is in a separate room off the main floor. There isn't any place to hide in the gallery."

"What made you think he had a west Texas accent?" Detective Sharp asked.

"I have relatives in Midland, which is where the artist lived, and the man talked like they do."

"Did you know the artist?"

"No, but I wish I had. She was certainly gifted."

"The doctor said they're keeping you overnight, but I'll need to be in contact when you feel you can draw the portrait, and I may need to ask you some more questions. Will you give me your home address, phone number and email?" Detective Spencer asked.

"Of course. Write down your contact information and I can email the picture to you."

An eternity later I was transferred to a regular hospital room. I was bored, but the only show on TV that I could bear to watch was the Cupcake Wars, probably because my cooking skills leave much to be desired. My vision was still a bit distorted. The cupcakes probably weren't oval.

A nurse's aide came in with a pitcher of iced water. "It's best not to watch TV with a concussion," she said as she turned off the TV.

I must have dozed because people were sitting in my room when I woke up. When I got my eyes focused I recognized the company. "Aunt Mattie, Uncle Jim, what are you doing here? How did you get here?" I was so happy to see my elderly neighbors that I began to sob which didn't help my headache.

"We're here because you can't stay out of trouble," Uncle Jim informed me. "And Leroy brought us. Please stop crying. Even when you were a little girl, I couldn't bear to see you cry."

"We were worried about you, dear," Aunt Mattie, said. "Leroy has gone to get you some flowers. Clean clothes are in the duffel bag Jim shoved into the closet."

"I'm so happy to see you, but how did you know I was in the hospital?"

"Zach's mother, Natalie, called me so upset I'm worried about her, too. She called Zach in California and since he finished his shoot, he should now be on his way back to Indianapolis," Aunt Mattie said.

About that time, Leroy Andrews, a childhood friend and Monroe County Sheriff, walked in carrying a basket full of roses, lilies, tulips—so many flowers I couldn't see all the varieties—an arrangement so huge it completely covered the bedside table.

"I've talked to Detective Spencer and got most of the story so you won't have to repeat it," Leroy said. "We won't stay long since you no doubt have a bad headache, but your neighbors weren't going to rest until they could see with their own eyes that you were alright. We'll take care of your animals and be back tomorrow to take you home if you can be released. The doctor said she thought you'd be fine, but need to take it easy so your head can heal."

"Thank you for coming. I'd be fine if this headache would stop, but I know it's going to last for a long time. Kind of puts in perspective those holes I've had to fill in on skulls whose faces I've reconstructed in clay. I was lucky. Hope they catch the jerk. Can't imagine why he wanted that painting so badly."

We said our goodbyes and I felt exhausted. I squirmed around, trying to make myself comfortable on the pillows, but nothing stopped the pain. I tried to think about my neighbors who had just left. I've known them all my life, since I grew up down the road from where we all live now. They're both well into their nineties, but like to think they take care of me. I call them aunt and uncle out of respect, but they're not blood relatives.

I had barely shut my eyes when someone spoke my name. It was my friend, Natalie, Zach's mother.

"I've been terribly worried about you, Lettie Sue. There was a lot of blood."

"Lots of blood vessels in the head. I'll be fine."

"I was bringing you lunch since you were there all by yourself and have been so nice to help out, but I found you on the floor. I didn't know if you were dead or alive."

"Zach needs to put a buzzer that sounds when the door is opened and a lock on his studio door. I'm sure the thief snuck in while I was in the back and hid in there."

"It should have been me there. I feel so guilty."

"Don't feel that way. I want to know what's so special about that painting that would prompt someone to steal it."

"I can't imagine. Let's hope the police catch the thief. But I'm not going to stay. You're awfully pale and I'm sorry they had to shave your head. You had such beautiful long brown hair."

"You mean I'm going to be bald, too?"

"They had to treat the wound. The doctor said it's only a bald patch under the bandages. It will grow back in no time."

"Thanks for coming to cheer me up, Natalie," I chuckled. "See you later."

I dozed between nurse checks during the night and thought morning would never come. But it did and after I ate a light breakfast and had a quick check by the doctor, I was released. My friends arrived to take me home about eleven A.M. I was positive they had come by horse and buggy, but was assured they were held up by a traffic accident.

* * *

The pain in my head was annoying, but bearable, and I was anxious to sketch the face of the man who had been in the gallery prior to the attack and theft. Bailey and Catcher, my chocolate Labrador and black cat, clung to my side like pirates guarding their treasure.

"I'm happy to see you guys, too," I said, "but I was gone for less than two days. Give me a break. I need to sketch while the memory's still fresh."

The sketch pad was on my easel and as I picked up my pencil to draw, the phone rang. It kept ringing and I muted the sound. While I appreciated the "how are you" calls, they broke what little concentration I could muster.

Fueled by a headache, the itching of the bald spot and wound on my head, and plain, unadulterated anger, my hand moved quickly across the paper. When satisfied I'd captured the likeness of the man, I scanned the picture into the computer and emailed it to Detective Spencer in Indianapolis.

Leroy called a couple of days later to tell me the IMPD had asked the FBI to help with the investigation of the art theft, but that was all the information he had been able to learn. Since it wasn't a high profile case, he said I shouldn't expect it to be solved anytime soon.

* * *

About three weeks later, as I was putting the finishing touches on a facial reconstruction I was completing for a client, Detective Spencer called to tell me the painting had been recovered and asked if he could drop by to tell me the fascinating story connected to the theft. It was his day off and Leroy had invited him to go fishing since the two had become fast friends. They thought it would be a good time to fill me in on the story. I told him to come on out.

The men arrived in Leroy's SUV a short time later with Aunt Mattie and Uncle Jim in tow.

Detective Spencer told the story. "The Maloney relative who consigned the painting to the gallery had told several friends in Midland the painting was for sale since he knew Randy Maloney's art was well known in the area and he was hoping for a quick sale. The FBI interviewed those people and showed them your sketch. One of them recognized the man as Jim Baxter, a dealer in Native American artifacts in west Texas and southern Arizona. Baxter was easily located. He had an apartment out toward Seminole. While checking his records in Arizona, we learned he had been a person of interest in an unsolved murder in Mesa, but there had not been enough evidence to arrest him. When confronted in Texas, he had *The Shepherd Boy* painting in his possession. It had been removed from the frame and Baxter had been examining it with high powered magnifying equipment. He claimed he had purchased the painting from a man he met in Oklahoma, but wasn't given a receipt. The equipment was for studying the artist's painting techniques."

"Oh, come on," I said. "He actually expected the FBI to believe his story?"

"I'm just getting to the interesting part," Detective Spencer said. "After confessing to stealing the painting and transporting it to Midland, he also owned up to killing the man in Mesa. It seems the friend had told him a tale originally told to him by his father, about an old prospector named Jack Maloney, a great-uncle of Randy Maloney's husband, who had a cabin up in the hills. The old man was a legend in that part of Arizona. He used to rob the train to steal tobacco. Anyway, the old man said his niece had painted a picture of a shepherd boy in which she'd hidden clues he had revealed to her about the location of the Lost Dutchman Mine. These two good ol' boys decided to track down the painting and get the gold. They got drunk and started arguing about how they were going to divide the riches. In a fit of rage, Baxter hit the other man on the head with a geode and killed him. Then he started tracking the painting. The ole boys obviously weren't the brightest stars in the sky. You were lucky he didn't kill you, Lettie Sue."

"If the statue had been bronze instead of terra cotta, he might have. Will the Maloney's get the painting back? I'd still like to buy it."

"Yes, they'll get it back, but they're not in the market to sell it anymore. Zach, your gallery owner friend, made a film about the attack, the heist, and the legend of Jack Maloney and put it on YouTube. It's gone viral—a million hits so far—and people from Europe, Australia and New Zealand want to buy the painting. The price being offered is astronomical, but the Maloney's think with the family legend and heist, they need to keep it in their family for posterity," explained Detective Spencer.

"Well, has anybody checked out what might be in that statue of the shepherd boy?" I asked.

"Oh, no, Lettie Sue, you leave that mystery alone," Leroy said.

Author's note: Randy Maloney was a real artist who lived in Midland, Texas. She painted *The Shepherd Boy* and it hangs in her son's house. Jack Maloney, a great-uncle of the artist's husband, was also an actual person who lived in Arizona and about whom many legends have been told. The rest of the story is from the author's imagination.

Alberta Rehm Miller Shulz (1892–1980)
N. W. Campbell

Alberta Shulz admired the beauty of nature and, according to her cousin, "She revered all life, even the existence of the birds and the bees. For her, there was so much in Nature to admire and learn." Her paintings of Brown County established her as one of Indiana's most gifted landscape artists.

Born **Alberta Rehm Miller** in Indianapolis, she studied music from the age of six, but turned to art when she realized she could not sustain a music career. She enrolled in the arts program at the University of Texas. There she married, gave birth to daughter Emilie, and later divorced her husband. In 1922, Miller and her daughter moved back to Indiana to join the Brown County Art Colony. She rented a cabin from fellow artist Mary Murray Vawter and studied with various Brown County artists and at the John Herron Art Institute in Indianapolis.

Miller's most important instructor was Albert Robert Shulz, a landscape painter and founder of the Brown County colony. His style would powerfully influence Miller's work. He was married to artist Ada Shulz at the time, but in 1926 made the decision to divorce her and marry Alberta Miller. This set off a scandal that plagued the new Mrs. Shulz for the rest of her life.

Miller Shulz's work is characteristic of American Impressionism, and her subject was the rural landscape of Brown County. She and her husband spent winter months in Sarasota, Florida, where she continued her studies at the Ringling School of Art and added Florida and Georgia landscapes to her body of work. Prior to her death in 1980, she donated the land for the Brown County Art Gallery, where several of her works are on display.

Pride and Patience
Shari Held

Charles Hartford Clarriage III stood in the middle of the magnificent library. It had been his father's center of operations until 12:43 that morning. He stroked the top of the enormous, polished mahogany desk. Then he eased into the butter-soft leather chair, propped his legs up on the desk, smiled like a Cheshire cat, and lit a cigar.

Mine, all mine—the estate, the investments and the business—now that dear old Dad is gone. He blew smoke rings with more abandon than he normally allowed himself. And he poured an indulgent slug of Macallan sixty-year-old scotch from its Lalique crystal decanter, closing his eyes as the heat of the peaty concoction reached his belly.

Charles was roused from his state of near slumber when he heard Clarisse, the prettiest girl in the county—maybe the whole state—and the one he'd decided he'd marry, speaking to someone on the other side of the library door. The housekeeper must have let her in. It sounded like—no, wait. It couldn't be. What was Daniel doing in the house? He certainly couldn't be making a social call. He was their gardener's son, for God's sake. Correction: their *former* gardener. And while Charles knew his estate was no Downton Abbey, it was the gem of the county, and that put him a step or two above the help.

"Oh, Charles, I'm so sorry to hear about your father," Clarisse said as she rushed into the room and wrapped her arms around his neck. "You look dreadful. How are you holding up?"

Charles unfolded her arms, rubbing his thumbs down the length of her arms before he relinquished them. When he looked into her eyes, his face expressed nothing other than the pain of a grieving son. "I'm doing as well as can be expected," he said with a slight quiver in his voice.

She grabbed his hand and patted it. "If there's anything you need—anything at all—you know where to find me."

Was that an open invitation? It certainly sounded like it. Well, well.

She was coming round at last. Amazing how owning an estate could open doors. And the heart of a greedy woman.

"Please accept my condolences as well," Daniel said. "I know what it's like to lose a father. Your father was a good man. Always treated everyone well."

Treated everyone the same, no matter who they were, you mean.

His father had encouraged, and then financed, Daniel's artistic endeavors, down to letting Daniel use one of the buildings at the edge of their property as a gallery—for free.

Oh, how I look forward to seeing Daniel's face when I pull the plug on that.

But for now Charles must appear to be the bereaved son.

"Charles, why don't you come to Daniel's show tonight?" Clarisse asked. "It isn't good for you to sit in this big, old house alone with your thoughts. It'll do you good. Please say you'll come." Clarisse looked at him expectantly like a spaniel begging to be walked.

Well, why shouldn't I go? Daniel's art show may not be my first choice of venues, but if Clarisse wants to fuss over me, who am I to deny her the pleasure?

"Thank you, Clarisse," Charles said. "I think a little diversion *would* do me some good. What time should I pick you up?"

"Oh, no need to pick me up. I'm going to the gallery early to help Daniel set up. But why don't you come around six-ish. We'll see you then."

Daniel put his arm around Clarisse to guide her through the door. Then he turned and said, "Yes, Charles. *We'll* see you there."

* * *

Charles hadn't set foot in the building since Daniel started using it. The current exterior was washed in a gray-blue that complemented the pale blue walls of the interior. The inside glowed with thousands of inviting twinkle lights and whimsical sayings were calligraphed on the interior and exterior walls.

Charles frowned. He'd arrived late and the gallery was well-attended. Neither Clarisse nor Daniel were in sight. Then he heard a lilting laugh and they emerged from the back room, Daniel's arm around Clarisse as he bent and gave her a kiss.

"Hello, everyone," Daniel said. "Thank you for attending the show. If you haven't been here before, I specialize in portraiture—paintings of wives for husbands, husbands for wives, children—and I've even been known to do paintings of the family dog. Although I charge extra for that! But this evening it's all about my miniatures. In our ancestors' time, it was quite the rage for a woman to commission a miniature to give to her lover or for a husband to carry a pocket-sized version of his wife. Of course that was long before the iPhone!

"Miniatures are much more intimate, and make a statement of permanence and intent. That's why I'm on a personal, one-man quest to bring them back. The miniatures are in the side room of the gallery." He nodded to a woman who stood in front of the closed door. "We'll open the door in just a minute. But first," he began. He put his hand on a black cloth that covered a display on a pedestal, then swooped it off. "Here's one of this beautiful lady beside me. Doesn't it capture her very essence? A miniature is like a meaningful caress. An iPhoto is like an impersonal handshake."

The miniature in the display case was projected on two TV screens at opposite ends of the room. Clarisse's miniature was bathed in shimmering light. And amid the "oohs" and "ahs," Clarisse and Daniel embraced and kissed once more.

* * *

Charles survived the evening through sheer willpower. No one expected him to be gregarious, for God's sake. He was sure his tamped-down anger appeared as nothing more than heartfelt grief. Perfectly natural, given his recent loss.

He wadded the program he'd picked up at the door until it was the size of a walnut.

How dare that money-mooching loser think he could capture Clarisse's heart as easily as he captured her likeness. Girls like Clarisse respond to one thing. Money. And I have that in spades now that dear old dad is no longer around.

Of course, Charles had helped that along by adding the medication to his father's drink. A simple suggestion to the coroner that his inebriated father had accidently taken the azithromycin instead of his heart medication was all it took. Everyone knew his father was prone to partaking too much upon occasion. And everyone adored his father and didn't want to sully his reputation.

The Z-Pak an obliging doctor had prescribed for Charles while he was vacationing at Lake Tahoe was on the kitchen counter along with all the other vitamins and medications. Right there in full sight.

The big question now was, what to do to get Daniel out of the picture?

His fingers traced the delicate pattern on the Limoges vase in the study. Then he threw it at the opposite wall and watched as it smashed into bits, the shards raining down like deadly raindrops from the sky.

* * *

"What a surprise to see you here, Charles," Daniel said, looking up from his desk in the back room of the gallery. "I hope you're enjoying the excellent weather we've been having. And all the beautiful summer flowers. Those showy yellow lilies were your father's favorites, you know."

Like I care about the blooming vegetation.

"Let's dispense with the small talk, Daniel. We've never been, and never will be, friends."

"Then why are you here? And why'd you come to my show?"

"I came to your show because Clarisse invited me. You didn't think it was because I wanted to support our up-and-coming community artist, did you? Not a chance. You've received all the support from the Clarriages you're going to get. Trust me on that."

"You didn't enjoy the show?"

Daniel's wide-eyed look of innocence didn't fool Charles. No matter how naïve he appeared, Daniel knew how to play the game. When Charles's father was desperate for attention, he'd turned to the gardener's son instead of Charles.

"You hoodwinked my father into letting you use one of our properties for your gallery," Charles said. "He even paid to have it outfitted just to serve that purpose. I bet you enjoyed having him chip away at my inheritance to finance your little whim."

Daniel's expression didn't change. He said nothing.

But that wasn't the most pressing issue Charles had at the moment. This business with Clarisse was what concerned him now. Clarisse, whom Daniel had publically embraced and kissed in a tawdry display of affection. Clarisse, who should, by rights, belong to him—not Daniel. Daniel was trying to take her away from him, too.

Charles pulled himself together. "But that's history," he said. "Despite our differences, I do recognize your talent. That miniature you made of Clarisse was exquisite." Charles pulled his checkbook and pen out of his jacket pocket. "How much do you want for it?"

"It's not for sale," Daniel said.

"Don't be ridiculous. Everything comes down to money in the end. Name your price."

"No, really. It's one of my best pieces. I've booked five commissions for miniatures just from that one show. It'll be good for business. That's something you should understand."

"You can paint another subject that can serve in that capacity." Charles uncapped his Mont Blanc pen, scribbled something on a check, tore it out, and dropped it on the desk. "This should change your mind."

Daniel picked up the check. It was for twenty thousand dollars.

"Seriously?"

"When have you ever known me to not be serious about money?"

"You've got a point, but I'm afraid I can't accept your money. In case you didn't notice, Clarisse has become more than just my muse. We haven't announced our engagement yet, out of deference to your father's recent death, but Clarisse and I are getting married. And, somehow, I don't think selling a miniature of my future wife to another man would be appropriate."

Daniel rose from his chair, tore the check in two and tossed the pieces in the air.

"It will never work, you know." Charles was seething, but he kept his face controlled as he smoothed his coat. "Clarisse is used to a lifestyle far better than you can ever give her. She'll soon tire of taking long walks through the woods and watching old movies in front of the TV. Girls like Clarisse long for designer dresses, fine dining and heirloom jewelry. I'll wager you'll never even make it to the altar."

"That's one bet I'll take you up on," Daniel said. "Oh, and not that I don't trust you, but after I spray Clarisse's miniature with a protective coating and let it dry here overnight, I'm putting it in my safety deposit box. Better take a good look at it on your way out. It's the last time you'll ever feast your eyes on it."

* * *

If anyone was going to possess Clarisse's miniature, it was Charles—not Daniel. Clarisse was a vain woman, and when Daniel painted the miniature of her, she fell for his charm. What girl wouldn't have her head turned by something like that? But money and a prestigious lifestyle was a faster and more reliable route to a woman's heart.

Charles picked up the phone. "Clarisse, it's me. I know it's last minute, but I was wondering if you could meet me for lunch at the Club today. I could sure use your help on some of the things concerning the estate. I've got a good grasp on the finances, but for some of the other things it would be nice to have a woman's input.

"11:30, then? I can swing by and pick you up at your office. And, Clarisse, thanks. You've always been there for me from the time we were kids playing hide and seek. You don't know how much your help means to me."

* * *

The luncheon had gone exactly as planned. He might have overplayed the sympathy card, but Clarisse didn't seem to mind. She'd agreed to help him and was coming over this weekend. Ostensibly she'd only be there during the day, but Charles knew he could remedy that. After all, who could refuse a bereaved son—especially when he was rich, eligible and a long-time friend. If that ruined any of Daniel's plans for the weekend, all the better.

And speaking of Daniel, Charles wasn't going to let that artist son of a gardener have that miniature. If Daniel was going to remove it tomorrow, he'd take it tonight. He had the keys to all the buildings on the estate, and he was pretty sure Daniel wouldn't have changed the locks. If Daniel had, well, that's what crowbars were for. He'd toss the place and make it look like vandals had done it. That might be fun.

Anyway, he'd have the miniature in his possession by midnight, one way or another, and Daniel out in the street by the end of the month.

* * *

Charles decided to walk to the gallery. It was barely within walking distance, but he didn't want to chance that anyone would see his car. His Jag was well-known in the community.

He dressed down in a denim shirt, jeans, and hiking boots. The material felt coarse to the touch, but the woods were dense and held all manner of flowers, vines, and vegetation. Daniel's father, Ben, had been responsible for all of it, with Daniel helping him as a child. But after Ben died, only the formal gardens were tended by a landscaping service. Everything else had run amuck. Charles just hoped he wouldn't run into any poison ivy.

The gallery lights were dimmed. *Good. I can get the miniature and get home at a decent time.* Charles tried his key. It worked. It was almost too easy.

He stepped inside, and sure enough, the miniature sparkled on its pedestal. Charles removed it from the glass display and stroked it reverently, then brushed his lips across it before putting it in his pocket.

As he turned to leave, a figure emerged from the shadows. It was Daniel.

"I suppose you're going to ask me to return this?" Charles asked as he drew the miniature from his pocket.

"No. It's all yours, Charles. In fact, I made that one just for you."

"Really? I thought you said. . . ."

"That was before I realized you'd stop at nothing to get it."

"Smart man."

Daniel looked up at the wall clock. "You should begin to see, and feel, just how smart right about now."

"What are you talking about?" Charles felt peculiar, like a war was raging within him that no one was winning. He slumped down on the floor.

Daniel plucked the miniature from Charles's outstretched hand with a pair of tongs, and placed it in a liquid-filled jar. The liquid began bubbling, and the miniature disappeared before his eyes.

"What did you do? What's happening to me?" Charles asked as he grabbed his stomach and groaned.

Daniel ignored his questions until he'd replaced the destroyed miniature of Clarisse with the original.

"Well, Charles, I may only be a gardener's son, but at least that taught me to stay away from the deadly monkshood in your woods. I coated the miniature you attempted to steal from me with monkshood root—the most deadly part of the plant. You did the rest. All it takes is a touch, and you didn't just touch it. You stroked it and kissed it. An unexpected bonus! Right now it's attacking your internal organs. Soon it will get into your blood stream. And, if you're thinking this is a prank, let me assure you, it's not. Monkshood's fatal in the dosage I gave you. As fatal as that shove that killed my father."

"I don't know what you're talking about."

"I saw you," Daniel said. "There wasn't anything I could do at the time, but I'm patient. I was willing to wait until you had the most to lose. The money. The estate. The business. They'll never be yours to manage. Now, let's get you to your feet."

Charles could hardly piece together what he'd heard. But he offered no resistance when Daniel helped him stand.

Maybe if I walk a bit, I'll feel better. Surely Daniel's joking. He can't possibly have seen me, and even if he did, the gutless twerp doesn't have it in him to carry this out.

Daniel walked Charles deeper into the woods, then pushed him into a clearing filled with beautiful purple flowering plants. Charles staggered, then fell. He felt paralyzed and unable to concentrate. His breathing began to slow.

"Too bad you don't appreciate flowers," Daniel said. "They'll be the last thing you see." He turned away.

"This one's for you, Dad," Daniel said softly as he walked back to the gallery.

Gabriel Lehman (1976-)
Shari Held

Indiana native **Gabriel Lehman** didn't take up art until 2009. At the time, he lived in Wilmington, North Carolina, a city known for celebrating art and fostering artists.

Lehman worked hard, laying carpet during the day and perfecting his craft at night. The self-taught artist's fanciful artwork is his own unique concoction of surrealism, impressionism and the cartoon world.

He reached back to his childhood in Elkhart, Indiana, for inspiration. Lehman has conceptual dyslexia, so as a child, he took up drawing for escapism.

"I wasn't that good at it," he says. "I did a lot of cartoon characters."

He counts the rather unlikely trio of Rene Magritte, Norman Rockwell and Bill Watterson—the cartoonist/author of the Calvin and Hobbes comic strip—among the artists whose work he most enjoys. While you can see elements of each in his work, his pieces are truly original.

"Surrealism is fascinating to me," he says. "That's why you see giant teapots that fly around in the air with a bunch of balloons attached to them—and bowler hats and top hats. It's very cartoony and it lends itself to the type of colors I like to use."

In August 2014 at the Noblesville Art Fair on the Square, Lehman got his first big break. He gave an attendee permission to take some photos of his artwork, which were then posted online. "My work went global overnight," Lehman says. His website almost crashed several times, and he had his hands full just shipping orders.

He now has an international distribution deal. His work no longer shows in art galleries but is available on line through Gabriel Prints.

The Last Great Heist
Janet Williams

Meg couldn't believe what she just heard.

"You want me to do what?" she asked. Her cousin, Tom, gave her the kind of slight, knowing nod that one might see in a spy movie.

"Let me get this straight. You want me to rob Grandma's house?"

Again, the slight tip of the head toward Meg.

Is that a yes?

She turned her attention to Tim, the slightly smarter twin, who sat across the table beside Tom.

"Listen, we know you're good with . . . ah. . . ." Tim struggled to find the right words. "You're good with things that require a light touch." Tim reached across the table, stained with coffee and cigarette burns, to grab hold of Meg's hands.

She pulled back, crossing her arms as she balled her hands into fists.

Light touch. Nice way of saying I'm a thief. But a thief who's never been caught.

"You better spell out exactly what you want from me," Meg said.

Tim and Tom looked at each other. Tom cleared his throat as he reached into the breast pocket of his shirt to pull out a pack of cigarettes and put one to his lips. Unfiltered Pall Malls.

As he began flicking the lighter, Meg said, "You really going to smoke that? Smells bad enough in here."

"Hey, my place, my rules," Tom said, flicking the lighter one more time. But before the flame reached the cigarette, Tim grabbed the lighter.

"You can wait," Tim said.

Tom hesitated, then dropped the cigarette onto the table.

In truth, one more cigarette wouldn't have made much of a difference. The ashtray in Tim and Tom's garage apartment overflowed with cigarette butts, and the tabletop was smeared with grease and remnants of ketchup, making Meg want to gag as soon as she walked into the place.

Why did I even agree to come here?

After another knowing sideways glance at Tom, Tim spoke, "We need you to get in and take that chair painting Grandpa did." Meg must have looked as puzzled as she felt because Tim followed with, "You know, the one hanging over Grandma's organ."

Meg knew exactly what he was talking about—a watercolor painting of a simple tan arm chair with dark brown trim and brass buttons where the wood met leather. It sat alone against a bluish-green background and hung in a plain wood frame on the living room wall. Underneath was Grandma's organ, untouched for nearly a decade.

"You want what? That old painting? For heaven's sake, why?" she asked.

Tom opened his mouth like he was about to say something when Tim interjected, "None of your business. We need you to get it for us."

"Look, if you guys want that chair, why settle for the picture? Grandpa gave me that chair, the real chair, before he died. If it means that much to you, just take it."

Tim shook his head no, then Tom followed, a wave of head shakes. Tim and Tom did that a lot—one gestured and the other echoed.

"Ain't gonna work," Tom said.

"It's the painting we need," Tim said, as if he and his brother were completing a single sentence. "And only you can get it for us."

"Why don't you just ask Uncle Karl for it? What can that old painting matter to him? It's not even one of Grandpa's best."

Again, the twin heads swayed back and forth, telling Meg no. "He ain't gonna give us nothing." Tom again.

Meg should have figured that. Uncle Karl and his wife, Freda, moved in with Grandma after Grandpa died. Grandma had Alzheimer's and needed round-the-clock care, so Uncle Karl and Aunt Freda volunteered, much to the astonishment of the rest of the family.

In retrospect, it shouldn't have surprised anyone. They now controlled Grandma and therefore her late husband's considerable estate. That included a collection of original watercolors painted by Grandpa, who was a respected, if unknown, artist at the time of his death.

"Why not wait until after Grandma. . . ." Meg started to say.

"You mean . . . dies?" Tom asked.

"Yeah, I guess that's what I mean."

"Can't wait," Tim said, pulling a piece of paper from his pocket. It was a clipping from the local newspaper about an auction at the city's most exclusive gallery, featuring the work of the late Benjamin Klein.

"The Frick? They're auctioning Grandpa's paintings at the Frick?"

This has to be the work of Karl and Freda, but why and how?

"And they'll be picking up Grandpa's stuff from the house next weekend," Tom said.

"Which means we have to act fast," Tim added.

"Let them sell the stuff. Why should we care?"

Tom opened his mouth to speak but Tim stopped him, saying, "That don't matter. We just need you to get in there and get it out or else we. . . ."

"We tell that ritzy boyfriend of yours about how you used to do these break-ins all the time for Grandpa." Tom jabbed his finger at Meg's face.

The words felt like a slap.

"You can't really expect me to do this," she said, weakly pushing the finger aside. "And you can't tell Brian. I mean, this affects you, too."

"But we ain't got nothing to lose," Tom said.

Right. I'm screwed.

* * *

It had been months since she'd been inside the house, so Meg decided to pay Grandma a visit, or, as she told her cousins, she needed to do a little recon. It was the middle of a sunny afternoon and the shades were still drawn. A trashcan, which sat next to the driveway at the rear of the house, overflowed with garbage, and the lawn, always immaculate in Grandpa's day, was so long that it was beginning to go to seed.

Meg picked up the bundle of mail that was jammed inside the door as she knocked and listened for a sign of activity. Nothing. After a minute or so she knocked again, this time a little harder. Again, nothing. She pounded a third time when finally she heard a thud and then footsteps lumbering to the door.

Meg noticed one of the window shades slowly moved and she thought she caught a glimpse of Uncle Karl. Then a brittle female voice said, "Get back. Get away from there."

"It's the kid. Let me see what she wants." Meg recognized that grunt-like whisper of Uncle Karl.

"Make it quick," hissed a voice, which Meg presumed to be Aunt Freda.

Slowly, the door creaked open, but only enough to reveal Uncle Karl's face through the crack.

"What are you doing here?" Karl asked, with a grunt.

"U-u-ncle Karl, I-I just wanted to see Grandma." Meg wedged her foot inside the door so Karl couldn't shut it on her.

"Your grandmother can't see nobody. It just upsets her," Karl said.

"I won't upset her. I promise," Meg said, pushing her foot against the door, forcing Karl to open it a little wider. As he did, she tried to scan the living room through the slim opening and in the reflection from the mirror over the fireplace mantel.

"Please," she added after a moment when Karl didn't respond.

"Look, Meg, I'm sorry. But I can't let you in. Ain't nobody seeing her." Karl sounded almost apologetic.

"Just a few minutes?" Meg tried to push the door open, but Karl pushed back.

"No," he said firmly, shoving her away as he closed the door.

What the hell is going on in there?

Meg fought the urge to bang on the door and force her way inside, but that was a battle for another day. Today, she got what she needed—confirmation that the painting still hung on the wall opposite the fireplace and above Grandma's organ. She saw, too, that the rest of Grandpa's paintings were there, stacked haphazardly against a crate next to the organ.

* * *

Two nights later, Meg found herself in the alley outside Grandma's darkened duplex with a cheap wooden ladder that she leaned underneath her point of entry. She didn't have Grandpa to give her a boost like he did when she was a gangly preteen learning the fine art of burglary. This rectangular window above the mantel and next to the fireplace was Grandpa's favorite for teaching her how to break into houses. He taught her to hoist herself to the window ledge and then, while hanging onto a crevice in the stone facade with one hand, use the other to jiggle open the window latch with a putty knife. It would swing open into the room and then she would slide across the mantel and lower herself to the floor below.

It was practice, he told her. Move slowly, as quietly as possible and listen, always listen. She mastered these lessons and moved on to slipping into the houses of some of the wealthiest residents of Wittenberg and stealing paintings so valuable they had no real price tag. But that was a long time ago, before her conscience began bothering her so badly that she told her grandfather she couldn't steal for him anymore.

"Hope I remember," Meg muttered as she slowly mounted each step of the ladder, pausing as it shifted slightly in the soft, rain-soaked grass. She felt every step, too, through the thin soles of the ballet slippers she wore. They left no tread, Grandpa had told her as he outfitted her with the slippers, tights, a cap, and thin nylon gloves for her night's work. She remembered.

As she reached the window she felt the facade until she found a stone she could hang onto. She removed the putty knife from her jacket pocket and gently pressed it into the latch as she had been taught.

Nothing happened. As Meg examined the window more closely she could see it had been painted shut.

Shit. Okay. Deep breath. That's why you have a putty knife.

With swift, even strokes, Meg chiseled around the window frame, bits of white flakes floating to the ground. Then she tried the putty knife on the latch. This time it moved and, with a slight creaking sound, it opened.

Hearing nothing but the slight squeak, squeak, squeak of the window hinge, Meg pulled herself through the opening, crossed the mantel, and dropped to the floor. She paused to listen but heard nothing except the hum of a car's tires on the brick street in front of the house.

Faint yellowish streaks of light from the street lamps filtered in through gaps in the drawn shades. Meg closed her eyes and began to breathe deeply to steady her nerves. The smell caught her as she sucked in her second breath.

What was it? Urine? Vomit?

She immediately thought of Grandma lying in her own sickbed, but as she strained to see around the room she saw a shadowy mass sprawled across the hardwood floor.

At first it looked like a pile of blankets or pillows strewn across the floor, but, as her eyes adjusted to the dark, she could see it was neither.

Grandma? But where were Karl and Freda?

She crept closer, bending down to touch the shoulder of the crumpled figure. As she turned it over, she saw the dark liquid pooled by the head, and then she saw the face, eyes wide open in horror.

"Aunt Freda!" Meg said aloud, stepping away from the body.

Okay, calm down. Maybe she's not as dead as she looks.

She pulled off a glove to feel for a pulse, but there was nothing. The flesh was cold.

"Oh my God, Freda, what happened!" she said in a choked whisper.

She looked around the room, half expecting to the find the body of Uncle Karl or worse—Grandma. Meg couldn't see anything else, but she didn't want to go exploring, either.

What do I do?

She wrapped her arms around herself, shivering as she stared at Freda's battered body. *They'll think I did this!* Her grandfather had prepared her for a lot of things, but never anything like this. *Okay, Grandpa. Now what?*

"Breathe, little one. Take a deep breath. You aren't caught yet." It was Grandpa's voice, as clear as if he were speaking out loud to her now.

She breathed deeply and listened for several long seconds. That's when she realized it. She didn't even hear the wheezing hum of Grandma's oxygen machine. Then, as she slowly surveyed the room again, she saw the crate and stack of paintings were gone.

Her eyes moved again around the room. She spotted some kind of statue with a thick, bulbous base lying in the pool of blood near Freda's head.

Uncle Karl's bowling trophy?

She paused again and then continued scanning the room. And then she saw it—the painting she came to steal, the twenty-four by thirty-six watercolor of that damn chair. Only it wasn't hanging above the organ. It was leaning sideways against the sofa on the other side of the body.

Meg stepped gingerly over Freda's body and as she did, she felt her foot slip.

Shit! Blood!

She ripped off the slipper and jammed it into her jacket pocket. As her heart pounded and bile rose in her throat, she swallowed hard and took a deep breath.

Just get the hell out of here. Fast.

But not yet. She picked up the painting and moved away from the body as she scanned the room. There, on the table by Grandma's chair was the telephone. She picked up the receiver, punched in 911, and then dropped it onto the chair. The voice on the phone repeated, "What is your emergency?" and Meg tucked the painting under her arm and slipped out the front door.

* * *

Last night. Was it even real?

Meg's stomach churned as the dark image of Freda sprawled across the floor flashed through her mind. She huddled under the covers staring blankly at the ceiling when she heard the bang, bang, bang at the door.

"Meg! You in there? Open up!"

Tim. He'd come for the painting. Meg scrambled to get out of bed and wrapped herself in her bathrobe before heading for the door.

Tim hammered again before she could get there. "C'mon, Meg. Open up!"

"Hang on. I'm coming." As she brushed her hair back with one hand she opened the door and Tim pushed past her into the room.

"Where is it?" he demanded, scanning the living room of the tiny, one-bedroom apartment.

"And good morning to you, too."

"Cut the crap and just give me the painting."

Before Meg could say anything, Tim marched into her bedroom, scanned the room and then looked behind her dresser and under her bed. Meg grabbed his arm to stop him, but he shook her off as he opened her closet and shuffled through her clothes in search of the painting.

"It's not here," she said. "You think I'm crazy enough to bring that thing here?"

Tim eyed her, trying to figure out if she was telling the truth.

"Okay, where is it? And where the hell have you been? We've been trying to reach you for hours."

"Asleep. I was asleep. Late night." She tried to control her hard, angry tone.

Before Tim could utter another word, his phone rang. "Yeah, she's here," he said after a moment. And then, "Oh, my God. Seriously? She's dead? Are you sure?" He hung up a minute later and turned, wide-eyed, to Meg.

"What was that about?"

"That was Tom. He said the police came by looking for Uncle Karl," he said, dumbfounded. "They said Aunt Freda was dead."

"Dead?"

"Yeah. Dead."

"What else did they say?" She clenched her jaw as she tried to maintain a stoic expression.

"Nothing. Just that she was dead and Uncle Karl and Grandma were missing."

Grandma missing too?

Before she could say anything, Tim pressed her about the painting.

"It's in a safe place," she said.

"Listen, you screw with us and we'll make sure everyone knows about you."

"I don't even want that damn painting, but do you really think it's smart to drag it out now?"

Tim thought for a moment, then nodded. Meg ushered him out the door after a few more exchanges with a promise to connect later. As she closed the door behind him, she was astonished that her cousin never asked whether she knew anything about Freda's death.

Not too bright, thank heavens.

Meg's mind spun to last night. With one foot covered only by a sock, she had limped to her car several blocks away. After securing the painting in the trunk of her car, she briefly considered returning to remove the ladder and close the window.

Too risky. Police on their way by now.

It was a mess, she knew, but she couldn't undo her mistakes. She just better be sure she didn't make any others. She released the brake on the car and engaged the clutch, letting it roll down the hill before starting the engine.

Meg drove less than a mile to a row of old garages off an alley. She opened the second garage door and stashed the painting inside, covering it with an old tarp. This was Grandpa's lair and few people knew of it. This was where he had hidden their stolen artwork years ago, but now all it held were old paint supplies, bent and broken easels, and battered canvases.

Meg wasn't done yet. She still had to get rid of the bloodied slipper and her jacket, too, because of the blood smeared in the pocket. She sorted through the pile of damaged canvases until she found some rags and an old roll of duct tape. She bundled the slippers and jacket, wrapping them with stained rags and then bound them with the tape. She grabbed a football-sized chunk of concrete that lay in the alley and wrapped it and the bundle with more layers of tape.

Good thing Grandpa saved all this crap.

Meg then drove to the aging, two-lane bridge that crossed the river running through her small town. Pausing to check for traffic, she edged across onto the bridge and stopped in the middle. There, she got out, and after a quick glance around her, dropped the bundle into the water below. As she heard the splash, she got back into her car and headed for home and maybe, if she was lucky, a few hours of sleep.

* * *

Grandpa had told Meg that the most difficult part of any heist was waiting. Waiting for the right time to do the job and waiting afterwards to see what the fallout might be. What did Grandpa hear through his art world sources? Would the victims call the police? Unlikely, since she and Grandpa—and one time, Tim and Tom—only stole works of art that had been stolen from museums or private collectors. A few of the works had been looted by the Nazis.

"Those sons of bitches are getting what they deserve," Grandpa would say to justify the thefts.

Eventually, that justification wasn't enough for Meg and she refused to steal for Grandpa. He drafted Tim and Tom into the business, but on their first and only job they were nearly caught. Grandpa decided it was a sign he should retire. He left that business and pursued his own painting with a renewed vigor.

Meg never knew what became of the paintings they stole. As far as she was concerned, their whereabouts died with her grandfather and that was fine with her.

Now Meg was waiting. Waiting to find out what happened to Uncle Karl. Waiting to learn what happened to her grandmother. Waiting for the police to figure out that she was in the house the night Aunt Freda died. Waiting.

She only had to wait until that evening when there was a knock at her door. Tim or Tom, she thought as approached the door.

"W-who is it?"

"Ma'am, I'm Detective Sam Browning here with my partner, Detective Angie Santorini."

"Ah, just a minute." Meg tried to sound calm, but her heart began pounding and her hands trembled slightly. Her first instinct was to back away from the door, toward her bedroom and a window that led to a fire escape.

"Ms. Klein, we just need a few minutes." It was a woman's voice.

"I'm coming," Meg replied.

Maybe running's not such a bright idea.

She slipped into the bathroom and flushed the toilet before opening the door. "Sorry, I, ah, was in the bathroom."

The female detective, tall and thin with short dark hair, gave her a slight smile while the other, short, stocky, and bald, pushed his way in. They both flashed their badges.

"What can I do for you?"

"You Margaret Klein?" Browning asked.

"I'm *Meg* Klein," she replied.

"Sorry, ma'am, but we have a few questions about Karl and Freda Klein. They're your uncle and aunt, right?"

Meg nodded, plunging her still shaking hands into her jeans pockets.

"And you heard about what happened to your aunt, right?" Browning was doing all the talking.

Meg nodded again, breathing slowly and deeply to keep the rising panic at bay.

"Well, we understand you might have been the last person to see them."

"Me? The last person to see them?" Her voice was calm even as she pictured the detectives leading her out of the apartment in handcuffs.

"Yes. Your cousins told us. . . ." It was Detective Santorini.

"Tim and Tom?"

"Yes, we talked to them earlier today," Santorini said.

Oh, God, what did they say? Breathe. Breathe. You haven't been caught yet.

"And they said you went to see Karl and Freda a couple of nights ago," Santorini continued.

"A couple of nights ago?" A wave of relief washed through her. "Yes, I stopped by to see Grandma but they wouldn't let me in."

"Who wouldn't let you in?" Browning asked.

"They, both of them. No, wait. It was Uncle Karl at the door but I could hear Aunt Freda in the background. I think she was the one who didn't want to let me in."

The detectives asked Meg a few more questions about the encounter before stepping closer to the door.

"Can I ask you a question?" Meg asked and the detectives nodded. "How did Aunt Freda die?"

"Can't tell you that," Browning said.

"Okay, then. What happened to Uncle Karl? And where's my grandmother?"

Santorini looked at Browning, who gave her a quick nod before she answered. "It seems your aunt and uncle moved your grandmother to a nursing home about two weeks ago. It looks like they were planning to sell off your grandfather's paintings when. . . ."

Browning cut her off but Meg finished the sentence, ". . . when Karl killed Aunt Freda?"

"You didn't hear that from us," Browning said.

Santorini nodded knowingly at her, adding, "But we've got a lot of loose ends to figure out."

"A lot of loose ends," Browning echoed as they headed out the door.

Yeah, and I bet I know just what they are.

Meg closed the door, slumping against it in relief.

* * *

Uncle Karl wasn't on the run very long. He was caught two weeks later in Brownsville, Texas trying to sell one of Grandpa's paintings to a local art dealer for enough cash to escape into Mexico. He was back in Wittenberg within the week, and the rest of the artwork was auctioned off at the Frick as Karl originally intended. Only the proceeds went into a trust for Grandma's medical care.

Almost as soon as Karl was back in town, the cousins were at Meg's door demanding the painting.

"No. Not now. Not yet," she told them as she closed the door behind them.

"What do you mean not now?" Tim asked.

"Hand it over or we go to the cops," Tom said.

"And say what?" she asked.

"They might be interested in knowing you were there that night." Tom was in her face.

"Yeah, and who planned it? If I'm in deep shit, then so are you."

Tom opened his mouth to lash back but Tim raised his hand to stop him. "Okay, so what do we do now?"

"We wait some more."

"And what? You steal our painting?" Tom growled.

"Right. I *steal* a worthless painting." Meg shook her head. "Listen, I don't want the painting. I never wanted that painting. But if it shows up now it will raise too many questions."

"It ain't gonna show. . . ." Tom started to say before Tim cut him off.

"Maybe she's right. Wait until this thing with Karl blows over," Tim told him.

Tom was ready to argue when Tim gave him a knowing look. Tom relented, saying, "Yeah, okay. We wait."

* * *

The case was settled faster than she expected. Uncle Karl admitted hitting his wife with the bowling trophy but maintained he was defending himself against one of her tantrums. Prosecutors didn't buy his story, accusing him of staging a faux break-in to cover up his crime and pointing to the ladder and open window as evidence. They were prepared to charge him with murder, and the threat of a life sentence was enough to convince him to plead guilty to voluntary manslaughter. He got twenty years.

Before Tim and Tom could make another demand for the painting, Meg summoned them to her apartment. The first thing they saw when they entered was the object they sought for so many months, perched on the very subject of the painting.

"Okay, you were right. She didn't screw us," Tom said to Tim as he rushed to grab the painting.

As Tom held the painting, Tim pulled a bottle of rubbing alcohol from his pocket, and after dampening a rag, he began gently rubbing a corner surface. The paint began to rub off onto the rag, but Meg couldn't see what was revealed underneath.

"C'mon. What's it show?" Tom said.

"Just hang on a minute. We don't want to ruin it," Tim replied as he continued to gently rub the surface of the painting with the alcohol.

"Ruin what?" Meg asked, trying not to choke on the alcohol fumes that filled the room.

"Just you wait," Tom said.

"You may as well know," Tim said, facing her. "That last painting Grandpa stole, you know, the one you wouldn't help with?"

Meg nodded.

"It was a Monet. Grandpa knew the guy we took it from got it on the black market," Tim said. "Grandpa said it belonged in a museum."

"That's what he said about every painting we stole," Meg said.

"Yeah, well about a week after that, me and Tom went over to see Grandpa. He was in that little studio of his painting this picture over the Monet," Tim explained.

Meg's eyes widened and her jaw dropped in astonishment. "That's a Monet under that ugly painting?"

Tom nodded as Tim returned to removing the layer of paint, slowly erasing bits of the chair and the background. But his work only revealed plain white canvas, and as it did, Tim began wiping the surface more vigorously. Still, only more white canvas. He had removed about a quarter of the paint and with nothing more than the plain canvas showing.

"What the hell is this?" Tom turned to Meg in a fury. "You swap out our painting?"

"Don't be ridiculous. This is the same stupid painting I took that night."

"Then what? Where is it?" Tom asked.

Tim began softly laughing as he tossed the rag to the floor. "Grandpa. He must have done something else with it, especially if he thought we saw him paint over it."

"Damn that old man!" Tom picked up the painting and slammed it onto the chair, tearing the canvas and breaking the frame.

"Hey. . . ." Before Meg could say anything else Tom charged out of the apartment with Tim close behind.

"Thanks guys. Leave me to clean up the mess," she said as she tossed the alcohol-soaked rag into the kitchen sink.

She picked up a piece of the shattered frame and peeled away the torn and paint-smeared canvas. The frame was hollow, she was surprised to discover, but one piece appeared to have something wedged inside.

Some kind of scroll?

She spent a couple of minutes trying to pry the document loose with her fingers when she gave up and got a pair of long-nose pliers from her toolbox. Gingerly, she slid the pliers into the hollow of the frame and snagged the document.

What in the world is this?

It was a piece of canvas that Meg carefully unrolled.

What else were you up to, Grandpa? Some kind of message?

She recognized her grandfather's precise cursive writing on this slender document, so she poured herself a glass of wine and sat down in that same tan chair to read it. Not a message, but a list, she realized. And then it dawned on her. This was a list of every single painting the old man had done over the years. But that wasn't the surprising part. Next to each title was a dash followed by the name of one of the works they had stolen.

"All this time. Those paintings were right in front of us all this time. You painted over every single one. And now they're gone."

Meg smiled and raised her glass. "To you Grandpa. To your last great heist."

T.C. Steele (1847-1926)
Stephen Terrell

Perhaps the greatest tribute to the importance and influence of Hoosier artist **T.C. Steele** came sixty years after his death. In 1986, two Indianapolis art dealers were charged with dealing in forged paintings. The New York Times reported that it was the first time a state's forgery statutes were used for paintings. And the artist whose work was forged was T.C. Steele.

Born Theodore Clement Steele in 1845 in Owen County, Indiana, Steele was educated around the Midwest, including at what would become DePauw University. In the 1870s, he eked out a living in Indianapolis, painting portraits and commercial signs. But in 1880, a patron saw Steele's potential and funded Steele's study at the Royal Academy in Munich. Five years later, his talents honed, he returned to Indiana.

In 1890, Steele published a book of twenty-five paintings. His work drew the attention of national art critics. Over the next quarter century, his paintings were included in prestigious international exhibitions in the United States, Europe, and South America.

Steele purchased two hundred acres of wooded land in Brown County. At his "House of the Singing Winds," he focused on his landscapes, working with light and shadow amid the tree-covered hills of Brown County. However, Steele continued to paint portraits on commission, including poet James Whitcomb Riley, President Benjamin Harrison, and the official portraits of several Indiana governors.

Steele was the most famous of the "Hoosier Group" of American impressionist painters, which included J. Ottis Adams, William Forsyth and Otto Stark. Steele's Indianapolis studio became the first Herron School of Art. His works grace many private and museum collections in Indiana and throughout the United States. His Brown County home is now the T.C. Steele State Historic Site and is open to the public.

Callipygian
MB Dabney

"Wrap your lovely lips around this."

Taken aback by the sudden and unwanted flirtation, Kendall Hunter turned. And despite her government training, her heart nearly stopped. She was face-to-face with the most gorgeous man she had ever seen in person. As she opened her mouth to voice her indignation, a fork full of cake passed between her lips. The frosting was a delight to her taste buds and the man a delight to her eyes. Both were a creamy chocolate. She imagined his face, with its light-brown bedroom eyes, full lips and well-defined cheek bones, was chiseled personally by the gods.

Kendall took all this in in the span of two seconds, and hoped he didn't notice her brief bewilderment. "It's delicious. Thanks," she managed after swallowing.

His smile was charming and his white teeth were a perfect counterpoint to his dark skin. "My name is—" he started.

"Hampton Simmonds," she finished for him, having recovered her composure. "It's you we're all here to celebrate."

"Ah, yes, well, I suppose you are right about that," he said, sounding modest and nearly embarrassed as he looked around the art gallery at the crowd of beautiful people in their best formal attire. Men generally look good in a tux. But Hampton Simmonds's six-foot frame looked positively spectacular.

He handed the plate with the remains of the cake to a passing waitress. "You can just call me Hamp," he said to Kendall.

She wore a form-fitting blue evening dress with a modest neckline and spaghetti straps. Her white pearl necklace and pearl earrings were her only accessories. "I'm Kendall Hunter."

Hampton smiled again and his right hand engulfed hers in a strong, confident, but not crushing grip. "It's nice to meet you." He didn't release her hand, but guided her toward the wall to her right. "Let me personally escort you through the gallery."

When Hampton released her hand, he seemed to carry her along through the force of his personality. They moved into a room of contemporary paintings. One wall was dominated by a ten-foot-wide painting in off-white with five diagonal splashes of deep red. Kendall stopped, stared, and frowned, but felt Hampton observing her.

"You don't like?" he said.

"I can't wrap my mind around what it's supposed to mean," Kendall said. She studied the information card on the wall next to the painting to avoid looking at the luscious man next to her.

They started walking again and took the stairs to the second floor. "I don't get it, either," he said with a chuckle. He lowered his voice to a conspiratory whisper. "I've never liked that artist. She's tremendously overrated."

Kendall began to relax as they continued, with Hampton pointing out bits of information as they passed more art. Occasionally, someone would catch his eye and nod but no one interrupted them. Kendall's sister's eyes bugged out when she spotted them together but Kiara quickly turned back to a sculpture of a pair of steepled hands.

"Are you a collector?" Hampton asked. "I think I've met all the major black collectors here in Indianapolis. But I don't think I've seen you before."

"I'm originally from here, but I live in Philadelphia now," she said. They entered the main room on the second floor. On the opposite wall were three abstract paintings.

"And what do you do in the City of Brotherly Love . . . and Sisterly Affection?" he said, flirting directly once again.

She didn't skip a beat. "I'm a special agent with the FBI. I specialize in criminal profiles."

That stopped him in his tracks. "Really?"

Kendall smiled and started them moving again. In social situations such as this, she loved revealing her occupation, as if being a tall, attractive black woman *and* an FBI agent were mutually exclusive.

"I'm home for a short vacation. Visiting family. As a matter of fact, you know my sister, Kiara. She works for Mitch, the gallery owner. Does the PR. She had an invitation, of course." Kendall held up the embroidered invitation in her left hand. "I'm her plus one."

"Oh, yes, Kiara. I do know her," Hampton said, turning to look back over his shoulder to where Kiara had once stood, then back at Kendall. "And I'm certainly glad you're her plus one. Otherwise, I might have been bored out of my mind this evening."

The waitress appeared again, this time carrying a tray of hors d'oeuvres. Her presence was announced a second earlier by the fragrance she wore. The waitress offered them sausage-stuffed mushrooms, which Kendall declined. Hampton popped one into his mouth as the woman moved on.

"Those are your paintings, aren't they?" Kendall asked.

Hampton reached around her waist in a particularly intimate way and pulled her toward the wall where the paintings hung. "What do you think? This is my series celebrating the female form."

Kendall stared. "I'm not sure what to think."

"The one on the left is called *A Woman's Eyes*," Hampton said.

It was an abstract with bright primary colors and broad, yet soft brush strokes for the facial lines. In the profile facing to the right, both eyes appeared on the same side of her face.

"The one on the right is simply called *Bosoms of Love*," he commented.

Like the others, it was in a simple dark frame. But it didn't look like the breasts of any woman Kendall had ever seen.

"You can see the outline of the torso from the neck down to the narrow waist." Hampton continued. "But see how the painting draws your eyes to the center of the female form. It's not sexual but it encompasses the wholeness of womanhood. Do you see that?"

Kendall wanted to say no, but just nodded instead. Finally, Hampton brought her attention to the painting in the middle.

"This is *Callipygian*. My masterpiece," he said, almost as if in a dream.

"*Callipygian*? What does that mean?" she asked.

Hampton smiled and scratched his shaved bald head. "You'll just have to figure that one out."

While it was still abstract, Kendall was able to discern the curve of a woman's back, from just below the neck down to the round, full hips, sweeping inward again to reveal muscular legs. The brush strokes were soft and feminine, the colors bright and vivid.

It was obvious Hampton was a man who loved the female body. He put his hands on the curve of her hips as he leaned in to whisper into Kendall's ear, "You should model for me sometime."

The man's breath in her ear warmed Kendall much farther south. And it surprised her. But then she sensed, rather than noticed, someone approach from their left.

"Hampton, darling, you're ignoring the other guests," said a woman in a silver dress, who glided up with such stealth she could have been a ninja. Of average height and build, she wore a smile that contained neither humor nor warmth.

Hampton pulled away from Kendall. "Oh, I'm sorry. How thoughtless of me," he said, ever the charmer. "Kendall, this is my wife, Celine. Celine, this is Kendall Hunter of the FBI."

Celine appraised Kendall in a not-too-subtle way before extending a hand. "It's a pleasure to meet the FBI," she said. Kendall couldn't determine whether she was cold by nature or circumstance. But she was territorial. Celine effortlessly positioned herself between Kendall and Hampton. "I hope my dear husband isn't being too much of a bore. When he's talking about his work, he gets that way. Loses all sense of the moment."

"No, he's been fine," Kendall tried to reassure.

"Hampton, you need to mingle," Celine said, taking his arm just below the elbow and pulling him away. As an after-thought, she said to Kendall, "You don't mind, do you?"

"Of course not," Kendall said as they moved away. "It was wonderful meeting you both. And thanks, Hamp, for the art lesson."

Hampton waved a hand to her as he departed. Celine steered him into the center of a group of men and deposited him there. Kendall grabbed a glass of champagne from a passing waiter and downed most of it. With one last glance at *Callipygian*, she moved on.

As the evening was winding down, the waitress suddenly arrived at Kendall's side, handing her a card with a name written in platinum. It was raised and embossed. "He wanted you to have this," the waitress said.

Kendall looked at the card, then around the room until she saw Hampton. She turned the card over and saw handwriting on the back. There was an address and cell phone number. *Give me a call and come by for a Private Lesson.* She looked up at Hampton, who winked.

* * *

"Oh, God, my feet are killing me," Kiara said from the passenger seat of Kendall's BMW. Kiara reached down to unfasten the ankle straps on her black, five-inch heels.

Kendall took her eyes off the road only briefly to see Kiara wiggling her toes, a luxury that would elude Kendall for the twenty-five minute drive back to Kiara's house.

"I saw you talking to Hampton Simmonds."

A bit of anger rose up through Kendall's chest but she was able to clamp it down before it escaped her lips. She swerved into the left lane at the last second to avoid hitting another car as she passed it. "So? I talked to a lot of people tonight. And besides, the event was for him. Of course I talked to him."

"He's a player and everybody knows it, Kendall," Kiara said, adjusting her seat to lie back. "He's hit on me several times, even though he's a married man."

"Married, I know. I met Celine. Charming woman," Kendall said. She didn't know if Kiara caught her irony. But the car seemed to speed up as the tension inside the vehicle increased. "He gave me his personal card."

"And you took it?" Kiara said, alarm in her voice. She sat up. "I would think you, of all people, wouldn't want to go there."

Kendall faced her sister. This time, she didn't hold back her anger. "Because my husband couldn't keep his fucking dick in his pants and ran off with some fucking woman. Is that what you are saying, Kiara? That I shouldn't be a whore like that bitch and screw some married man? For your information, it's none of your business whomever I choose to fuck."

There was quiet in the car. Finally, Kiara said, "I'm sorry. I didn't mean. . . ."

Kendall looked over at her dejected sister and then down at the speedometer. She slowed. "All men are dogs, you know. The entire species. They're all dogs."

"Not my Perry," Kiara said timidly but with sincerity. "My Perry's a good man."

Knowing she had wounded her sister more than she'd ever want, Kendall reached over to take Kiara's hand. "You're right. He's a great guy and a wonderful father. And I'm glad you're together and happy." Kendall squeezed her sister's hand tightly and then placed both her hands back on the wheel. "But all the rest are dogs."

She smiled at her sister. Kiara smiled back, closed her eyes and within moments, was asleep.

* * *

Perry looked up from his morning paper as Kendall entered from outside, carrying a cardboard tray with three tall cups of coffee. It was 8:10. Kendall wore running pants and her top was pasted to her body by her perspiration.

Kiara entered the kitchen wearing a thigh-length pink robe. Her hair was a mess, her eyes barely open. "Coffee. I need coffee." As she headed for the coffee maker on the counter, Kendall handed her a cup. "Ah, thanks," Kiara said, taking a sip. "When did you go out for some coffee?"

"I didn't want to wake you guys. I went for a run on the Monon Trail around six and stopped at a coffee shop on the way back."

"You slept in your pearl earrings?" Kiara noticed, reaching up to touch Kendall's ears. "Isn't that uncomfortable? I could never do that."

"Uh. . . ." Kendall hesitated to reply. She touched her ears. "I guess I was too tired to notice when we got in. It was a long evening."

"Kiara, you'd better hurry. You'll be late for work," Perry said.

The wall-mounted telephone rang and Kiara walked over. "It's all right. Mitch said after last night, I could sleep in and get into work around 10:30," she said as she grabbed the phone from the wall. "Hello."

Perry and Kendall looked over at Kiara when she nearly dropped her coffee. "What? Oh my God. When? They took all three? The cops are there? I can't believe this. Yes, yes, I'm com-

Fine Art of Murder

ing. I'll leave immediately. If you need me before I get there, call my cell."

"What's up?" Kendall asked.

"The gallery was burglarized. They took all three Simmonds paintings. They're worth more than a million dollars," Kiara said. "I gotta go in right now."

Kiara headed out of the kitchen but then turned back. "Kendall, back East you guys probably get cases like this all the time. But not here in Naptown. It's a rarity. Why don't you come along? The local cops could probably use your insights. I know Mitch won't mind. He likes you."

"As long as I'm not in the way," Kendall said.

They took quick showers and dressed. Kiara pulled out of the driveway in under thirty minutes.

"Kendall, I can't tell you how much I appreciate you coming. With you on vacation and all," Kiara said.

"No problem. It'll give me something to do."

* * *

The August Gallery was in a two-story building on Indiana Avenue, just a block southeast of the historic Madame C.J. Walker Building. The block was closed off with police cruisers and unmarked law enforcement cars. Kendall recognized the FBI vehicles. But she expected that. Art theft was a federal crime.

Kendall was in jeans and a white blouse, but her FBI identification got her through the door while her sister went off looking for her boss.

"Who's in charge?" Kendall asked a man in a blue FBI jacket. She was directed to see Agent Arthur Dennis on the second floor. When she got there, she saw a short, older white guy in a dark suit and white shirt. Kendall knew the type. Old school FBI.

Agent Dennis stood in front of where the Simmonds paintings had once hung, talking to two local police detectives and a woman. Kendall pegged her as an insurance investigator. They'd speak, occasionally look at the empty wall and then up to the ceiling and skylight.

They all turned as Kendall approached.

"Special Agent Dennis? I'm Special Agent Kendall Hunter of

the Philadelphia field office," she said, showing her ID once again. "Is there some way I can help?"

"Philadelphia?" the two detectives said.

Dennis looked puzzled and shifted his weight from side to side. "Why's someone from the Philadelphia office interested in this theft?"

Kendall explained the circumstances of her being at the scene, including the fact that they would want to interview all the guests from last night.

They all seemed to accept her logic and offer of help. "I'm glad to have your help," Dennis said, although Kendall wasn't sure it was sincere.

"What do we know?" she asked.

One of the local detectives, a man named Jefferson, picked up the thread.

"Sometime in the wee hours of the morning," he said, "someone by-passed the security system, probably entered through the skylight—there was evidence of that on the roof—took the three pieces, and exited, also probably through the skylight."

"The artist, Hampton Simmonds, is a fast-rising star on the national art scene," the insurance woman interjected. Beads of perspiration dotted her forehead. "We're carrying a million-dollar policy on those three paintings."

"Who discovered the theft?" Kendall asked.

"Mitchell August, the gallery owner. He got in early and turned off the security system but noticed the lights didn't come on. He walked through the gallery to investigate and discovered the pieces were missing," Dennis said. "He called the police and they called us. We're interviewing him and some staff members downstairs right now."

"Is that all that's missing?" Kendall asked.

"As far as we've been told," Detective Jefferson said.

Three metal pieces the size of dimes were on the floor at their feet. They looked like small watch batteries.

"What are those?" Kendall said.

"There are sensors on every item in the gallery. If a painting or sculpture or whatever is moved, an alarm goes off," Dennis said. "Somehow, the thieves removed the sensors without setting off the alarm."

Kendall walked around the room, looking for evidence and examining the other works, how they were attached to the wall. Then she looked up at the skylight. Finally, she turned back to the others.

"And you said the security system was on when the owner arrived? Uh-huh," she said, looking down as if in thought, then back to the others. "That's curious." She headed for the stairs, with the officers bringing up the rear.

"How so?" Jefferson asked.

"Where's Mitch August?" Kendall asked the first officer she encountered. Turning back to those trailing her, she said, "Your current theory on the theft is flawed because of the security system. My sister went on and on about it. She says it can't be hacked or bypassed."

Mitch August was standing in his office while an FBI agent seated at the desk questioned him. They turned as Kendall and the others entered the office. "Mr. August, tell us about your security system," Kendall said.

"Who are you?" the seated agent asked, but backed down after noting the expression on Agent Dennis's face.

Kendall introduced herself and addressed the gallery owner again. "Your security system?"

August looked at the insurance woman as he spoke. "It's a state-of-the-art system by the Nightwalt Corp. The insurance company wouldn't write the policy on Hamp's paintings unless I upgraded," August said. "The payments are a killer."

Dennis stepped in front of Kendall to face August. "Tell me about the system."

But it was the insurance investigator who spoke.

"The NW5000 is a civilian version of a system the government uses. It uses a ten-digit encryption algorithm of randomly selected numbers and letters. It changes daily. Only through a biometric monitor can you gain access to the encryption to turn off the system. Access to the monitor is limited."

"How many people had access?" Dennis asked.

"Myself," Mitch said, touching his chest, "my assistant, one other staffer and," he paused before continuing, "Hamp Simmonds."

Glances were exchanged throughout the room.

"Can the system be activated—turned on, that is—without access to the monitor?" Kendall asked.

"Yes," August said. "There is a much simpler code to turn it on but you have to leave immediately once the system is set. Most of the staff knows the code to turn it on when I'm not here."

"Any evidence left in the ceiling skylight is a ruse to throw us off track," Kendall concluded. "You can't disable the system that way. Someone with access disabled the security system and probably let someone else in. Since walking in and out the front door would be too obvious, they probably entered and exited through a large vent."

A commotion greeted them from outside the office. It grew louder as the source got closer to the office, and erupted when Celine Simmonds entered the room.

"Who stole my paintings?" Celine said in a loud voice. When she noticed Kendall, she added, "What are you doing here?" There was quiet for the second it took for the recognition to kick in. "Oh yeah, I remember. You're FBI," Celine said with a disdain she made no attempt to hide. "Well, you'd better find my paintings."

"Your paintings?" Kendall said, stepping closer to Celine.

"Yes. They belong to me," Celine said defiantly.

August introduced Celine before the questioning resumed.

"Do you know where your husband is, Mrs. Simmonds?" Agent Dennis asked.

"No, I do not. He didn't come home last night after the gala," she answered, but immediately returned to her original concern. "So, what are you doing to find my paintings?"

"Is that unusual that he wasn't home?" Detective Jefferson asked. "You don't seem that alarmed. You're more concerned with the art."

Celine turned to the police detective. "We live separate lives. He's not always at home." Then, to Kendall, she asked again, "What about my paintings?"

Kendall looked at Dennis before answering. "The FBI is doing everything it can to recover the stolen artwork. But tell us, how did you know about the theft?"

"One of Mitch's people called the house this morning," Celine said and started to leave.

"Hang on a minute, please, Mrs. Simmonds," Dennis said. "We might have more questions for you."

She looked around the room. "Questions? What questions?" The faces of law enforcement were impassive. "You think I'm involved in this?" she said, taking a chair in the corner. "The paintings belong to me. I own them. Why in the world would I steal my own property?"

"Because you and your husband are broke and you need the insurance money," Kendall answered.

"What? That's outrageous. How dare you, you government hussy."

Kendall's eyes narrowed on the woman. Outwardly, she remained under control. Inwardly, she felt her body temperature rise. But she was an excellent investigator—and liar.

"My sister works at the gallery," Kendall started. "And she told me about the financial arrangement you made to have the art displayed here. So don't try to hide that. We'll find out sooner or later when your financial records are checked."

Celine muttered "bitch" under her breath, although everyone in the room heard it. But she settled down.

Using Mitch August's laptop computer, they checked the video feed for the room with the Simmonds paintings and discovered most of the cameras throughout the entire gallery were shut off shortly after 11:30, just as the catering crew finished the clean-up.

Dennis addressed one of his agents. "We'll need to interview all the waiters from the catering company who here last night." To August, he asked, "What caterer did you use?"

"Buona Cucina Catering. It's on Massachusetts Avenue. Just past College Avenue," August said.

Although it seemed obvious, Kendall added, "And interview the women, too. The waitresses."

From the seat in the corner came, "There were no waitresses."

"Of course there were," Kendall said, dismissing the comment.

"No, there were not," Celine said, pushing herself up from her chair and heading toward Kendall. "I hired the caterer for the event last night and I insisted that there be no women. You met my husband. He came on to you. I saw it, too, so don't try to deny it. He can't keep his hands to himself. Didn't your *busy-body sister* tell you that? Everybody else in the city knows it. I insisted no females."

Kendall's eyes focused on the empty space in the middle of the room, as if it could provide an answer. "But there was at least one waitress. I saw her. A couple of times. She was wearing too much fragrance."

"Yes, I remember a waitress," August chimed in.

Kendall headed over to the desk and turned the laptop around. She checked the video feed from earlier in the evening. She found a clear shot taken from a camera on the second floor of the woman carrying a tray full of champagne flutes.

"There! There she is," Kendall said. "Does anyone recognize her?" Everyone said no. She reached into her back pocket and pulled out her cell phone. "I'm going to take a picture of this image, send it to the bureau, and have a tech run it through our facial recognition software. Perhaps we'll get a hit."

"Just what I was thinking," Dennis said.

As she was transmitting it, a uniformed police officer entered the office and whispered into Jefferson's ear. "Agent Dennis, there's been a development," the police detective said. "You're gonna want to know this."

Jefferson and Dennis left the room after giving the underlings instructions on what to do next. Kendall followed them. "What's happening?" she said as she reached Dennis's car on the street in front of the gallery.

"Simmonds's body was just found. He's dead. Shot a couple of times. It's in his art studio-apartment near here. Why don't you come along?"

It was a short ride to a four-story yellow brick building on Senate Avenue. It was a former factory converted into an artist colony for musicians, writers, painters and photographers. Two uniformed police officers stood sentry on either side of the doorway to a top floor studio suite. Inside was a rather large room where the artist must have done most of his work. Officers were busy taking pictures and fingerprinting everything in the studio, which was filled with art supplies alongside paintings and drawings in various stages of completion.

Kendall paid close attention to a couple of the drawings and photos but continued with Dennis and Jefferson into a bedroom just off the studio. Sprawled out on a bed was Hampton, tieless but still in a tux, his open eyes staring blankly at the ceiling. His starched white shirt was marred with two red spots on his chest where he'd been shot.

In the background, Kendall could hear the police officers briefing Dennis and Jefferson as she stared down at the victim. While Hampton Simmonds was still an attractive physical specimen, death took his captivating charm.

"Officers investigating the art theft came to the studio looking for Simmonds," someone said. "They found the door partially open, and upon entering discovered the deceased on the bed. Based on body temperature, the coroner estimated he'd been dead seven or eight hours—since about three or four in the morning. There were no signs of forced entry, so the victim must have known the assailant and let him or her in, or the assailant had a key."

"She was here," Kendall said, still looking at Hampton. "And they were having an affair."

"Pardon?" Dennis said, turning to her.

She walked over to the officers. "Notice the faint smell in the air?" Kendall asked. "It's the same fragrance the waitress wore at the event last night. I noticed it then. Plus, follow me."

They headed back into the studio and over to Hampton's work area. Taped on a board were pictures of the waitress, including several nudes. On a table were sketches of her and some early sketches of his three stolen paintings.

"The missing paintings were of her, the waitress. One of her eyes, one of her breasts. And callipygian," Kendall said.

"Calli-what?" Jefferson asked.

"Callipygian. Look it up. Means having shapely buttocks. The man obviously loved women with big butts," Kendall said. "Typical."

Kendall rubbed her forehead for a moment and then pointed at one of the sketches as she continued. "My guess is the artist helped this woman steal his paintings. Probably for the money. He shut off the security, she took the paintings and stashed them in a car or van, probably parked in back. One or the other of them turned the system back on."

"Who killed him and why?" Dennis said.

"Hard to tell without further evidence. But he was a married man cheating on his wife. That often doesn't end well for the parties involved," Kendall said.

"Yes, but generally not with murder," the detective said.

"True, but if she hated him for cheating . . . it could happen. The wife could have learned of the affair and killed him. Or the mistress could have decided Hampton had outlived his usefulness when all she wanted was his artwork," Kendall said.

Her cell phone beeped and she pulled it out of her jeans pocket. "Yeah, Hunter here. Yeah, hold on a sec." Holding the phone to her ear with her right shoulder, Kendall reached into her back left pocket for a black pad and a small pencil. "Go ahead."

Everyone watched as Kendall grunted and took several pages of notes. She finally ended the call and looked at the notes before she spoke.

"The bureau got a hit off that picture I emailed. Her name is Isabelle Binoche, French-Canadian, thirty-one. Was arrested in Paris six years ago for art forgery with a Frenchman named Jean-Pierre Garnier. She did time, two years. Garnier escaped and is still at large. Interpol is searching for him. Could be anywhere."

Kendall flipped a page and kept reading. "Binoche came to the United States three years ago. Lived in New York, then moved to. . . ." She looked up for effect. "Indianapolis. Two years ago. They have an address. 49th and Washington Boulevard."

"Let's go," Dennis said.

The apartment building where Binoche lived was less than fifteen minutes away. Dennis called ahead and was met there by another car with three FBI agents. Behind the building was a blue truck with white lettering that said Buona Cucina Catering. Two agents entered the back of the building, while Dennis and another agent took the front. Since she did not have her gun, Kendall stood outside.

Five minutes passed before an agent stuck his head out the front of the building and signaled for Kendall to come in. The apartment was messy, evidence of untidy living as opposed to someone having searched the place.

Wearing casual street clothing instead of her waitress pants and white shirt, Binoche was on the floor next to a coffee table, shot once in the head. On the sofa were two of Simmonds's missing pieces—*A Woman's Eyes* and *Bosoms of Love*. An empty picture frame was on the coffee table.

"They must have cut the third painting out of the frame," Dennis remarked.

"*Callipygian* was the best and most valuable of the three," Kendall said.

* * *

Kendall stood next to the coroner's truck. They hadn't yet moved the body from the second-floor apartment, but she'd probably be gone by the time they did. No reason for her to stay. She'd called Kiara to come get her and her sister was waiting in her car.

"Thank you, Special Agent Hunter. Your assistance proved invaluable," Dennis said as he shook her hand.

"No problem." She turned toward Kiara's car.

"I wonder why whoever killed her didn't take all the pieces," Dennis said.

Kendall stopped and turned back. "Difficult to say. But I think there are two main possibilities to track down. One, Celine Simmonds. She can't account for her time last night and their need of money is a good motive. But so is anger. Spousal infidelity can be a powerful motive for murder.

"The other possibility is that someone else killed them. My guess would be Garnier, Binoche's old partner. In any event, Binoche was possibly not the only thief working the gala last night. Someone else probably drove the van. Someone connected with Binoche killed Simmonds out of jealousy or monetary gain, then killed Binoche for the same reason and took the painting.

"Those are the areas of investigation I'd start with," Kendall said.

Dennis opened the passenger side door for her. "Thanks again for all your help."

"I've enjoyed working with you, but I head back to Philadelphia tomorrow. I'm due back in the office on Monday," Kendall said. "Please keep me up-to-date on your investigation. Find the person with the painting and you'll find the person who killed Binoche."

"Won't they get rid of it? Sell it or what-have-you?" Dennis asked.

Kendall shook her head. "It's too hot an item. Certainly right now it is. They can't sell it."

"Maybe it's for a private buyer. They arranged it ahead of time."

"Doubt it. I think the killer wants to keep it for some reason. A souvenir of the killing, perhaps. A reminder," Kendall said, looking at Dennis. "Figure that out and you'll get the painting and the killer."

* * *

Kendall rose early the next morning, wanting to hit the road for her ten-hour drive to Philadelphia. Despite the length, Kendall enjoyed the drive. She drove a convertible and when the top was down, the wind violently whipped her hair. Since her hair was often pulled back off her face into a ponytail when she was working, having it blown about in the wind was a sort of luxury—one her hairdresser repeatedly told her to avoid.

After a light breakfast, Kendall hugged Kiara and Perry and went to the car, putting her purse in the trunk out of sight of her sister.

"Call me when you get in, okay?" Kiara asked.

Kendall nodded and blew one more air kiss to her sister. Then she got in, started the car and drove away without once looking back into the mirror.

It was sunny and just a tad chilly, so Kendall wore long sleeves and rolled them up as it warmed. With her sunglasses on, she looked like a movie star out for a drive.

Even with the top down and the increased drag co-efficient, the BMW had good gas mileage and an incredible range. She was more than four hundred miles from Indianapolis before she stopped for fuel. At the Somerset rest area on the Pennsylvania Turnpike, Kendall pulled up to the gas pump. Despite wind-swept hair and sunglasses, a guy at the next pump offered a flir-tatious smile. She wasn't sure if the smile was for her or her car but she didn't care.

Kendall walked around to the back and opened the trunk. Her credit card and a hair scrunchie were in her purse, and she got them both out. Pulling her hair back into a ponytail, she glanced back down into the trunk. In the furthest reaches was a black shipping tube. She smiled at the tube. Inside it was a souvenir, a remembrance of the trip home.

After getting a suitable frame, Kendall planned to hang *Cal-lipygian* in the walk-in closet in her bedroom. The deadly souvenir would complement her other such remembrances. No one would ever see them because no one ever went into her closet. No one but her.

Kendall fell in love with the painting the moment she saw it, though that wasn't the reason the adulterer and his mistress were dead.

Infidelity, like that committed by her ex, was a powerful mo-tive.

Eyeing the tube again, she smiled and closed the trunk. Ken-dall swiped her credit card, pumped the gas, and got back on the road to Philadelphia.

Hoosier Salon
Stephen Terrell

The **Hoosier Salon** is Indiana's oldest annual juried art exhibition. For more than ninety years, it has served as a showcase for Indiana artists and an outlet for their work.

Ironically, the Hoosier Salon's birthplace is in Chicago. A group of women artists from Indiana, but living in Chicago, formed themselves into the Daughters of Indiana. In 1925 they organized the first Hoosier Salon exhibit at Marshall Fields Department Store in downtown Chicago. Participating artists were required to have lived at some time in Indiana, a requirement that still exists.

Nearly one-third of the original exhibitors were women, an unheard of number for that time. All four living members of the Hoosier Group (T.C. Steele, William Forsyth, Otto Stark, and J. Ottis Adams) exhibited at the inaugural Hoosier Salon, with Covington artist Eugene Savage winning the top merit award for his painting *Recessional*. At the second exhibition, Wayman Adams won top prize for his painting *The Art Jury*, a group portrait of the four surviving members of the Hoosier Group.

After two years, Hoosier Salon Patron's Association was formed. The nonprofit organization still operates the Hoosier Salon. In 1942, the event moved to Indianapolis where it has since been held in various local locations, including the Ayres and Blocks department stores, the Indiana State Museum, and the Indiana Historical Society.

Notable participants include William Victor Higgins of New Mexico's "Taos Ten," *Little Orphan Annie* cartoonist Harold Gray, and *Abe Martin* creator Frank McKinney "Kin" Hubbard. Recent artists have included K. P. Singh, Floyd Hopper, Nancy Noel, and Martha Slaymaker.

The Hoosier Salon now operates year-round galleries in Carmel and New Harmony.

Sketches in Black on White

C. L. Shore

January 21, 1991

New decade, new suit, new city, new digs. My sister helped me find this apartment. It's in a part of Indianapolis that used to be pretty swank, but it isn't now. I can afford it, that's the main thing. Definitely more space than I've had for the last twenty-plus years. More privacy, too. And I can catch the bus in front of the building. You can't say that about every place in Indy.

I actually had a few household things my sister's been storing for me all this time. She's had the space since she inherited the parental home. I took my cut in cash. Guess she deserves the house, and she needs it more than I do, with three kids and two dogs. Oh yeah, and a husband. He and I never got along very well. In the new lingo, I didn't see male bonding in our future.

But, thanks to Sis, I have a settee, a chrome table, and two chairs, and what they used to call a hi-fi that still plays the twenty vinyl albums I own that didn't warp. And a couple of wall clocks that even tell time. Heck, I'm domesticated. But I need a bed. Sis lent me an air mattress and a sleeping bag. It'll keep me warm 'til twenty below, so I'm set even if the heat goes out in this fourth floor walk-up.

My location on Meridian Street is not far from the Herron School of Art building. They're thinking of moving the school, I hear. What a crying shame that would be. I loved the old place, the studios up on the third floor letting in the natural light, the smell of paint thinner when you walked in the door. If I hadn't been drafted, who knows, maybe I'd be an artist today.

For the last couple of decades I've been limited to pencil on dime-store sketch pads my sister sent me. And now, charcoal. There was a box of sketching charcoal in my stash of things in storage. I'll start trying to reacquaint myself with it, practice a little here and there.

Tonight, I'm going to enjoy peace and quiet. No yelling down the block. No clanging metal doors. A leaky faucet? Not gonna bother me.

January 28, 1991

Finally got around to walking to Herron School of Art. It was quite a walk in the cold, but I'm in pretty good shape. The smell of paint thinner and linseed oil greeted me when I opened the door, just like it did decades ago. I breathed deep and started coughing. Too many unfiltered cigarettes over the years. Some of the kids walking back and forth on the first floor turned and looked. One stared.

The aroma brought back memories and I wasn't gonna let a punk kid spoil it.

I took a drawing class back in the day. Wasn't thinking of a career in art, but just taking the class for fun my freshman year. Then I got drafted, and spent the next few years in Nam after becoming an Army medic. I picked the role because of the relatively long training, hoping the war would be over by the time I finished it. No such luck. I was never in battle but saw the bloody messes afterward and heard horror-filled stories that made my skin crawl. I still can't believe I was medically discharged. Army doc said I would go psycho and harm myself or others if I stayed in. Not true, but I was glad to get stateside. I looked up some guys I knew in basic training. A few of them were back home, too.

A few of us vets moved to Philly together. I learned a little about crime there. I guess you could say it was a crime school with an internship. We all had jobs, but we dabbled in drugs and stolen cars. I didn't get arrested until I moved back to Indy and a simple car heist went south. I'd earned myself a multiple year stint at a lakeside resort, one without a view. But I did get a degree, courtesy of the state. BA in General Studies. Maybe someone will overlook my record now and hire me. Ha!

I took the stairs up to Herron's third floor where the sketching studios were. All of the doors were closed. Class was probably in session. Probably naked women behind a couple of those doors. Might be worth it to scrape up tuition money just to look at those women. A buzzer went off, doors opened, and the halls were filled with people, young kids mostly. Like on the first floor, I attracted a couple of stares. Did I look that bad, that old? The idea was depressing. I headed home. Maybe I'd come back another day.

January 29, 1991

They say the sense of smell is closely tied to memory, and I think that's true. The aroma of paint thinner took me back to the more innocent self I'd abandoned long ago. I'd slept a deep sleep with many dreams. Most I don't remember, but in one, I dreamt about being in art class, a sketching class, and drawing a hot girl named Lorraine. In real life she'd been in my class and sat next to me while we sketched the nude models in front of us. It came back to me, how her face and the body of one of the models became the headline feature of my late adolescent dreams. Lorraine appeared engrossed, studious, and even business-like in our classes together; but my dreams, then and now, were far from studious. I woke up in a cold sweat.

I'd forgotten about Lorraine after I'd been drafted. But now I saw her in vivid color, even texture and smell. I remembered her face: it was heart-shaped, which was considered the ideal back then. Her hair was a light brown, almost blonde, and fluffy. She wore it pinned back from her face, drawing attention to her hazel eyes and her perfect mouth. I'd fantasized about messing up her shiny pink lip gloss. She had great legs and wore her skirts on the short side. She was an art student as well, as I remember. I think her specialty was sculpture.

I shook my head and stumbled to the kitchen, searching for the blue can of Maxwell House. I'd make a full pot. One thing about life on the outside, I had my own kitchen and could drink as much coffee as I wanted. I plugged in the percolator and headed to the bathroom to shave and shower while it was brewing. So far, I'd never run out of hot water. Another blessing, something many people take for granted.

After a couple cups of joe and a stale donut from the grocery store, I found my box of charcoal and a cheap, but decent sketch pad I'd bought at a Walmart. I started to draw Lorraine's face. I worked on it for about thirty minutes, and the developing picture looked pretty good, I thought. I'd captured her innocent look, the spacing of her eyes, and her fluffy hair. Her eyes looked directly at me. I decided to set it aside and continue to work on it later.

I needed to put a few bills in the mail, so I got my jacket and walked the four blocks to deposit them. When I reentered the lobby, an old man was struggling to keep a hold on his groceries while opening his mailbox.

"Here, let me help," I said. I caught the bag just as it slipped out of his hands. Everything stayed within the brown paper except a tube of toothpaste. I picked it up and put it back on top. "Why don't you throw your mail on the top of the sack, then you'll only have one thing to carry?"

"I will. Thanks, young man." He took his brown paper sack and headed up the stairs. It looked like he was having trouble. I caught up with him in three steps. "Here, I'll carry this to your apartment. You'll have both hands free for the key."

"Okay," he said as he continued to climb. "I'm glad my place is on the second floor. Don't know how long I'll be able to live here, though. Probably will need a place with an elevator soon. Or an apartment on ground level." He found his keys and fumbled a minute before he found the right one. "Come on in. You can put the stuff on the table, there."

His apartment had a different floor plan than mine. His was larger. We entered a dining room, which my smaller apartment lacked. His living room was bigger, too, with a nice window looking out on Meridian Street. My living room faced a littered alley and the dull windows and bricks of another apartment building about thirty feet away.

I put the sack on the dining room table. It looked to be a nice piece of furniture and had six matching chairs. His sofa was in good shape, too. Kind of odd. In this building. I suspected most tenants probably had Goodwill-type furnishings, like mine.

"Well, thanks," he said after catching his breath. "Name's Sam. Sam McCutcheon."

For some reason, I didn't want to give him my last name. "I'm Max," I said. "New guy, fourth floor. Seems a nice place."

Sam shrugged. "It's okay. I used to have a home in Meridian Hills. But I moved here when I could no longer drive. I like to be close to the School of Art."

"Really?"

"Yes, I used to teach there. Sculpture. But can't do it anymore. Requires a fair amount of physical strength. And a studio. I had one for a while at Herron, even after retiring. Professor Emeritus, you know. But like I said, I no longer can do it. Sometimes I sketch a little."

I looked at the pictures on the walls. They were actually photos. Photos of sculptures. "Are these pictures of your work?" I asked.

"Yes." The old man backed up to a recliner and sat down.

I took a quick look around. There was a male nude in one, a soldier in another. A female nude in the third. She had a heart shaped face. *Lorraine.* I could feel my heart rate double. I'm good at the poker face, though.

"Well, nice to meet you," I said. "I've gotta run. Stuff to do." I needed to get back to my own place and ponder these new facts about my neighbor. It seemed almost spooky. I mean, I'd just been thinking about Lorraine, and I'd been handed a connection to her. Seemed like fate the more I thought about it.

It was eleven thirty and I was hungry. I heated up a can of chili on the stove and wolfed down every last bean. Then I went back to work on my charcoal sketch of Lorraine. After finishing the portrait, I started another sketch, a full-body view this time, based on the photo I'd seen downstairs. It was like I was inspired to take back Lorraine. Take her back from the old man. Maybe I should say *older* man. I mean, I'm no spring chicken, but I can walk up four flights of stairs without getting winded.

January 31, 1991

For the third day in a row, I awoke thinking about that heart-shaped face. Had it changed over the last twenty years? Would she remember me? I needed to stop this obsession with a memory. After clearing my mind of Lorraine's image, I looked at the square of sky visible from my bedroom window. Clouds gave it a dark gray appearance and tree branches whipped back and forth. A good day to stay inside. Maybe a good day to sketch. If I could get her face right maybe I could exorcise this obsession. Or maybe I could find her, make contact with her. Maybe the old man could tell me about Lorraine's whereabouts. At least give me a clue. Then I made a plan.

I pulled on a sweatshirt and jeans and started the percolator. In spite of the weather, I made a brief neighborhood run, north of 38th Street. I passed a hardware store just beyond the intersection. Good to know it was there, but I was going to try my luck at a resale consignment shop I spotted right across the street. I found what I wanted, a four-cup and a two-cup thermos. A buck each.

I made the purchases and jogged back home through the wicked, damp wind. I'd only been gone eleven minutes. I washed both thermoses at the sink. Poured myself a cup of coffee, filled the larger thermos for refills during the day. I'd take the smaller one downstairs to the professor. I wasn't sure if he was a coffee drinker, but I'd bet he was.

I knocked on the door. There was a delay and I heard shuffling. After a minute, the door opened. The prof appeared wearing wrinkled pants, a dingy white shirt, and a cardigan. His sweater had dried stuff on it, looked like oatmeal. I wondered if he'd slept in his clothes in his recliner.

"Oh, hello neighbor," he said. "How are you?"

"I brought some coffee." I hoisted the thermos. "Can I interest you in a cup? I thought we could talk about art. One thing I didn't tell you a couple of days ago. I was an art student at Herron for one semester. Until I joined the Vietnam War effort."

His eyes widened. "You don't say! Well, come in! Never thought I'd meet an art student in this building." He backed up from the door, shuffling his feet in reverse. "I do drink coffee, although I prefer tea. Or whiskey. A little early in the day for whiskey, though." He started to laugh, but ended up coughing. "But as long as I have sugar on hand, I'll drink coffee." He pivoted and started shuffling forward this time, toward the kitchen.

I expected to see him locate sugar in a bowl, but he struggled with a five-pound bag of the stuff, bringing it down from a cupboard. After rummaging through two drawers he located a spoon. He took two teacups from a shelf and I poured coffee into each. He loaded two heaping spoons of sugar into his cup, stirred, then sipped.

"Ah," he said. "Been a while since I've had coffee that tasted this fresh. I could get used to it." He moved a pile of envelopes to one side of the dining table, clearing a place for the cups. I kept my eye on the one with the sugar because I didn't want it placed in front of me. "Here, have a seat. We can talk about Herron. Whose classes were you in?" He pulled out the chair closest to the kitchen.

I sat and took a tentative sip. I had the right cup. "You know, I can't remember my teacher's name. It was a beginning drawing class. He was a tall, skinny guy. This would've been the fall of 1970."

The prof considered this as he sipped more coffee. "Probably Reasonor. He taught beginning drawing and painting then."

"Sounds familiar. I only took the one art class. And English 101. Art, because I thought I might want to pursue it as a major. English, because it was required for all freshmen." I set my cup down. "But I was drafted. Couldn't say I minded too much. Getting a degree as a part-time student just seemed like that could go on forever."

"Yes. Yes. I guess it could seem so, particularly to a young man."

I was relieved the prof didn't bring up the GI bill, or what I'd done after the service. "Anyhow," I began. "I think I recognize the model in one of your sculptures." I gestured toward the living room. "The woman, there. I think her name was Lorraine."

"You have an impressive memory, Max. Yes, her name was Lorraine. Lorraine Yoder. Came from the Berne area, Mennonite stock, but I think her family had left the fold. She was the stereotypical pure and innocent farm girl . . . until she came to my class, that is. Earned part of her tuition by modeling for me privately." He sat back and started laughing. A small, high-pitched, weaselly laugh. Not meant for my benefit. "Lorraine really earned her tuition." He sat back wearing a satisfied look and brought the teacup to his lips. "Those were the days. Great job with satisfying benefits, if you know what I mean."

I wanted to leap from my chair and grab him by the throat. I knew what he meant—sexual harassment. Abuse of authority. With a strong display of willpower I didn't know I possessed, I remained in my chair and concentrated on maintaining a neutral expression. A blank canvas.

"The times have changed," I said, after I trusted myself to speak.

"Oh, yeah." The old man sighed. His more serious expression returned. "She was a lovely girl, a lovely girl."

My original plan was to suggest we could do some sketching together. Now, I couldn't stand being in the same room with the man. My cup was empty. I stood.

"Well, I hope you enjoyed the coffee. Maybe I'll come back with more, the next cold, windy morning we have."

"Thank you, Max. You're thoughtful. The coffee was good, as was the conversation."

Well, that's your opinion. I picked up the thermos and let myself out of the apartment. When I climbed the stairs to my own place, I paced my small living room for at least a half hour. The nerve of the guy, the nerve. . . . He was a dirty old man, pure and simple. I couldn't let go of my need for some kind of retaliation. He couldn't get away with something like that. It wasn't right. He'd made it clear he didn't have any regret. He needed to pay. Pay up.

A new plan started to take shape. Hazy at best. I needed to do a little legwork first. I bounded down the stairs to street level and walked to the nearest bus stop. After studying the sign, I mentally sketched a schedule for the following day. I'd head to the downtown commuter campus of the state university. I might have to walk around a little, but I think I could get enough information to put my plan into action. After walking back upstairs to my own place, I realized I was hungry. It was noon, and all I'd consumed so far was three cups of coffee. I opened two cans of Campbell's chicken noodle soup and dumped them into a pot.

February 1, 1991

I was at the bus stop at nine the next morning and boarded a southbound bus within five minutes. I got off seven stops later and walked four blocks to the medical school library. I easily found the toxicology section, located a couple of textbooks, and made a few notes in my sketchbook. I looked at my watch. Only ten-thirty, and I had enough background information to make my phone call.

A woman's voice answered. "Poison Control. How can I help you?"

"My name's Jeffrey Black," I began, using the author's name from the textbook in front of me. I consulted the list of notes I'd made while I told her my story. I was concerned about an uncle who'd started to develop a tremor. He'd taken up gardening the previous spring. The tremor became more pronounced. Were any of his fertilizers or insecticides contributing to his problem? The symptoms had peaked around September, but were less obvious now. What should I look for in his garden shed?

The woman was extremely helpful naming several specific products I should be watching for. I'd accomplished everything on my list. At least, everything on my campus list. I still had one more errand to run.

I retraced my route and took the return bus back to north Meridian. I decided to complete my last task before returning to my apartment. I crossed 38th Street and walked two blocks to the hardware store. I found two products mentioned by my Poison Control advisor.

"Getting a head start on the gardening this year, eh?" the mustached cashier asked.

"You bet," I said. "I'm hearing that the groundhog won't see his shadow this year. Early spring."

"Hope you're right. An early spring would be good for business."

I thought of one more item and stopped at the convenience store on the corner, where I bought a tube of toothpaste.

Once back in the apartment, I threw my purchases onto the kitchen counter and collapsed into a chair. Tomorrow, I'd put the plan into action.

February 2, 1991

The sun was hiding on Groundhog Day. I put on the coffee pot and poured four cups of the brew into the large thermos. I added a powder concocted from my purchases of the day before. Then I added water to what was left of the dry powder. I took the toothpaste and squirted out a small amount into the sink. Then I took my solution and used a straw to transfer it into the tube. I kneaded it a little, but didn't want it to look too manhandled. I put the toothpaste into my inner jacket pocket and picked up the thermos before heading downstairs.

After I knocked, I heard the shuffling before the door opened. "Max! I was hoping you'd come back. Do you have any more of the good coffee?"

"Indeed I do." I hoisted the thermos. "May I come in?"

"Of course, of course. I'll get the cups."

It looked like the same cups we'd used were waiting further use in the dish drainer. He brought them to the table. This time he placed a sugar bowl in the center of the table cloth.

I poured from the thermos into the two cups, the prof's cup close to the brim, my own less than half full. "I've already had two cups this morning," I explained.

We took the same chairs we'd used two days ago. "You know," the prof began, "After you left, I kept thinking about Lorraine Yoder. I think she's married now, of course, and teaches art at Wayne Township. High school."

"Is that right?" I felt my heart beat a little faster. I hadn't even considered whether it would be possible to find Lorraine, although he'd mentioned her maiden name—Yoder. "How did you find out?"

"Well, she did graduate. The school keeps track of their alumni."

Interesting. *Maybe I could find her, too.* I wanted to ask if he'd tried to track her down, but couldn't bring myself to do it. I didn't think I could handle it if he answered yes.

"Do you mind if I use your bathroom?" I asked. "All of a sudden, this coffee's running right through me."

"Sure." The prof said between sips. He gestured with his thumb, behind him. "Just down the hall to the right."

I turned on the light and ran water into the sink to cover the sound of opening the medicine cabinet. Sure enough, his toothpaste lay inside on a shelf. I removed the tube from my jacket pocket, and pressed on it here and there to make it look like the one I removed from the shelf. I put the professor's tube in my pocket. Then I flushed and returned to the dining room.

"Well, about this Lorraine . . . were you in love with her?" I sat down again.

"Nah. I was married at the time. Lorraine was just a flirtation, an amusement."

"Is that how she looked at it? Your relationship, I mean."

"I don't know. She didn't seem to mind, I guess," he said.

Was that any way to treat a woman like Loraine? "Seems like she stands out to you, though. You haven't forgotten her."

"She was a beauty. And the sculpture of her was some of my best work. I thought so, and my critics thought the same."

"Would you say you owe her something? Lorraine, I mean."

"No. She was paid. I didn't owe her anything more."

Really. "Well, I'd best be going." I stood. "Keep the coffee. You can enjoy it the rest of the afternoon. I'll come back and get the thermos later."

"Okay." The old man didn't make a move to get up. "Thanks."

February 3, 1991

The prof was still alive the next morning. I went to the lobby to get my mail and saw him standing there. I didn't want to talk to him, but I didn't need to worry. "Oh! I gotta run," he said, and scuttled out the door. I saw a yellow taxi waiting at the curb.

The Poison Control lady said the effects of the garden substances would accumulate over time. I'd carried out my plan and decided not to change anything. But I experienced a few seconds of panic when I got back to my room. What if McCutcheon was going to a doctor who would pinpoint the exact substances? I realized the thought was close to ridiculous, and got out my charcoal and sketchbook. I looked over the six I'd drawn so far. I'd started with a sketch based on the photo of Lorraine on the prof's wall. I added more sketches of the same pose, but from different angles, constructed in my mind's eye.

February 12, 1991

An ambulance with a stretcher pulled up yesterday. I saw the attendants on the sidewalk, but they weren't rushing. I sighed. It was over. I would keep my distance. Sooner or later, I'd hear who found him and the circumstances.

The prof's obit made today's paper and it was a long one. A lot about his career. His wife's name was Martha and she'd been dead for six years. I felt sorry for the woman, God rest her soul. A daughter and a married son survived him. Funeral would take place on Valentine's Day at a downtown church with interment at Crown Hill cemetery.

I resolved to go to the graveside service. For one thing, I could take the bus to Crown Hill. The cemetery was a beautiful and historic place. James Whitcomb Riley has a picturesque tomb on the crest of a hill. In high school, my buddies and I dared each other to stand on Dillinger's grave on Halloween night. Yes, I'd go.

February 14, 1991
About an inch of snow fell before dawn. I put on my new suit and the coat I'd bought at the consignment store and headed for Crown Hill. I allowed myself enough time to find the grave. Crown Hill Cemetery is a big place. I discovered they had an office, and a helpful person pointed me in the direction. I timed my arrival just about right—the pallbearers were carrying a stainless steel coffin to the gravesite as I approached.

A dozen people clustered under the canopy. Two women and a man sat in folding chairs nearest the grave, the rest gathered behind. Everyone was wearing a black or gray coat. Even the pine tree needles sticking out from under the snow looked more gray than green. It occurred to me a black-and-white sketch of the scene would look no different than a color photograph.

A man stood near the grave and read a few Bible verses. He gave a final blessing, and it was over. The people standing near the grave began to turn around.

A woman wearing a black beret caught my eye. It was the scarf around her neck, and a pin attached to her lapel that got my attention. Both were bright red, welcome dots of color. Her hair was loose and was graying, now a faded brown. She'd combed it back from her face, and her beret held it in place. The face was heart-shaped. *Lorraine.* In spite of the years, her eyes held the same intensity I remembered.

I closed the distance between us in four steps. "Lorraine? Hi, I'm Max. I sat next to you once in a sketching class. Years ago.

Freshman year. 1970, actually. You probably don't remember me."

I could see her eyes retreat for a second while she searched for a connection to the name. "Max! I do remember you. You were so shy."

"Well, you know what they say. Have to watch out for those quiet ones."

She laughed.

"So, you were close to the professor?" I asked before her laughter ended.

She looked down and shook her head before meeting my eyes again. "No, I wouldn't put it that way, exactly. But I did learn a lot from him. I came today for a sort of closure."

Closure. I liked that new lingo.

"Life treat you well, Lorraine?"

Her smile returned. "Yes. A beautiful family, a chance to teach art to talented students, and a few commissioned sculptures around the city. How about you?"

I lied to her, of course, and watched her walk away toward the line of parked cars.

Robert Indiana (1928-)
Stephen Terrell

Robert Indiana was born Robert Clark in 1928 in New Castle. Early on, teachers recognized his artistic talent. In 1942, he graduated from Arsenal Technical High School in Indianapolis. Despite later adopting his home state's name, Robert's education was anything but provincial. After three years in the Air Force, he studied at the Art Institute of Chicago, the Skowhegan School of Sculpture and Painting in Maine, and the Edinburgh College of Art in Scotland.

In the mid-1950s, Robert Clark joined the hotbed of modern American art in New York City. When he found too many other artists named Clark, he changed his name to that of his native state, and Robert Indiana was born. Within a decade, he drew recognition as a rising star in the arts, working with various media and dramatically using numbers and short impactful words at the center of his work. In 1964 he was commissioned to create a twenty-foot electrified "EAT" sign for the 1964 New York World's Fair.

In 1965, his LOVE painting was selected by the New York Museum of Modern Art for their Christmas card. As they say, the rest is history. In modern jargon, LOVE quickly went viral, even appearing on a best-selling U.S. postage stamp. The Indianapolis Museum of Art purchased one of Indiana's LOVE paintings in 1967, and later acquired his 1970 LOVE statue, which graces the IMA grounds and is the most recognized piece in IMA's collection.

Robert Indiana's work is now displayed in dozens of museums throughout the United States and around the world, as well as in numerous private collections. In a 2014 article, he said that he felt ignored by the art world after the overwhelming success of the LOVE paintings, prints and sculpture. In 1978, he moved from New York City to Vinalhaven, a remote island in Maine, where he still resides.

James Dean and Me, Martha
Sherita Saffer Campbell

I was gliding along on my skis, riding on the tiptop of the waves as they rolled up high on their way to shore. No panic, no fear. I had never felt so free. It was like flying. I felt something slide down my leg like the softest touch of a breeze, or like fish when they slide down a part of your skin trying to nibble and see what kind of food you are. Then it was soft, finger-like tendrils, and they began to move slowly upward, soft tiny nibbles moving up my body, tasting. Then little flicks of tongue.

Damn, was it a fish or a snapping turtle? Then it reached my waist. Damn, that wasn't a fish!

"Holy shit!" I struggled for air. Tried to move my arms in a butterfly movement to reach the water's surface, fighting with everything I could muster.

"Hey, surfer girl, take it easy. You are in the shallows."

I felt heavy breathing and the faint smell of Artemis, which began to stir my senses a bit. "What the hell? Dear God!" I fell back against the pillows. "James Dean, it *is* you. Really you. It's not a dream."

"You bet your sweet life it isn't."

I looked up at him as he looked down at me—he apparently was well on the way to the top. "It's morning, isn't it?" Then came a long thoughtful kiss.

"You bet your sweet you-know-what it is."

We kissed again. It had been a long time since I had a kiss like that.

I opened my eyes wide, pulled him tighter. He didn't seem to mind. We sort of collapsed together. I could barely breathe. I wondered if he needed a nitroglycerin tablet. He raised an eyebrow. "No, do you?"

I just smiled.

"Been a while, hasn't it?"

"For me or you?" I asked.

"A lady never asks," he said, giving that wicked smile.

"Neither does a gentleman."

"Then I gather neither one of us is a lady or a gentleman." There was another slow and very tender kiss. I looked at him for a long time. He slowly moved to his pillow then looked at me for a while.

"I'd offer you a cigarette, but I can't smoke anymore."

"Me either. You make a good whiskey sour. It's an art form if you can do that."

"You know I'd rather have a comment on my studly behavior than my drink making abilities." He handed me a Lifesaver pack.

I took it. "My breath bad?"

"No, just if you unwrap it slowly, it takes the place of a cigarette."

I started laughing, and unwrapped the Lifesaver. Strong mint.

He pointed across the room. "Shower."

I stretched and headed to the bathroom. He followed. We hit the shower almost together after a pit stop. Two toilets, small glass panel between. He was a cad. A well prepared cad. And a nice one, I thought, as we stepped into the spray. The shower was up-to-date James Bond, but advanced James Bond. It even had a comfortable seat, which came in handy. The shower was warm, bordering on boiling. The soap was probably mixed by elves in a magic woods in a secret garden. We stepped out of the fragrant rain forest, and he held up a fluffy white robe. Honey, I mean fluffy terry cloth robe. He held both doors open and pointed me to a small glassed-in breakfast room.

Someone was there. A butler? Servant? I had no idea. "What will you have ma'am?"

Isaac, I thought. *Isaac.*

"How about a veggie omelet?"

Isaac looked me in the eye. "Good choice," he said as he looked at my chubby little self.

Gay, I thought.

"No, I am not. Just psychic," he said as he disappeared into the kitchen.

I could smell the food as he brought it in. I devoured it without looking up. Drank the orange juice. Fresh squeezed, of course.

"Dessert?" Dean asked, his hand on a bell.

Good Lord. Was I dreaming my secret desire? "I think I had it already."

He choked on his juice. "Then I suggest coffee and a meeting of our minds about our respective lives and desires."

Good Lord, I thought, as Jeeves—no, Isaac—poured my coffee and set down a small pitcher of whole cream and diet liquid sugar. I looked at Isaac. He smiled evilly. I was beginning to like ole Jeeves/Isaac. He laughed this time.

"I want to make you a proposition," Dean said.

I sat down my cup. Gave him a long, hard look. "I thought you already did."

"Not unless you think I'm going to pimp you out or. . . ."

"Or I'm pimping you out," I said.

"That's settled. I need a business associate."

I raised my eyebrows. "What kind of business?" I don't know why I asked, if it meant time with him.

"I am sort of in the same kind of business you are, sort of. . . ."

"And which business would that be?"

"Well it's hard to define. I do research. And I write . . . articles, after I do research."

"As do I."

Isaac came back carrying an Indiana's Hollywood version of a French phone. I raised an eyebrow. He shrugged.

My cell phone rang.

"I have to go," Dean and I said at the same time.

I jumped in my car, headed to a designated drive-in, pulled in and ordered a Coke.

The deep voice that seemed to control too many minutes of my old-aged life, spoke.

"The art studio at the Oaktree Crossing. They need students who want to learn to paint and be in their show later on. Be there. Twenty minutes ago."

"But. . . ."

"I understand you were busy last night and might be tired, but you could use some art instruction."

"Listen you. . . ."

He hung up.

I wanted to rip the phone apart when it rang again. It was he-who-knows-all again.

"You know where it is. You should be driving there now instead of talking and looking at the road."

"You. . . ."

But he hung up with, "Tsk, tsk."

I looked around, saw nothing, heard the passenger door close, no person in sight, but a complete paint case was lying on the seat with a thermos. I looked around. Not a creature was stirring. I picked up the thermos, opened it, and smelled the contents. Whisky Sour. My drink of choice since ninth grade. Closed the lid. "How the hell did . . . ?"

My check came. I looked around. A car left. My Coke came. I sipped it slowly as I backed out of the parking space and headed to the gallery.

When I walked in, the attendant nodded at me and I went to the station with my name on it.

"We reserved it as soon as your assistant called. He gave us your name and needs, charged to your account of course," she said.

I smiled. Of course.

"Thank you," I said. Mentally, I understood how Alice felt when she fell down that rabbit hole.

There was a canvas before me and I stared at it for a minute, picked up the brush and paint palette, and began to paint what I always painted when I was disturbed or looking for an answer. I swished my brush in the dark green and began to make tiny leaves. I felt Dean pass behind me rather than saw him. Surprised he used the same gallery I did as I'd never seen him here before. Maybe it was the first time for him. Maybe he had been following me longer than I thought. Maybe I was crazy. But, why, if he was a regular, had I not noticed him before? Not too many people knew about this gallery. You had to turn off the highway, chug down this squiggly road, and park beside a faded wood and glass building that appeared to be hiding in a magic grass circle surrounded by woods. It concealed the budding and professional artists within from the view of glaring strangers. And from the view of all the cars buzzing down the highway. Maybe we artists were indecent.

Then the thoughts quieted down, my brain switched to another channel, and I began to paint green leaves—teeny tiny leaves, middle-sized leaves, and bigger leaves. I mixed paint on my palette with diverse shades of green and brown contrasts, starting wrongly from the top instead of letting the tree grow from the roots through the trunk. I felt the breeze and the wind blowing through the forest enter my mind and body and whisper softly to my soul as the tree grew and covered my canvas. I was standing in the forest as I continued to paint, and as I changed colors and shading, I smelled the musty odor of herbs and flowers growing around my tree. Heard the birds. And felt the wolves walking over crushed leaves. I sensed, as I always did, the shadow behind me. Then I started to scream but only squeaked.

A hand touched my shoulder and some place my cell phone was ringing. I turned around, tears running down my cheeks. Jimmy, eyebrows raised, pulled me to him.

"That must be some tree you're painting."

"Rendezvous at road park, now."

Jimmy gave me a hug. "Forgot I have a damn board meeting. See you later."

He almost ran to the door. I cleaned my paints carefully. Placed everything in its place then beat it out the door. Watched Jimmy head for his car, then watched him leave as I sprinted for my car. Turned the lights so they would not switch on automatically, and drove toward the road park.

Jimmy flew down the highway. I followed. We had to be going to the same place. We pulled into the park, him first, me in the shadows of the shelter. I shut off the engine and coasted, then parked.

He got out of his car and walked toward a bunch of trees.

I slid out my door and closed it without a click. Carrying my purse, I reached my hand inside and rested it on the gun. A man walked out from under a big maple, and he had a gun pointed at Jimmy. I pulled my gun out and shot the same time Jimmy did.

Both shots hit the man. I ran ahead and dropped to my knees and checked. He was dead.

"What the hell?" Jimmy asked as I opened my switchblade. Jimmy got there as I was digging out the bullet. I placed a spent bullet from an old crime scene in the wound. Jimmy did the same. I hid our bullet casings in a tampon carton. We pulled our gloves off, slipped them into my secret pocket, and I said a prayer to Saint Anthony as five unmarked cars pulled up.

I turned on the tears as a plain-clothes detective got out of the car. "He was trying to rob us. He shot at Jimmy."

The detective took the gun out of my hand. Another started to read the infamous Miranda as he looked at Jimmy and me. I don't think he could read the Miranda to Jimmy with a straight face, so I was going to get the full treatment to ease his confusion. *How do you read the Miranda to someone who is supposed to be dead?* I thought.

"Don't you understand she's with me? She's one of us," Jimmy said.

"Shall we adjourn this little meeting, lady and gentleman? To your diner, James?"

We went to the diner and straight to Jimmy's office, the back way, with special parking and all. I had reached into my pocket and flipped on my recorder. After all, someone on my side needed to have an idea where I was. I still didn't know how I got into these messes.

Jimmy explained everything. The Captain just listened and watched me like I was going to fly away. The lieutenant took notes.

"Comments? Anyone?" the Captain said.

"No, sir," I said.

Jimmy said the same.

"It took me a while to get a report on you ma'am. Any comment on that, ma'am?"

"No, sir."

"Like why you don't officially exist?"

"No, sir."

"Or why you used to exist? Or knew that was a drug drop? Or that that art studio was somehow a drop in some way I or anyone else can't fathom?"

The Captain looked at me, at Jimmy, waiting.

"We have been watching that gallery, studio, as a possible drug drop," he added.

We both nodded.

He stared and drummed his fingers. His phone rang. He glared at us. Then said, "Yes, sir. Right away, sir." He hung up. "Could you men step outside for a minute?" he asked the detectives. They looked a little surprised, but left.

"Could I see the cards now?" the Captain said to us.

Jimmy and I looked at each other, reached into our billfolds, and handed him our pretty charge cards. He looked at them, turned them over, reached into his pocket, pulled out a lighter and held our cards one by one over the flame until the Agency's symbol popped into view. He flipped the lighter shut and gave the cards back.

"Okay. We've been checking that damn studio for months. Could never find anything. Where was it? In the paint?"

"That was my first choice," Jimmy said. "But, it's in the frames. They sell the paintings to certain buyers. Who. . . ."

"Sell it on the street," I said.

"They said I could ask why . . . both of you . . . why?"

"Why I do this?" I asked. "I had a son. Someone introduced him to drugs. I found him after a long search. But I didn't get there in time. He was dying. I made a pledge as he died. Whatever it took, I would find the sons of bitches."

"And did you? Find them?"

"It took a while. But I did."

"And?"

"I shot them all. The whole bunch. Hunted them down. Like mad dogs. Killed everyone I could. With a .22 rifle when I couldn't get close enough to use a German Luger."

"And?"

"They caught me, of course. Offered me a deal. Work for them or go to prison. It was a no-brainer. I went to work for them."

There was silence. He looked at Jimmy.

"I wasn't driving my car that evening everyone thought I died. My friend was and he was higher than a kite. He wrecked. I climbed out. Slept it off in a cheap motel. I thought no one saw me, but it was reported in the papers that someone was seen running away from the crash. The Feds found me. Offered me a chance for a new life with a mission. I took it."

The lieutenant walked in. "Their rides are here."

We got up and walked to the door. Jimmy and I shook hands with the Captain. We rambled to his new car and new assignment. There was a long silence.

Then he said, "And?"

"And what?" I asked.

"Why do you always paint trees with all those tiny individual leaves?"

"Every little leaf stands for a kid who died or whose life was ruined by drugs. If you look closely, you'll find a red circle on some."

He raised his eyebrows and looked at me very hard. Like he knew he was going to hear something a little weird.

"The leaves with the red dots are for the pushers I shot."

Then I walked to my new car. My driver told me the house had been cleaned out. All traces of me erased. He handed me a new identity.

"Your new paint supplies and canvas are in the trunk," he said. I knew he was watching for any reaction.

"Thank you," was all I said. I sat in silence while he explained my next assignment.

All I asked was, "Will Jimmy be there?"

The Richmond Artists Group
N. W. Campbell

In 1870, a group of largely self-taught artists came together in Richmond, Indiana, to form the Ramblers' Sketch Club, later the **Richmond Art Group**. Richmond's rapid development from a pioneer community to a center of industry and commerce attracted many artisans—architects, pattern-makers, printers, builders, interior decorators, stone masons, and mechanics. Many were attracted to the *en plein air*, or outdoor, practice of sketching landscapes and nature scenes, a movement that developed in France at the Barbizon colony during the 1830s.

The Ramblers camped on weekends and holidays to sketch, paint, encourage one another in their work, and share music and entertainment. Many were Quakers who, unlike others of their faith who saw the visual arts as frivolous, embraced their talent and sought outlets for its expression. The establishment of Earlham College's arts department led many Ramblers to seek formal arts training and to develop their skills as painters. They developed a distinctive impressionistic style that Ella Bond Johnston would show off to Indiana and the nation in the first of several Richmond Art Association traveling exhibitions in 1910.

John Elwood Bundy, a North Carolina Quaker by birth, is considered by many to have been the most influential leader of the group. Bundy's work is widely exhibited in the US and abroad. With him was the sketch artist and painter Marcus Mote, who lobbied the Indiana legislature tirelessly to have arts education included in the public school curriculum.

Shaun Thomas Dingwerth's *The Richmond Group Artists* (Indiana University Press, 2014) is recommended reading. Works by Richmond Group artists are on public display locally at the Indianapolis Museum of Art and the Richmond Art Museum.

The Presumption of Value

B. K. Hart

Felicity stretched from her place on the step stool, reached across her mantle, and finished the last few wipes with her dust rag. Outside, the engine of her half-sister's sports car revved as it made its way down the drive, past Felicity's cottage, and up to the main house. Constance, the perpetually tardy. The reading of the will was scheduled for ten. It was half past and the estate attorney, Doc Jamison, had arrived nearly an hour ago.

She sighed, lifted her chin, and squared her shoulders. How long could it possibly take? An hour? Then Constance would leave and Felicity might never need to see her again. She could do this. Gramps would expect her to be civil. He called it good breeding. Certainly the Donovans could claim some good genes, but Felicity wasn't sure she could take credit for any of the 'good' part of the breeding. And, what happened to Constance? She was half Donovan, and she sure didn't show much breeding, unless you measured it by the cost of her handbag.

Felicity rubbed her hands down the sides of her grubby jeans, tossed the rag onto her coffee table, and picked up a pair of box cutters, slipping them into the side pocket of her pants. If she remembered, she'd cut some of the pink roses in front of the mansion on her way back to the cottage.

She wandered up the drive to the front entry of the main house, stepping out of the way of auction assistants and holding open the door for two of them as they dragged in more staging equipment. It was disconcerting to think new owners would be taking over the estate now that her grandfather had passed. Still, it was what the old house needed. Certainly deeper pockets than she had to keep up on repairs.

Her sister's agitated voice echoed from the den two doors down on the left. Disturbing. Felicity wished the lawyer had picked a different room, the study perhaps. The den doubled as the TV room and was filled with years of kindness and familiarity. It would now be tainted with the final encounter. Not that

Felicity would be spending any future evenings here, but it was a shame to ruin the memory all the same.

"Finally, Lecia, you'd think you could show up on time, since you live here," Constance said.

"I was here, Connie. Doc told me to come back once you'd arrived so I wouldn't be in the way of the auctioneer."

"You know I hate that name." Constance, pristine in a white tennis skirt, tank top, and matching Puma tennis shoes, turned away from her and started in again on the attorney.

Yes, Felicity did know the nickname was hated, just as Constance knew that Felicity hated being called Lecia.

"I just don't think it's prudent," Constance continued, "that the auctioneers have first rights to paw over the antiques before the will is actually probated. Don't we have any rights as the heirs?"

How convenient. Now, 'we' have a common enemy.

Felicity rolled her eyes and took her usual position in the corner of the leather couch. She turned her attention toward the fireplace, watching the fire crackle and pop as she tuned out her sister's whine. She already knew the contents of the will. They all did. This meeting was a formality. Gramps knew it would be necessary so Constance understood the will was non-negotiable. Felicity expected no surprises.

Twenty minutes later, Constance started in again. Or, more accurately, had never really stopped.

"I understand Grandfather's thinking, it's that I hardly see how this is a fair distribution to his heirs. I get two lousy antiques," Constance said throwing her hands in the air.

"The will stipulates that you get your choice picks of the antiques. The items that hold the most sentimental value to you, I am sure, will be set aside by the auction house and arrangements made to have them delivered," Doc replied, sliding his glasses off to polish the lens with a piece of cloth.

"What if one of the items I have sentimental attachments to is that painting?" Constance said, pointing to a replica of Van Gogh's *The Lovers: The Poets' Garden IV*. The painting was the sole item Felicity had been left in her grandfather's will. *The Lovers* depicted a couple, a man in pale blue clothing with a yellow hat and a woman in a pink shirt with a black skirt. The scenery was lined by a row of green cypress against a pink sky and a pale lemon crescent. With signature Van Gogh flare, the foreground was only a vague landscape sprinkled with sand and thistle.

Doc Jamison pinched the bridge of his nose and took a deep breath. "The instructions are clear. The painting goes to Felicity. You, Constance, may select any two *other* antiques. A small cash bequeath is to be delivered to several small charities and the remaining proceeds and estate grounds are being left in the care of the National Arts Foundation."

Constance swept a long blonde strand out of her eyes, her long, graceful neck red from heightened irritability. "The rest of the *estate*, but Felicity gets the gatehouse. That's hardly fair, either."

"If I recall correctly, Gramps paid a half-million dollars for your home to be built upon your twenty-second birthday," Felicity pointed out. "After which, he felt obligated to even the distribution and spend the same amount on me for a house. I refused and he insisted I take the cottage. I could hardly turn him down since I was already living there but I can assure you it's not anywhere near the same value. And this is ancient territory. The cottage hasn't been part of the estate for almost five years."

"Still," Constance dismissed Felicity with a wave of a manicured hand and turned on the attorney again. "How could you have allowed him to pass the estate out of family hands? I think we need to question whether there was a competence issue here. Do I need to retain my own lawyer in order to protect my inheritance?"

Felicity nearly laughed aloud. Poor Constance, poor little rich girl.

"Both Doc and I can vouch for Gramps's competency, you know that. He explained why he was handling the estate this way in his letter, Constance. Give it a rest. You and I both have trust funds from our father. There is no hardship here."

"And you are perfectly fine with this?" she demanded, pointing again at *The Lovers*. "It's not even an original, it's only a replica. But you don't care? Gramps screwed your inheritance too, but you don't give a shit. And I look like the bitch because I think I deserve more than the National Artist Society."

"It's the National Arts Foundation," Doc corrected.

"Whatever. The point is, what did they ever do for him?"

Their grandfather and Carleton Smith had created the National Arts Foundation together. Charley Donovan would have been a recognized co-founder with Uncle Carleton except that he chose not to have his name on any of the foundation documents, preferring to remain anonymous. He made a substantial contribution to the foundation every year of his life. Constance would know this if she had ever cared to inquire.

It was just sad. The entire scene made Felicity sad. She leaned her head back on the couch, propped her feet up on the coffee table, and stared up at the painting. It held a prominent position over the fireplace. The plasma screen was to its left. How many nights had she come up to the house and watched *Wheel of Fortune*, or Friday nights watching a movie? Gramps was always partial to action-adventure or war flicks. How many times had he insisted they watch *The Monuments Men*? She smiled. You can never go wrong selecting a movie with Clooney in it. She'd drool, Gramps would make commentary.

"This movie is supposed to be based on all those documents they released from WWII, but they made up most of it."

"I know, Gramps, you told me. A real Monuments Man wouldn't have told anybody about any of these art retrieval projects. But what you never tell me is, how do you know that?"

"I was in the service during the war. I know these things."

It was a familiar exchange. Felicity's gaze drifted away from the blank screen back to the painting. The soundtrack of their discussion had worn a groove in her mind, in a good way. *The Lovers* had been ripped on the bottom left corner from a moving accident Gramps once said. The jagged tear noticeable now only if you had an artist's eye and knew what to look for. Gramps had been a master conservator, a plastic surgeon for art. Everything Felicity had learned over the years about art restoration was due to Gramps. He had been a wealth of information, and yet, she would never match his skill level.

Once, Felicity had caught him staring above the fireplace at the Van Gogh on the mantle, a far off look in his eye and a half smile on his lips. She wondered why it evoked such a look of adoration. She knew the story behind the original painting. The real Van Gogh had been lost during World War II, assumed to be one of the pieces Hitler had destroyed. The replica itself was reportedly created from a letter to brother, Theo Van Gogh, describing the canvas in minute detail. It seemed impossible to Felicity that anyone could create such a remarkable likeness simply from a letter.

"How am I supposed to know which ones are worth anything? Felicity, are you paying any attention at all?" Constance asked.

Felicity turned her attention back to Doc and Constance. "The auctioneers are marking what they think is a probable value on the placards attached to the item. Why don't you roam the house and see which ones have big dollar signs on them? Or better, ask for Roman MacAllister, he's the owner of the auction house, and he can probably take you directly to the more valuable items."

"I'll do that," she huffed off, speaking over her shoulder as she disappeared. "But the baby grand technically belongs to me and I better not get any grief."

Doc's head was in his hands, his shoulders shaking slightly. Felicity feared he had been overcome by emotion brought on by Constance's nagging. She rose from the couch. Doc snorted and lifted his face. There were tears in the corner of his eye. He snorted again, hiccupped, and managed to stifle a guffaw.

"Having fun?" she asked.

"Charley predicted this. I just never thought. . . ."

"Yeah, she's a piece of work, eh?" Felicity said.

Doc Jamison reached a gloved hand into his breast pocket and retrieved an envelope of cream parchment paper. It held the initials CED in the corner, curled in a neat script, her grandfather's personal stash of stationary. He handed it across the desk.

"Charley asked me to make sure you got this separately. Go on and read it."

Felicity took a deep breath and blew it out between her lips, slid one finger under the flap and gently pulled the envelope open to the familiar scrawl.

My delightful Fe,
I have spent my life doing the "right" thing, or trying to, at any rate. It's easy to see the mistakes of youth when you wear an old man's clothes.

Still, I would have done little, if anything, differently. Someday, may you understand that a decision made in a moment can limit the choices afforded us in later days.

You and your sister share the Donovan name and blood. It is difficult, but don't let her make it impossible. I have faith in you. There has been no way to even the distribution between you girls as I know material things mean so little to you. I can never express how much your company has meant to the heart of this old fool. Time, in so many ways, makes all men equal—each life holding a finite number of minutes in a boundless world of possibility. Yet, we find value within ourselves that match our spirit's highest calling, always.

Look beneath the surface for true value. You will know when you find it.

With much love,
Gramps

Felicity folded the sheet of paper and slid it back into the envelope. Her finger traced the flap.

"Why don't I help you get that painting down so you can get it home?" Doc asked.

"It doesn't matter if it stays here for a few days, though I cleared the place over the mantle where it used to sit. The cottage is ready to receive it back in its original home."

"He loved that gatehouse. I never understood it."

Felicity chuckled, "It was his escape from Grandma. She was hell on wheels and that was on a good day. He didn't bring all his things up to the big house until after she died. It was sad, really. I think he missed her, but didn't know how to show her he loved her when she was alive. Or maybe they had a special understanding, who knows. I was young still."

"He worried about you spending so much time with him. Not getting out and having your own life. He loved it too, though. He loved you, Fe."

Fe, Gramps's nickname for her. She winked at Doc and kicked the footstool over toward the mantel, stepping up for the painting. No time like the present. She would never spend another evening here with Charles Evan Donovan. She wiped the back of her hand across her eyes, squeezing the corners dry with her finger tips.

"Maybe I should leave it for now. I walked from the cottage." Felicity said, eyeing her inheritance.

"Nonsense. I'll drive you down. Surely between the two of us, we can get it up on your mantle," Doc declared.

They each took a corner, lifted it from the mantle, and began walking the long trek through the home to place it on the backseat of Doc's black Lexus sedan. Felicity hesitated and looked back toward the home. She wanted to say her goodbyes to the house, but it would have to wait until there were fewer people. It wasn't as if the Arts Foundation would keep her out. She was on good terms with their director. She needed to make a strong, clean break, but maybe not right now.

And then there was Constance to consider.

She took a deep breath and leaned into Doc's car, "Constance?"

"She won't even miss us."

True. And, she knew where Felicity lived, if she cared to stop by.

She climbed into the Lexus and Doc drove them up to her cottage. They got out of the car and carefully maneuvered the painting from the backseat and walked it up her front steps.

"I don't remember this painting being so heavy. I helped move this once before, you know, many years ago," Doc said.

"Not so heavy, twenty-five, thirty pounds. It's a nice frame, but it adds to the weight. Are you the one who ripped the canvas?" Felicity teased.

"Ha, nope, that was a bayonet." Doc huffed, shifting up the last step and waiting while she opened the front door.

"Bayonet? I thought it was damaged during a move."

"Bayonet? Did I say bayonet? I meant bassinet, isn't that what they call those baby things? Smacked right into the corner and tore the canvas," Doc said.

Felicity laughed. Why hadn't Doc spent some of those evenings with her and Gramps? She might have gotten more out of the old war stories. Bayonet, bassinet, indeed. She set her corner on the floor and helped Doc prop it against the wall so she could assess the height and width to be sure she had cleared enough space.

"Gramps used to love those old war movies. Used to go on about *The Monuments Men*," she commented, watching him discretely from the corner of her eye.

"That movie's a bunch of hooey," Doc said, running a hanky across his forehead. "No Monuments Man would have talked about being a. . . ."

". . . Monuments Man. Yeah, so he said." She nodded. "But he never said how he knew that. I have my suspicions, though."

"Do you now, Missy?" Doc lifted his edge of the art piece and dropped his chin toward her. They lifted together and set it on the mantle, sliding it to the middle of the dark wood shelf. "In a few years, those suspicions won't mean anything to anybody. All those men, if they ever did exist, will be dead and buried. Don't you think?"

Felicity folded her arms across her chest and studied her grandfather's old friend. "You served with Gramps and Uncle Carleton in the same unit, right?"

"And?" he said, his face wrinkled, eyes twinkling. "Carleton would tell you the same thing old Charley would have told you."

"Huh?"

"Things ain't always how they look. You remember that. I'm an old man. I believe some secrets are best left kept," he slapped his hands together as if he was knocking dirt from his hands. "You give me a holler if you need anything. I'm going to check in with the boys at the house, then get on out of here, assuming they'll let me leave."

"You can always stop back by for coffee if they tell you to stick around."

She'd forgotten to clip roses, she thought, as she watched him park his Lexus next to the thick row of bushes. She closed the front door and retreated to her den. She studied the painting, patted her pockets, and withdrew the box cutter, placing it back on the coffee table. She unfolded the letter from Charles Evan Donovan and scanned it again.

Look beneath the surface for true value. You will know when you find it.

With much love,
Gramps

Felicity stepped back up on the stool and gripped both sides of the painting, wrestling it down from the mantel. She rested it on the floor and studied the paint, the way the light fell across the angles. She thought about words in the letter *look beneath the surface*. The echo of Doc Jamison's words resonating in her ear—*heavier than I remembered it*. She squinted at the old wound in the canvas expertly repaired by her grandfather years ago. She reflected on Doc's comment about the bayonet, wondering if the painting had become collateral damage during its rescue. This only made sense if the painting was authentic, of course.

She tilted the painting forward and looked at the thickness of the frame. The backing was a brown paper wrap. Felicity picked up the box cutter and carefully ran the blade down the edge of the back, separating the brown wrap from the edge of the wood frame. She delicately peeled down the paper wrap and jerked her head back in surprise. Probing with her fingers, she tore paper away dropping multiple tightly-wrapped bundles of one hundred dollar bills onto the floor.

A cream colored-parchment envelope lay amid the green bundles. Felicity looked nervously over her shoulder and reached for the envelope. She unfolded the contents and began to read.

My dearest Fe,
You wanted the story for years, but being stubborn and fearful of consequences, I could never bring myself to tell you. It doesn't matter so much now, I suppose. About the painting. . . .

She neatly folded the parchment and slipped it back into the envelope. *Well, Gramps, this certainly isn't information that should be left lying around.* She leaned down and set the envelope carefully into the flames, watching as the fire burned away all evidence of the painting's history. The day would come when the painting would need to be restituted. For a while, though, it would be Gramps's legacy and would sit in honor over her fireplace as it had for most of the last fifty years. Time enough later for the painting to find its way home.

Still Life with Profile of Laval (1886)
B. K. Hart

The Indianapolis Museum of Art is full of treasures with unique and interesting backgrounds. In the case of *Still Life with Profile of Laval* from French painter Paul Gaugin, the masterpiece was not only saved as part of the Monuments Men's diligent work, but its rescue has been attributed to an Indiana native, Thomas Carr Howe Jr. The painting was acquired by IMA in 1998 with a generous contribution from the Lilly Endowment, and it now resides in the Jane H. Fortune gallery at the art museum.

Thomas Carr Howe Jr., an Indianapolis native, was born in 1904 in Kokomo. His father taught and served as Butler University president from 1907 to 1920. He tells the story of how the Gaugin masterpiece was retrieved in his book, *Salt Mines and Castles: The Discovery and Restitution of Looted European Art*, which was commissioned in 1946 by Bobbs-Merrill, an Indianapolis-based publishing company, and immortalizes Howe Jr.'s adventures in recovering looted art during WWII.

Still Life with Profile of Laval was retrieved during a solo mission in Bavaria where eighty-one cases of art were recovered from the Nazis. He was nearly thwarted in his mission by a Hungarian curator who had been charged with its safekeeping. However, Howe persevered and was able to get the painting to a central collecting point in Munich. The painting, looted from the famous Jewish Herzog Collection, was eventually restituted and returned to the widow of the Herzog heir.

The Making of a Masterpiece

C. A. Paddock

"She won't even see it coming," a hoarse voice echoes in his head. And with that encouragement, he raises his Bowie knife and slashes through her midsection. As the steel blade again cuts through the air and down the side of her porcelain-like face, he howls his disgust at her.

"You destroyed us. You destroyed our perfect relationship. Now you will pay for what you've done to me! I gave you my all for months and months and what do you I get from you? Nothing. Nothing, that's what. You lead me on with your beauty and your charms and your teasing perfection. But you betrayed me with all of it!"

He lifts the knife with even more fervor and slices her over and over, carving out his anger and fear, until he stops suddenly and falls on his knees. His hand, so gnarled and cramped from holding the weapon, gives out and he drops the knife. He stares down at what he has done and knows that she would have screamed out, if she could have, because the pain had to be unbearable. He feels it himself, the small burning sensation that soon engulfs him in a full-fledged roar of flaming agony. He waits and listens, half-expecting to see her rise up and cry out.

The only sound he hears is the moan that escapes his lips.

It all started, this obsession of his, when he attended his new show at the Galeria Blanca in Chicago. The well-respected gallery was known for hosting the most evocative contemporary artists from the national and international art scene. Over the years, the gallery had included a few of his pieces in its shows, but this was the first time it held a solo exhibition for his celebrated art. The gallery had received so many requests from patrons to see more of his work. The curator had contacted him to arrange a special viewing of his newest creations, a mixed-media collection of artistic amalgams of oils, charcoal and film that exemplified his unique talent.

It was during the opening of this special viewing that he first saw her. He was leaning against a circular white pillar describing his creative process to a group of ardent listeners, new and long-time connoisseurs of his work, alike. He was telling them how he enters his dreams—waking and sleeping—to actualize his creations, when all of a sudden his eyes caught a narrow band of darkness across the crowded, open-space gallery. A glimpse that made him stop in midsentence to focus on its blackness.

As he concentrated on the vision, he witnessed its transformation into long, silky locks of hair, slipping across and down a perfect porcelain face. In that second, he beheld her features—her high forehead, the straight slope of her nose, the slight curl of her lip, the soft curve of her jaw, the slenderness of her neck. At the same time, she turned to the hanging on the wall of his depiction of a grandmother and child. She moved just enough so the spotlight on the work sparkled in her emerald eyes. She cocked her head and smiled while she examined the work, and after a moment, as if she had made an important connection in her mind, her eyes widened, her smile stretched open and her hair fell forward with an emphatic nod of her head.

She is the most beautiful woman I have ever seen! Look at her. She is smiling at my work. She gets it, she gets me! he declared to himself.

"She is perfect for you," a low voice teased in his ear. And with that he knew he had found the muse for which he had been searching his entire life.

* * *

He took her back to his retreat outside of Nashville, Indiana. No matter where he traveled in the world or where his work was shown, be it Chicago, New York or London, he always returned to this hamlet where he felt most at home. Where he could create, to be a painter among painters, an artist among awarded and aspiring artists alike. It was a place where he could enter the local art store and buy his supplies without the stares or whispers.

When he needed inspiration, he could wander unacknowledged through the Friday evening farmers market in nearby Bean Blossom, listening to the music of local bluegrass bands and capturing moments of human expressions through his lens, all the while gathering the ingredients for his weekend meals. He could be himself in this quiet world. And he knew that this exotic, cosmopolitan woman could be herself here, too, in this idyllic town.

He would make sure she would love this part of southern Indiana and become a beloved part of the community.

"I know this isn't the bustling excitement of the city you're used to, but you will learn to love it here," he told her as he turned his '70s wood-paneled Jeep Wagoneer off the narrow, gravel county road onto the smooth pebble lane of his property.

"There are five acres of land here, mostly wooded as you can see. All types of trees—maple, walnut, oak, sycamore, and, of course, pawpaw trees. Oh, they are so beautiful in the fall! You won't believe there could be anything more stunning in the world. Except you, my love, of course. I grew up here in all this splendor. And, just think, you will be living in it, too!"

He paused so she could take in the towering trees and entangled ferns, wildflowers and common brush hugging the drive. A crunch, crunch, crunch sound of stone being mashed by rubber tires syncopated the moment.

"There used to be another eighty acres of farmland and woods when my grandfather owned it; but over the years, a little bit here and a little bit there was sold off to make ends meet. When my grandfather died, my grandmother sold off all but these five acres to pay for his funeral and help take care of me. After she died, I got it and redid the house. This is what is left," he continued to tell her over a squawking engine belt as the truck climbed up a hill.

When they reached the clearing at the top, he put the Jeep into park, turned off the key, and spread his arms wide. "This is all yours now. We will be so happy living here. And the most important thing will be the wonderful works of art we will make together. With you at my side, I can finally create my masterpiece! I have waited so long for this, waited so long to find you. Let's not waste another minute sitting here."

He hopped out and ran with her to his one-room, wood-sided home. It included a tiny living area and a large studio. A bed and nightstand, a sectional sofa, a closeted bath, a café table with two chairs, and a small stove and refrigerator were all that made up his living space. His work studio encompassed the rest of the immaculate room. White wood shelves housed cans and tubes of paint, neatly organized by color. A walnut cabinet held his cameras, lenses, tripods, and other photography equipment. A stack of unused, stretched canvas frames rested against a gray metal table covered with sketch pads and charcoal pencils.

"Isn't this grand! Our very own haven of inspiration and desire! You, *mi cara*, will make this place shine!" So enthused to have his muse with him finally, he set up his easel and canvas and began to sketch her outline.

* * *

Each morning, filled with hope and passion, started the same: he would stroke her sleek, black hair, brushing away any stray strands as he traced her alabaster chin and slid his hand down to caress her tight breasts. Staring lovingly into her green eyes, glistening in the early sunlight, he would whisper in her ear, "Your beauty and love inspires me today. I can see in your eyes your desire to fulfill my every dream. And, you are, *mi cara*, you *are*. You love me for me, and you understand me. What more can a man ask for?" He would then throw back his head and let out whoops of happiness.

For the first time in his life, he felt invigorated. He could accomplish anything. With her help, he began to feel as if he were talented and deserved the high praise he received in reviews of his work. He even dug out old newspaper articles, the few he still kept, and read them to her.

"Listen to this, *cara:* The Indianapolis Star once called my exhibition, 'mesmerizing by the sheer detail of emotions that exudes from his medium. He knows what his creations feel and exhibits this empathy in a way that forces one not to look away.' I can't believe I didn't realize they were calling me a genius at the time. At my next show you will be by my side, and then they really will know what an artistic genius I am!"

As the days went on and he realized she was not going to leave him, he revealed to her the struggle he had growing up in this house with only his grandmother, and the secrets he kept.

"When I was little boy, I would cower in the corner and close my eyes so tight that I imagined they would disappear into little lines under my brows. This way she couldn't find me to whip me with the switch she broke off of the maple tree out back. I never knew what I had done or what I said to make her so angry." He put his head in his hands.

"She'd yell the same thing at me every time, in that scathing, growling voice of hers, 'Boy, you'll never amount to nothin'. Just like your ol' mama. She thought she could play music better'n anyone else. Thinkin' people would pay to hear her play that guitar and sing. But the only thing they'd pay her for was a good time. And look'n what she got out of that—you! A ugly, bratty ball chained around her waist. No wonder she run off after seein' you come into the world.'

"That's when I would retreat into my little corner to draw and imagine how I'd escape this hellhole one day. I created this whole world where I'd become a famous painter with people telling me how smart I was and how my art was the best they'd ever seen. People would love me!" Tears slithered down his cheek as the memory played in his mind.

"Oh, don't look at me with those sad eyes. I survived—even thrived. Some folks from town even took pity on me when my grandmother died and helped me go to the Herron School of Art in Indianapolis. And look at me now—I AM a famous artist with the most exquisite woman and muse one could have."

While the days were filled with dreams and possibilities, the nights with her took on another sensation. The seed of doubt had started to grow again, and crept up on him to murmur in his ear. "Those folks are as dumb as a box of rocks if they think what you make is somethin' special. You're still the poor, stupid boy who couldn't paint himself out of this ol' shack your grandad built. You're a fool if you think she is going to change that for you. I ain't gonna ever let you forget that."

Now each time he looked at her, he glanced away, not wanting to see the disappointment in her eyes. In fact, the smile that once captivated him, now seemed to mock him wherever he went. He would curl up in the corner to hide from her penetrating stare, the stare he knew reflected the darkness in him.

For as long as he could, he tried to ignore her as if she were a sore on his side, aching and festering until he could not bear the incessant pain any longer. Then he would rush to her side to stroke her hair once more, to feel the passion he once felt for her. But all he could see were her cracked lips and flaking skin.

* * *

Still on his knees, he gapes down at her, her radiating beauty gone. His rage returns, bubbling up like the bile rising from his gut and explodes through his mouth.

"How dare you betray me! You weren't smiling at me when I first saw you because you got me, got my work. You smiled because it was the most hideous thing you'd ever seen. What a liar you are!

"You seduced me into thinking you were my muse. You stole the best time of my life from me, leading me on, all along knowing that I would fail again." He picks up the knife, still wet and sticky from his sweat, and begins to stab her once more.

"I hate you. I hate you. I hate you! I hate you!" he repeats with each stab.

Exhausted from his tirade, he pauses and watches as a drop of perspiration falls from his brow and lands on what would have been her cheek and slides down to her chin. It is in this moment he grasps with increasing horrific disbelief the magnitude of his actions. Not only did he destroy his dream, but also the perfect culmination of his work. As his angst overcomes him, he hears the whisper of his grandmother's voice, "Now look what you've done. You're a loser like you always been, and now a murderer to boot."

With one last look around his shambled studio, he turns his hand, still gripping the knife, and plunges the blade into his side, plunges it, plunges it, until the crimson completely covers his trembling hand and drips from his wrist. He registers its metallic taste as he collapses onto what is left of her mangled face.

* * *

A woman in her sixties wearing blue polyester pants and a red short-sleeve knit top covered with a flowered smock dries her hands on a towel hanging from the stove handle. A large silver safety pin holding a wad of material at her waist sticks out from the side opening of her smock. She saunters over to the kitchen doorway and looks into the paneled room where her husband sits in his green Lazy Boy chair, staring at the wide rectangular screen.

"Honey, did you see where that famous painter who lives down the road died? They say he killed himself. Can you believe that? They said on the television that the police found his place a mess. They said his body was laying on top of a ruined painting of a beautiful woman. They called it his masterpiece, his *Mona Lisa*, whatever that means." The woman leans on the once-white door frame.

Minutes pass before he responds. "What did you say, babe? I was watching the IU basketball game."

Harold E. Hansen (1943-)
Stephen Terrell

Nestled in rural Wisconsin, not far from the art community of Cedarburg, Hoosier native **Harold E. Hansen** lives with his wife in a renovated 1847 farmhouse. In his nearby gallery, he works amid antiques and books more than a hundred years old, creating his intricate artwork with a stone lithograph that dates to another time.

Hansen is a throwback to another time. Born in rural Rush County in Indiana during the midst of WWII, he graduated from Herron School of Art. He spent the first fifteen years of his career focused on painting before finding a desire to focus on printing and stone lithography.

Lithography is a labor-intensive art form with few practitioners. The heavy stones, creaking press, and intricate work are far more demanding than an easel and palette of oils. But Hansen's love of his subjects and the process of creating lithographic prints are evident in each piece. Hansen's meticulously detailed lithographs range in size from the massive prints of the lions that stand outside the Chicago Museum of Art to award-winning miniature prints of antique toys, fishing flies, old household items, and Scottish landscapes.

While printing, Hansen did not abandon painting. He has completed more than six hundred watercolors as well as his lithographs. In 1985, he published *Sketches of Cedarburg,* a book of lithographs celebrating the town's centennial. Recently, he created images from his travels to Scotland, Ireland, England, France, and Germany. Hansen's work hangs in private and corporate collections throughout the United States and as far away as Australia. One of his most recent exhibits was "Harold E Hansen: Paintings and Stone Lithographs, From Far and Near," at the Cedarburg Art Museum.

In addition to his art, Hansen has a passion for single malt scotches. His personal notebook lists more than 740 single malt scotches he has tasted—in order of preference.

Portrait of a Rainy Death
Claudia Pfeiffer

Rain is my favorite Durato painting. In keeping with her artistic style, she left much of the white canvas untouched. An indistinct cabin emerged from behind suggestions of bending trees and her signature spatters. In most of her paintings the spatters appeared in the lower realms of the canvas in wide sweeps from left to right. Sometimes there were a random few throughout the painting, but not many. Except in this work where they descended from top to bottom straight down. Like rain. Though semi-abstract and nearly monochromatic, life pulsed in this painting. The gray tones evoked a cold atmosphere. A subtle hint of pale orange suggested the warmth inside the cabin. The heavy downward strokes recalled the power of the rain. Its wetness in the glistening white pinpoints. The subdued spatters of earth tones at the base came down from the rain and flowed to the right, alluding to the hope of life-giving moisture. Yes, definitely my favorite.

"I see your husband was an aficionado of Celeste Durato. Three of her paintings in one room. Impressive," I said.

"Didn't you see the paintings before?"

"Yeah. Briefly." I scratched at the stubble on my jaw. "We met in the living room but took a quick tour of this office."

"Well, his love for Durato started with her." Janelle Lamb gestured toward an eloquent ballet dancer caught in a burst of varicolored floodlights, their oval radiance spilling over into droplets of color sweeping rightward. "Wes said she reminded him of me—of how I touched his heart when I danced." She dabbed her eyes gently with a tissue.

"So you were a dancer? Were you in the ballet company?" I set my briefcase down. Actually, it's a catalog case. It can hold a lot of files and stuff. Heavy son of a gun. I glanced down at the carpet, took a big step forward and looked up at the painting of the rain, now so close I could reach out with my hand and touch it.

"No. I had six years of ballet and jazz before college and enrolled as a dance major. Wes was my instructor for two years."

"But you're a corporate lawyer. That's a b-i-g step away from a dance major." My eyes continued to rove over the painting, stopping briefly at the warm, orange window and traveling downward with the rain to study the beginnings of life at the bottom.

"It was the sensible thing to do. Two years into the dance program, I realized I could never be the prima ballerina. At nineteen, I was already considered too old. And I wasn't interested in simply dancing in the corps or teaching children, so I switched my major to pre-law."

"Betcha Mr. Lamb was upset. No worry though. He obviously got over it. You were married quite a few years." I glanced around the room. Bookcases. Large desk. Filing cabinet. Small upholstered chair opposite where I stood. End tables on either side, one with a lamp and the other holding a bronze replica of Degas's *Little Dancer.*

"Yes, he was livid. I wanted to continue taking classes just for the exercise. He refused."

I studied her. In tee and slim yoga pants, her well-toned body was evident. She looked in better shape than me, and I'm proud of my physique. Between gym workouts and boxing at the precinct, I'm in good form. Can still run a mile in less than eight minutes. Faster when chasing a suspect. That's pretty good for a man of forty-three. But I've never run a marathon. This woman finished two, both times in the top third.

"Do ya dance now, Mrs. Lamb?"

"Yes. Jazz classes two nights a week."

"Jazz can build a body like yours?" I knew it was an offensive question but figured she was vain enough to answer it.

"Jazz is for fun. Weight lifting is how I keep in shape."

"Oh? Where do ya do that?"

"The gym on Castle. Four times a week." She lifted her chin with a look of arrogance then quickly dropped her head to dab at her eyes. "But what's this have to do with my husband's murder?"

"The painting of the tap dancer." I pointed to another Durato hanging behind the desk. "It's a grand one for its small size."

"I got it for Wes. To bribe him. He still wouldn't let me back in class but did invite me to move in with him." She tossed her head. "Two years later, we got married."

"Lemme figure. Hmmm." I tapped my lower teeth with my thumbnail, a habit my ex-wife hated. Tried to break me of it for five years. Finally divorced me. Not because of that. Because she hated being married to a cop. "Wasn't that about the time he took over Paravael Ballet?"

"Yes. Wes saved the company. Brought it from the brink of bankruptcy to one of the top dance companies in the nation."

"Made him a lotta money too, didn't it? But I guess he didn't really need it. You married a pretty wealthy man."

"Wes deserved every penny he inherited from his parents. They treated him terribly for going into the arts. And as for Paravael, they only paid him what he deserved. He was a genius when it came to dance."

"From what you say, he wasn't so smart when it came to drugs, huh?"

Her expression changed from condescending to grief-stricken widow in an instant. She wiped her dry eyes, then walked to the chair and sat delicately on the edge. "He couldn't help that. The arthritis got so bad." She sniffled, a dry sound.

"He didn't have a doctor?"

"Of course he did." She looked at me defiantly. "But the imbecile limited the number of pills Wes could have. The more crippled he got, the worse the pain. The doctor wouldn't increase his prescription, so he turned to the streets."

"He did? For sure?" I walked to the desk and leaned against the corner. Thought maybe if I acted more nonchalant, she'd break out of her controlled stiffness. I'd never seen a surviving spouse with such discipline. Especially a woman. I don't mean that in a patronizing way. Just an observation from being a cop for twenty-plus years. Nine of them detective.

"Yes," she stated. A look of aggravation flickered. "I thought we already had that established. His nightly forays I told you about. The baggie you found on his body. The ones I found in the bathroom trash."

"Yeah. Can you get them for me?"

"Right now? They're upstairs."

"If you don't mind."

She left the room. Was gone just long enough. Returned with

the baggies. I dropped them into my briefcase. "This one's got the dancers beat." I gestured toward the painting of the rain. "They're active. Dancing, leaping, while this one's a stationary building, but the rain gives it more dynamism than a whole passel of dancers."

"I disagree." She shook her head. "I've never liked that one. It's just a bunch of paint dribbling down. I like the realism of the dancers. Abstract background, but you can tell they're people."

I turned to face Mrs. Lamb. "I take it you didn't buy this one."

"No. Wes got it at a fundraiser. Paid way too much for it."

"Still, it's a powerful painting. I noticed it when we were in here last time. You ever get tired of it I'll take it off your hands." I laughed.

She continued to watch me with the same aloof expression.

"Your husband have any enemies?"

"I'm sure he did. Everybody has people who don't like them, Detective, even you."

"Oh, you got that right. I got more than my share. But I'm talking about someone who might wanna kill him."

"Well, there's Corrina Belle. She's been on his back for years about a dance number she claims he stole from her. Foolishness, of course."

"Tell me more."

"Wes developed a lovely *pas de trois* for his spring program three years ago. The critics raved about it. Corrina demanded Wes publicly admit he stole the piece from her. She claimed she did it for a class assignment. She harassed him by mail, phone, even personal contact. I told him to have her arrested. He thought ignoring her was the best way to handle the situation."

"So when was the last time you saw Ms. Belle?"

"Maybe two months ago. She banged on the door for an hour. When I went out later to get the mail, there was a dead rat on the front steps. I'm sure she left it there."

"Did you report it?"

"Wes wouldn't let me."

"I'll need her address and all," I stated. She walked to the desk and scribbled on a tablet.

I bent to study the statuette of Degas's *Little Dancer*. "I've always loved this sculpture. This is a splendid reproduction. Looks heavy. Bronze, is it?"

"Yes." She handed me a paper with Corrina Belle's contact information. "When will you release my husband's body? I don't like the idea of him being in cold storage. You're done with the autopsy—a terrible thing to do to him. Was it really necessary?" She stood ramrod straight. I only had her by a few inches, and I'm a tall guy.

"We found his body in a dumpster, Mrs. Lamb. That's suspicious. Autopsy was the best way to find out what happened to him."

"But that was obvious. You said blunt force trauma, right?"

"Yes'm. Back of the head."

"So, why an autopsy?"

"To clear up questions. Was he dead before or after he was hit? Did he have a heart attack and fall, hitting his head? All kinds of things."

"Detective, there is no reason to be facetious. People don't have heart attacks in dumpsters." Her voice was hostile.

"Yes'm. You got that right." I turned to go. She put her hand on my arm.

"You didn't answer my question. When will you release the body?"

"We will release *the body* when we're done with our investigation. Good day, Mrs. Lamb. I can find my way out."

The body? Did she actually say that? It seemed cold. Her husband of almost sixteen years was found in a dumpster with the back of his head ripped open. Well, like they say, it takes all kinds.

I ran to my car, slid behind the wheel, and wiped the rain from my face. I pulled out my cell. Called my partner. She answered on the third ring. Sounded like shit. I guess she wasn't fooling when she called in sick. Wasn't keeping her from working, though.

"You got anything on Travis Mallard yet, Rosie?" I unwrapped a piece of gum and popped it in my mouth. Then a second piece. Apparently I cracked my gum. Something else my ex didn't like and I couldn't change.

"Yep. The car we followed is one of five registered in his name." Sounded like she had a clothespin on her nose. She rattled off a list of the five vehicles.

"Tell me about him." I wondered what anyone would do with five cars.

"CEO of Crossman Oil. Owner of Parkway Airlines and Freedom Avenue Bank. Sits on the board of several big companies." A pause, a loud sneeze, a phlegmy cough. I felt like wiping my cell off. "You gonna go see him?" She cleared her throat with a loud rasp.

"Yeah, but not at home. I'll catch him at work. Gimme the address for Crossman Oil." I scribbled it on the palm of my hand. Another habit my ex hated.

I ditched the gum before approaching Mallard.

He was a big man. Had me by a couple inches and more than twenty pounds. Wore a three-piece suit. Vest pulled taut. Not fat at all. Just big boned and muscular. Looked like a brick wall. But he was gracious. Had his girl bring me coffee. Good coffee. Answered my questions pleasantly.

"How do you know Janelle Lamb?"

"She's my attorney."

"You always have dinner at expensive restaurants with your attorneys?"

"Nope. Just Janie. 'Cause she's my only attorney." He gave a jovial laugh. "Sometimes I prefer having a business meeting in nicer surroundings than a boardroom or an office. I can afford it. We relax, discuss things in comfort. How do you know where I go for dinner?"

"And her husband? How'd he feel about these little trysts?" I asked, ignoring his question.

"Trysts? C'mon, Detective. Business meetings. As for how her husband took it—he never came after me with a shotgun." Another jovial laugh. "Besides, it was only a couple times."

"Actually, six for sure. Three here in town at the Manchester Hotel and three at the bed and breakfast on the way to Tradford."

"Nothing suspicious about the Manchester. Have you ever eaten at the restaurant there? Trivoli's? Best Italian food in the city. And Harvey's, the little dining room off the lounge, has wonderful food. Then we met for business at the bed and breakfast for brunch once or twice. They make superb muffins and omelets the size of Texas. I don't know where you get three times though." He frowned. "Refresh my memory."

I gave him dates and times. He checked his calendar. Said the second date was impossible. He was out of state then. Must have him mixed up with someone else. Laughter. Jovial. I asked where he was the night Weston Lamb was killed. Said he was with a woman. He'd prefer to keep her name out of this. She was married. I insisted on the name to confirm his information even though it would be worthless. Obviously she'd be a hooker he paid to be his alibi. We already knew where he was that night. Before Rosie got sick, she and I were shadowing Mrs. Lamb. You know the saying—the spouse is the first suspect. Then Rosie pointed him out.

"Look who she's talking to. Watch. See how he brushed her hair off her face? And look how he touched her cheek, real gentle like?"

"So? That's Mallard. She's his attorney. Why wouldn't they be talking?" I frowned.

"I mean how he treats her. The hair. The cheek. Those are pretty personal gestures."

I studied them and began to nod. "I see. So there might be a little hanky-panky going on."

Lamb entered the building, and Mallard walked to a shiny red Ferrari parked at the curb. We were across the street. I eased into traffic, turned around in the alley and followed Mallard to his condo. That's when we spotted the gumshoe. He made me laugh. He pulled to the curb, snapped a picture of Mallard, and then propped a newspaper in front of his face. Talk about stereotype. While Rosie stayed with the car watching the condo, I walked to the PI's car, opened the passenger door, and climbed in.

"What the hell?" He turned toward me and dropped his camera on the floor, then bent over and retrieved it. I flashed my shield. He explained that Mallard's wife hired him to follow her husband.

"I'll need your notes and photos."

"No way, mister. I've got a license."

"And I'll pull it if you don't cooperate," I told him gruffly.

"Shit. This is the first decent paying gig I've had for ages. Why you wanna get in my face?"

"Tell you what. You give me copies of all your notes and duplicate photos, and you can stay on the job. Just keep that info flowing my direction. You don't? You'll be charged with interfering with a police investigation." I handed him my card and got out of the car. Walked back, got in with Rosie and pulled into traffic.

"What's up, Mason?" she asked.

"We've got a bulldog on the job for us. We'll go watch the widow." I explained things to her, and we had a good laugh. The setup worked out well for us. All kinds of surveillance done on someone else's time and dime. It's how we found out about the Manchester and the bed and breakfast. And how we found out where he was the night in question. It sure wasn't with some married woman.

When his body was found, Weston Lamb's wallet was empty. Possible robbery. A baggie in his pocket tested positive for residue of oxycodone. I talked with his doctor. He confirmed the arthritis and showed me Lamb's file. He was prescribing enough medication to treat an elephant. Lamb had no reason to be looking for more on the street.

I worked the case steady, checking my suspicions against times and possibilities. Running down the irate student, Corrina Belle. Having California police interview her. Studying her alibi. Comparing my notes with those of the PI. I worked some late nights. Hated doing that to Rosie, but she understood my work better'n the ex ever did. The test results I was waiting for came back just before suppertime. So did my partner. She called for me to pick her up. The cough was gone. No more sneezing. Just a sniffle now and then. Still, I was concerned because it was raining pretty hard. I didn't want her having a relapse. She said not to worry, she was pumped full of antibiotics. I was glad to have her back.

"Wanna grab something to eat? You can fill me in on the case," she said.

"Yeah. Mexi-Grill okay?" I asked.

She nodded. We got a booth and dug into our chili. "So, where are we on the case?" she asked.

"It's ready to close. I know who killed Weston Lamb. I know

where, why, and how. And I've got proof."

"What's up with that? You workin' the case alone? I thought we were partners." She frowned.

"You helped work it. You got the dope on Mallard."

"Big deal. The private guy did all the work. I simply checked his notes."

"What'd you want me to do? Sit in a corner waiting for you to get over the flu?"

"Walking pneumonia, not flu." She jabbed at the crackers in her chili.

"Okay, okay. Doesn't matter. You were sick. I wasn't gonna sit around doing nothing until you were back on the job. C'mon, Rosie, don't be mad. Let's close our case and get on to the next one."

"Next one?"

"College kid found at the reservoir right before the rain today. Broken neck. Don't have much more on it yet, but we'll hit the crime scene later this evening. So you see, there's plenty of work for you to do."

"Okay. So, who killed Weston Lamb?"

"We're meeting with his widow. Loverboy will be there too. I'll explain it all then."

"If you say so." She shrugged. Rosie was a good sport. "Where's the meeting?"

"The widow's house."

"So, we headin' there now?"

"We can finish eating. Maybe have some pie." I motioned to the waitress for more coffee.

"You sure the widow and Mallard are lovers?" She looked at me over the rim of her coffee cup, the hot vapors making her face look wavy.

"Don't know about love, but they're doing it. The shamus has photos. R rated."

"I thought I had all his files. I don't recall any racy photos. Just outdoor pics of Mallard and Lamb going into a restaurant." She blew on her coffee and took a sip.

"I leaned on our bulldog a bit more. Got him to give me the good stuff. He was holding some back. Probably thinking about blackmail. I told him I'd press charges if he didn't turn 'em over to me." I reached in my briefcase and pulled out a manila envelope. "Here." I tossed it across the table. "Don't blush too much when you look at 'em."

* * *

Janelle Lamb answered the door. She looked surprised. Normal reaction. I didn't call first.

"Detective, what are you doing here?"

"Evening, Mrs. Lamb. This is my partner, Detective Rosina Gage. We have a few questions. Mr. Mallard arrive yet?"

"What? Why?"

"Can we step in outta the rain?"

"Oh. Yes." She opened the door all the way. Rosie and I stepped inside. I dropped my catalog case while I hung up my coat. Rosie leaned her umbrella against the coat rack.

"It seems Mr. Mallard did arrive. He's there in the living room." I grabbed my case. "Mind if we meet in your husband's office? I want my partner to see the painting I like so much."

"Of course. I'll get him, but how did you know Travis . . . Mr. Mallard would be here?"

"Simple. I sent the message for him to come."

"You did what?" She looked at me, incensed. "What's going on here?"

"Let's talk, Mrs. Lamb. Ask Mr. Mallard to join us." I walked to the office. Rosie followed. I pulled the chair from behind the desk and placed it beside the one near the painting. Rosie and I stood, my case at her feet. Mrs. Lamb walked in with Travis Mallard.

"What's going on, Detective? Janie tells me you sent the text for me to come here. Why? And to use her name. . . ." His voice was strident. His face flushed.

"Would you've come if you knew the police were asking for your presence? I thought it best to get you here any way I could. Figured you'd want to be here while we discuss Weston Lamb's murder."

He paused then nodded. "Good thinking. I can give Janie moral support at this difficult time."

"Moral support? If that's what you wanna call it. Why don't

you both sit? You take the upholstered chair, Mrs. Lamb. Mallard, you can have this one. We'll stand." I turned to my partner. "So, what do ya think of the painting?"

"It's like the weather outside. I like the dancers better."

"Well, you haven't had time to study it. Okay, we need to get down to business." Mrs. Lamb was perched on the edge of her chair, ramrod straight, like the last time we met here.

"So, what's the deal?" Mallard asked.

"I have some questions tickling my brain about this murder." I paced in front of them. "Like this assumption that Mr. Lamb was killed for the oxycodone he was carrying and the cash he had for buying more."

"What do you mean assumption?" The widow's voice was indignant. "Somebody jumped him for the drugs and cash, killed him and tossed his body in a dumpster like a piece of trash." She dropped her head, dug in her pocket for a tissue and dabbed her eyes. "Like a piece of trash. He was such a frail little man. Crippled and bent. Maybe ninety pounds. He didn't deserve to be treated so heartlessly."

"You're right, Mrs. Lamb, he didn't. But we don't think that's exactly the way it happened, do we Rosie?" She shook her head and turned toward the widow. I knew she was in the dark but also knew she'd follow my lead and back me up. I paced in front of the chairs. Mrs. Lamb watched me closely. "In fact, we doubt Mr. Lamb ever bought drugs on the street."

"What? You said somebody killed him for his drugs and money and dumped him. Why are you changing your mind now? Oh, I get it. It was Corrina Belle."

"Don't think so." I shook my head.

"Then why aren't you out there looking for the murderer? It's been weeks, and you haven't done squat." She glared at me. Man, if looks could kill.

"Remember me saying some things were tickling my brain? One's the wallet." I stopped directly in front of her. "Why'd the murderer take the money and not the wallet? Why not take everything? ID's and credit cards are pretty valuable."

"Maybe somebody came along, so he grabbed the money and ran." She frowned and glanced at Mallard. He sat, hands clasped beneath his chin, not moving.

"Also, there's the baggie found in his pocket." I resumed pacing, hands clasped behind my back. "The question scratching at my brain this time is why the guy didn't take the baggie with him. You know, grab the bag of pills. Why dump them in his pocket or another container? And why return the baggie to Mr. Lamb's pocket? Why not toss it in the dumpster if he didn't want it?"

"Hmmm. Those are good questions." Mallard nodded, his chin bumping into his steepled hands. "Probably some young punk. Maybe his first robbery."

"Really?" I stopped pacing and raised my eyebrows, looking directly at him. "It doesn't look like a setup to you? Huh, I thought you'd see it right away. How someone wanted it to look like a robbery. Someone who doesn't know much about such things so just took the money. But the baggie adds to it. Looks like someone wants us to think this is drug related."

"Are you saying this whole thing was staged?" Mallard lowered his hands and tilted his head.

"It would seem so."

"That's clever. Corrina's certainly devious enough to have thought that up." Lamb nodded sagely.

"Again, I don't think so." I shook my head and paced.

"I don't understand." Mrs. Lamb stood abruptly, her voice angry. "You're just toying with us. I want you to leave. Don't come back until you can tell me who killed my sweet Weston. And why."

"But I can tell you that right now. Where he was killed. How. Why. I can even tell you by whom. Should I start with why?" I stood directly in front of her and engaged in a staring war. There was a definite tremor in her clenched jaw. She sat.

"Have you arrested him?" Mallard asked.

"No. Thought perhaps the widow would want to know how we solved this case first. Then we'll get right on it and make our arrest."

"Okay, I'll bite. Start with why." Mallard steepled his hands again.

"The envelope please." I looked at Rosie. She reached in my briefcase, removed the manila envelope and handed it to me. I looked from the widow to Mallard. "Who wants to take a peek?"

Portrait of a Rainy Death

Mallard reached up, took the envelope, and opened it. He pulled the glossy prints out far enough to get the idea and dropped them back in. He looked at Janelle Lamb.

"Photos." He held her glance. Her eyes widened.

"You don't mean. . . ."

"Yes, he does mean, Mrs. Lamb. The two of you at the bed and breakfast where they serve omelets the size of Texas. But you weren't interested in the breakfasts there. Only the beds." It looked like Rosie was having trouble keeping a smile off her face.

"That's an invasion of our privacy. How dare you." She stood indignantly and reached for the envelope. "These will be destroyed and any other copies you have. Do you understand, Detective?"

"Fine by me. They're not my photos."

"Whose are they?"

"The gumshoe tailing Mr. Mallard. Hired by his wife. He got these interesting pics of you two. They seem to point to a motive for the murder of your husband."

"Motive? What are you talking about?" Mallard also stood.

"If Mrs. Lamb got a divorce, she'd get nothing. On the other hand, she'd get everything if her husband died."

"Ridiculous." Mallard shook his head. "Janie could divorce him easily. She doesn't need his money. I have more money than we can ever use. You have no motive for either of us, if that's what you're getting at." He reached for her hand. She hesitated then entwined her fingers with his.

"I think you're trying to muddy the waters, Detective." The widow's voice was icy. "What have you found out about Corrina Belle? Or have you even bothered to investigate her?"

"Sure did. She's clean. Solid alibi for the night of your husband's death. For the week before it to the present, in fact. She's been in London. Scotland Yard confirmed. Besides, I think her allegations carry some weight. Why don't you both sit down? We can move past why to where and how."

"Actually, I think I'd like to have my attorney present." Mrs. Lamb lifted her chin.

"Fine by me, but it's really not necessary. I'm not going to ask you any questions. Just sit and listen. You can't incriminate yourself by listening. You know that." I shrugged.

She looked at Mallard. He nodded and helped her sit, then resumed his place and held the envelope on his lap.

"We examined the baggies from the bathroom trash can and the residue was oxycodone." I nodded at Mrs. Lamb. "Funny, though, the only fingerprints on them were yours. Maybe you put pills in them and dumped them out, leaving the residue."

"And why would I do such a thing?" Lamb's face flushed.

"I guess to make it look like he bought drugs off the street." I held up my hand as she started to speak. "Now for the next interesting fact in this case—the toxicology report. There was no oxycodone in Mr. Lamb's system."

"So? He bought it but got killed before he could take any." Mrs. Lamb straightened her already erect body.

"Conceivably." I nodded and paced a bit more. "More interesting was the high level of diphenhydramine in his blood."

"Whatever that is." There was irritation in her voice and, I thought, fear in her eyes.

"It's the principal ingredient in over-the-counter sleep medications. One of the most commonly used ones is *Nitey Nite*. I'm guessing there's an opened bottle in your medicine cabinet. The question is, why would Weston Lamb take a big dose of a sleeping solution before going out to buy drugs? I'd be scared to try to walk, much less drive a car if I'd taken as much as he had in his system."

"I don't get where this is going, Detective." Mallard sounded irritated. "Why don't you tell us the damn facts and get this over with. Who killed him? And why hasn't he been arrested?"

"Both good questions," I smiled politely, "but I said I'd tell you where and how the murder took place. This may make you feel uncomfortable."

"Why is that?" Mallard raised his eyebrows.

"'Cause we're at the murder scene."

"What? The murder scene? He was in a dumpster." Mrs. Lamb tossed her head.

"She's right." Mallard drew his eyebrows together. "Wes was found in an alley dumpster nowhere near here."

"Yes, and that *is* a crime scene, but it's not where he died," I said.

"Are you implying Weston was killed in this room?" Mrs. Lamb glared at me. "Preposterous."

"So, tell us, Detective, why you think he was killed here and how his body ended up in that alley." Mallard pressed his hands together beneath his chin. So tight his knuckles were white.

"The murder part's easy. He was struck over the head with the Degas dancer."

"This one?" Mallard turned his head and looked at the statuette on the end table beside him.

"Precisely. Only it wasn't sitting there at the time of the murder. It was over here." I walked to stand opposite Mrs. Lamb. "There was a chair here. That's where Mr. Lamb was sitting when he died."

"What are you talking about?" Mrs. Lamb's voice was shrill. "What. . . ."

"Why, he's right, Janie. There used to be matching chairs here." Mallard looked up, surprised. "They sat opposite each other. Wes's was there where the detective's standing."

"Shut up, Travis. I think it's time for the detectives to leave. I'm wearying of this charade."

"Wait, Janie. I'm curious. How'd you know about the chair, Detective?"

"Easy. The dents in the carpet. See, here and here? These four little round depressions show where it sat." I looked at Mallard and smiled. "And here is where the table sat. Smaller circles and less of an impression because of its lighter weight. The Degas was on the table. There was an oval rug here too, between everything. You can see the impression. Barely, but it's there."

"That's amazing. Whatever made you think to look for those things? And what does it all have to do with Wes Lamb's death?" Mallard leaned forward to look down at the carpet.

"On my first quick visit here, I saw something wasn't right. The hair rose on the back of my neck. That's my clue advisor. I got suspicious. Looked around. Noticed the impressions in the carpet. Saw the bronze dancer. Thought it looked like a good weapon. Next time I came, I brought my case with me. Sent Mrs. Lamb out of the room to get the baggies. Took a spray bottle from my case and sprayed a little bit of luminol on the statuette, put on goggles and switched the lights out. I could see where blood had been. I knew then I'd found the murder weapon."

I looked at Mrs. Lamb. Her lips were pulled into a thin, tight line. "Don't look so shocked," I said, barely able to keep from smiling. "You should know from TV shows that no matter how hard someone scrubs, labs can always find blood." I began to pace again. I always did a lot of pacing when my adrenaline got going. Another thing I did to annoy my ex.

"So, here's how it went down." I stopped briefly in front of Mrs. Lamb. She clutched her hands in her lap. Yep, there was fear in her eyes. "Motive? That's easy. Weston Lamb stood in the way of your freedom." I turned to look at Mallard. "You were getting a divorce to be with her. I suppose you think she killed her husband to be free to marry you."

"I think nothing of the sort. I don't believe Janie killed Weston. Why would she? She was going to get a divorce. Like I was doing. I already said I have more money than the two of us could ever use."

"But in a divorce Mrs. Lamb would lose this house. You'll probably say that doesn't matter. You've got three of them. But with no children, she's spent the last fifteen, sixteen years of her life pouring herself into this house. Remodeling. Creating each room. She loves this place. Probably more than she does you or Crandall Fry."

"Who? What are you talking about?" Mallard flung his hands up in irritation.

"Also, she'd lose everything else. The jewels. The bank accounts. The retirement funds. Everything. On the other hand, if he's dead, she gets it all. She's the only survivor."

"Who the hell is Crandall Fry?" Mallard raised his voice. His face flushed.

"If you'd looked through all the photos you would've met him. He and Mrs. Lamb liked the same B and B, too. And I think there's one of her at the elegant Towers with a Jeffrey Combe. I don't know how many others the PI got. I only asked for a couple."

"What the hell is he saying, Janie?" Mallard turned toward Mrs. Lamb.

"I don't have the foggiest." She raised her chin and looked him straight in the eye.

Mallard stared at Lamb, then opened the envelope and pulled out the glossy prints. As he flipped through them, his face got redder and redder. "What is all this, Janelle? What the hell's going on? We're getting married. Honeymooning on my island. What's with these other men? What about these suspicions of murder?" He stood suddenly. Threw the envelope on her lap and turned to me.

"What am I doing here? Am I under suspicion in this depravity?"

"You were for a while."

"We had to deal with the question of how Mr. Lamb's body was disposed of," Rosie popped up. She was giving me my next lead-in.

"We gave that a lot of thought. You're a big man. Perfectly capable of doing it. We had to see if you were complicit in the disposal. That was an easy question to answer." I held my hand to Rosie again, and she gave me our file. I took out two surveillance photos we got courtesy of the PI. They had date and time stamps. I handed them to Mallard.

"These photos show you were home the night of Weston Lamb's murder. From early evening to well past the time the body was found the next morning. Alone. These surveillance photos clear you completely." Mallard glanced at the photos and slumped into the chair.

"So, okay." I looked at Mallard and then at Lamb. "Time for specifics. We've got the where and the why. We've got the murder weapon. I guess next would be figuring out the who." I tapped my lower teeth with my thumbnail and paced, my head lowered. "It would have to be someone left-handed." I stood behind the spot where the missing chair once sat. "His head would've been hit like this," I swung my hands through the air as if holding a heavy object, "and forced blood that direction." I pointed.

"Left-handed? You're a lefty, Janie." Mallard looked at her with wide eyes. She stood and glared at him.

"Please sit down, Mrs. Lamb. I'm almost done here. Let's go back to the oval indenture," I pointed downward, "and the rug on top of the carpet."

She didn't answer. Simply stared, eyebrows raised.

"I'll tell you how I think things went." I held up my hand and counted on my fingers. "First of all, you drugged your husband with the sleeping medicine. Maybe in his tea? He was probably reading. When he fell asleep, he slumped forward. The back of his head made a good target." I held my hands in a circle about where his head would have been.

"You grabbed the statuette and slammed him with it. Right?" I held up my second finger. No answer from the widow, of course. I held up finger number three.

"You rolled him down onto the rug." I gestured, then held up the next finger, "and rolled him up in it." Next finger. "Carried him out to the SUV. Carried the chair out too." Time to move to the other hand. "Drove to an isolated alley. Tossed him in the dumpster."

"And how do you suppose a woman could do all that?" She sat and crossed her legs, lifting her brows in distain.

"Maybe most women couldn't, but you're not the average woman, Mrs. Lamb. You're in exceptional shape. A marathon runner. A dancer. A weight lifter. Taller and stronger than your frail, crippled husband who weighed so little." I was no longer counting on fingers. I was simply standing in front of the grieving, glaring widow.

"Yes, Mrs. Lamb. It was you who dumped him like a piece of trash. But not before you removed his cash and put the baggie in his pocket. That done, you disposed of the bloody rug and chair. We haven't found them yet, but I have no doubt we will someday." I shrugged. "Doesn't matter. We have so many other things with which to hang you. No matter how hard you cleaned, we'll no doubt find trace evidence in the SUV. We'll find spatter patterns on the wall in here. Maybe the end table. The book he was reading. Oh, you burned it? Well, we'll have to dig through the fireplace ashes." I paused and left some silence for her to think.

Mallard broke into the quiet. "So what made the hairs on the back of your neck go up, Detective?"

"This painting." I turned to face *Rain* and pointed. "The spatters at the bottom. Some are blood, not paint."

The widow's head came up fast. She peered around me at the painting. "What are you talking about? There's no blood on that painting." She stood and leaned closer. "There are no red spots."

"Not now, but there were. You never thought about blood spattering there, did you? It would've been red at first, but as blood dries it takes on a brownish tone." I pointed to flecks near the bottom. "Notice, they're not the same brown the artist used with her other earth tones." I straightened and looked at Mallard. "This painting has always been my favorite Durato work. I've pretty well got it memorized. She has a distinctive signature with her spatters. Always downward and to the right. First time I came in here, these spatters bothered me." I pointed to a section of the painting. "They go upward to the left. Consistent with blood from a victim sitting about there," I gestured, "and hit with a left-handed blow from behind." I pulled my handcuffs from my belt.

"Next time I came here, I brought cotton swabs and evidence bags with me. Got a sample off several of the flecks."

I reached out and turned Mrs. Lamb around. Brought her hands to her back and cuffed her. She pulled and twisted to face Mallard.

"Travis, are you going to just sit there and let them insult me this way?"

He ignored her. "What'd your tests of the flecks show, Detective?"

"They were all human blood." I nodded to Rosie. She closed the catalog case and picked it up. "You're free to go, Mr. Mallard. You can keep the photos or not. I have copies."

He glanced at Mrs. Lamb, then left. I heard the front open and close. I guided the widow toward the door.

"You have the right to remain. . . ."

Landmark for Peace (1995)
Stephen Terrell

One of the potentially most explosive moments in the history of Indiana took place at the intersection of 17th and Broadway in Indianapolis during the early evening of April 4, 1968. Robert F. Kennedy, campaigning for President, was scheduled to speak that evening to a large, mostly African-American crowd.

When Kennedy arrived in Indianapolis, he was notified that Martin Luther King Jr. had been assassinated in Memphis. A half hour later, against the advice of police, Kennedy was standing before the crowd on a flatbed trailer. In the recording of the speech, gasps and cries are clearly heard as Kennedy revealed the news of Dr. King's death. Kennedy then proceeded to give perhaps the greatest extemporaneous speech in American history and it was only five minutes long. Kennedy concluded: "What we need in the United States is not division; what we need in the United States is not hatred; what we need in the United States is not violence and lawlessness, but is love, and wisdom, and compassion toward one another, and a feeling of justice toward those who still suffer within our country, whether they be white or whether they be black."

Dedicated by President Bill Clinton in 1994, **Landmark for Peace** shows the bronze figures of King and Kennedy reaching out to each other across a walkway at the location of Kennedy's speech, now Martin Luther King Jr. Park. Indiana artist Greg Perry designed the Memorial from the idea of Hoosier politician Larry Conrad. Indiana sculptor Daniel Edward created the bronze figures. The memorial is made from confiscated guns that were melted down and reshaped into a symbol of peace.

How to Throw a Pot

Barbara Swander Miller

"Oh my gosh!" Marti gasped as she leaned her sturdy frame toward the glass museum case. "Will you look at that?"

Janice, her younger sister, whistled. "Those ancient Peruvians certainly were . . . lusty, weren't they? I thought they were just into silver and gold."

"We did see that incredible silver in the other room. But it takes a back seat to these figurines in their . . . uh . . . creative poses."

"I like the jugs that look like faces. Ha! That one looks like your neighbor, Leo!" Janice laughed.

Marti tore her eyes away from the graphic display and smiled. She glanced around the small, dimly lit room. "I'd hate to have my students see me in here!"

Janice smiled, "No worries. Remember, you're retired now. And it's art. Expensive, too, by the looks of these cameras and locks."

"Well, no wonder." Marti read from the typed sign on the wall near a display. "It says they are from 100–800 AD."

"Take a last look, sis, because where we're headed, we won't be doing much touring. I don't think they even have museums," Janice said.

Marti stepped out of the room of artifacts and into the gift shop. Amidst the colorful textiles and replica statuary, a book on Peruvian pottery caught her eye. She flipped through the pages and saw that it covered many periods of pre-Columbian history. "I think I'll get it. I need some reading material."

"*Gracias,*" she said, rifling through her wallet for a purple hundred *soles* bill. As her slim younger sister joined her at the counter, Marti said, "I'm guessing the people up north are probably more interested in basic survival than in preserving ancient relics."

Walking out into the courtyard of the mansion-turned-museum, Marti stopped to admire the cascades of vibrant fuchsia bougainvillea that tumbled down the stone garden wall. "Jan, take my picture, would you? I still can't seem to get a good-looking selfie."

Janice took her sister's phone and laughed. "It's not about your age, is it? I mean you are two years older than I am."

Marti made a face and changed the subject. "Seriously, Lima has been incredible, don't you think? I just want to get a few more pictures before we leave. I could use them in my class. " Marti stopped abruptly. "I mean, I love the bright flowers against the yellow buildings."

Janice sighed. "My favorite so far has been walking in Barranco and seeing the beautiful old homes. Who knows what those carved wooden doors are hiding."

"Well, it's time to head north," Marti said. "I hope this volunteer vacation will be a good blend of relaxation and helping others. I never thought I'd feel so useless when I retired."

The next day, after the exhausting bus ride from Lima to Huaraz and the cramped taxi ride to their host's house, Marti stretched her legs. She hated to leave their exotic bed and breakfast perched on the cliffs of the Pacific to head to the grimy downtown Lima bus station, but she brought her new pottery book to read on the winding trip. She was glad Janice felt comfortable admiring the changing scenery as they wound their way from the desert into the mountains.

Eight hours later, Marti steadied her rolling luggage on the sloping street in Huaraz, trying to get her bearings. The air was thin in the Cordillera Blanca mountains that loomed behind the low and jagged city skyline. Huascaran, the tallest mountain, jagged and dark, looked as if its peak had been hastily frosted by an impatient baker. A lazy dog looked up from a shady doorway.

Marti read the addresses painted on a stucco-covered house wall. "I think this is it," she huffed as she rang the doorbell. A little boy welcomed them to their temporary home.

After two days of volunteer teaching at the grade school, Raul, their host, invited the sisters to explore the open-air third floor of their lodgings. With no rails on the concrete steps, Marti was nervous climbing up to the bird's eye view of the town.

"I don't care if the scenery is gorgeous, Jan. I don't like this," Marti said as she gingerly stepped onto the top floor. Her arms spread out as if she were walking a tightrope. "I think I'll go hang out in the library and read my book about the Moche."

"I'll stay here," Janice replied adjusting her camera. "I'd like to get some shots of the city."

Later that week, Janice stopped by the library on her way to the rooftop. "How was your day at the school?" she asked her sister.

"I hate to complain and I know I shouldn't judge how they do things." Marti paused.

"Go on," her sister prodded.

"Well, learning English with worksheets is just not best practice," Marti said as she put several nonfiction books into a pile. "It's just so boring for these kids. It's hard to think I am making a difference here."

"Too bad you're not teaching theater. You probably never used a worksheet in your classroom. But I'm sure what you are doing is helping, even if it is short-term." Janice plopped into the settee to chat. "I know it's hard. At the community center where I'm working, everyone gets fed and no one is sick, even though their sanitation seems somewhat lacking. Maybe we have too many regulations and requirements back home."

Marti turned from filing books. "I don't know about regulations, but I know I'm ready to have some fun and not on that rooftop."

"What do you have in mind?"

"Well, for starters, I am tired of potatoes and rice. I suppose we could find a restaurant with something sweet."

"How about something a little more adventurous?" Janice suggested. She got up to look at the bulletin board on the wall above the yellowed Compaq computer. "It looks like there are day trips to the hot springs. Or how about an overnight mountain hike?"

"Not likely with this knee," Marti said, rubbing it. "It's been hurting ever since we got off the bus."

"You seem to love that pottery book. How about this?" She read from a flyer: "Pottery lessons—Mondays, Wednesdays, and Fridays. It says it's in a village outside of Huaraz. I'll bet you could catch a bus."

"That sounds different. But what about you? You'll come, right?

"No, I don't think so. You know I don't like crafts. I'll hang out here on the roof. I'm thinking about taking some pictures and writing some poetry to send back home."

"Oh, but think of how much fun it could be. When will you have the chance to see a real Peruvian potter's workshop?" Seeing her sister's hesitation, she added, "I don't think I'd want to go by myself."

"Well. . . ." Janice hesitated. "I guess I can take pictures anywhere. Okay. I'll go along for the ride."

Early the next afternoon, Marti lumbered onto a minibus heading to the pottery shop. She was eager to have her hands on something culturally tangible, not just English worksheets from a Peruvian school.

Marti counted twenty-one people, including an infant and two toddlers, crammed into a fifteen-passenger van that was colloquially called a mini bus. She was glad she found an open seat near the door and didn't have to climb over other passengers. She envied Janice, who nimbly shifted seats as passengers got out and others climbed in.

After several stops in town, the minibus headed for the highway and picked up speed. Fewer passengers were interested in heading out to the remote villages, especially right after lunch. By the time they reached the outskirts of town, the sisters shared the bus with two young men whose eyes were glued to their cell phones and an old woman wrapped in a purple striped blanket, loaded down with three bulging fabric bags. Marti leaned forward to confirm that the bus would stop in Santa Rosa.

"Sí, sí," the driver assured her, but Marti kept her eyes peeled for road signs.

"I'm afraid we'll end up in some remote village where no one speaks a word of English," she whispered to her sister. Over the past five days, some of Marti's Spanish had returned, but the verbs were only in present tense.

"Well," Janice laughed when Marti complained. "You'll just have to live in the moment. Otherwise, I can be pretty awesome at charades."

Finally, the bus jerked to a stop. "Pottery, here," the driver announced, looking at Marti. She smiled her relief to the driver as she and Janice bundled up their bags and followed the two younger men out the sliding door. She stopped and asked, *"Cuando autobus otra vez?"*

"A la hora y media," he replied.

Satisfied that they could catch the bus again, Marti gave the driver a ten *soles* bill and climbed out.

A crudely lettered sign that read 'pottery' pointed up a small hill from the bus stop. Most of the shops were closed for *siesta*. A trio of dogs, two multi-colored little ones and a larger gray one, trotted together down the center of the dirt street. "Quite a bit different from Lima, eh, Jan?"

"Yes, and perfect to get some non-touristy shots. I may wander around this area. Would you mind?"

"Nope, all I ask is that you help me get settled."

Marti noticed a woman opening a sliding metal door to an ice cream shop. "Maybe when we finish, we can get some gelato if the shop is still open. It might be a while until dinner." Huffing up yet another hill, Marti stopped to rub her knee.

Then they were upon it, tucked amidst some houses only three blocks from the tiny shopping district. Another sign hung precariously on the gate of a stucco wall. A large, yellow dog slunk over for a sniff and then wagged its tail as Janice reached out to scratch behind its ears.

Marti knocked on the gate door. There was no answer. "I think I hear people inside," she said. She cracked open the gate, peeked inside, then promptly pushed the heavy, squeaky gate fully open.

Janice hesitated before she and the dog followed her sister into the abandoned compound. Weeds grew as high as their waists in some places.

Intrigued by an adobe block well, Marti wandered over and peered into the dark hole. This was certainly no picture from a nursery rhyme book, she thought. It didn't even have a place to hang a bucket. Once her eyes adjusted to the dim light, she noticed bricks that protruded to form a spiral staircase. This must be the only way in and out of the well, she thought. Off to her right, Marti saw a large stucco building with a red clay tile roof. Through the open windows, she saw a few outlines of people moving from room to room. "That must be the place, Jan. I'm heading over there. Want to come?"

"Sure, I'll stay for awhile." She nodded. They picked their way through broken beer bottles scattered in the sand that flanked the stone walkway.

"*Hola,*" Marti called as she entered the dim room.

"*Sí, sí,*" she heard from inside an adjacent room. "Please come in."

"*Hola, Señor.* We are here for the pottery lessons."

"Yes, *sí.*" The rotund artisan dressed in a clay-stained apron motioned them toward a circular room with five pottery wheel stations. "I am Tomás. You make pot here. I show you." He pointed Marti toward one of the stations. When Janice held back, he said, "You, too, *Señorita.*"

"No, no," she laughed, pulling out a water bottle from her backpack. "I am just here to watch."

Scuffling noises from the nearby room stopped her laughter. Tomás scurried toward it as Marti turned to look toward the other room. She shrugged and settled herself on a wooden stool at the simple potter's wheel. "I wonder what is so important that he would leave a paying customer," she said.

"Do you even know what you're supposed to do at this thing?" Janice asked.

"Nope. Is this where I am supposed to put my feet?"

Just then, a pretty teenage girl entered the room. "*Hola, Señoras.* I am Silvia." She carried two balls of clay over to Marti's station and placed one of them on her wheel and the other on the wheel beside Marti. "Like this," she said, as she then demonstrated kicking the wheel beneath the stool.

Marti kicked the concrete wheel under her feet like Silvia had done. It glided easily, and soon, she had a smooth, easy rhythm that kept the turntable moving. "Now what?" she asked, looking at the girl.

"Use your hands, *Señora,*" she said. "Like this." The girl cupped her hands around the bottom of the mound of clay, making it more uniform as the wheel spun. She dribbled a little water from a dirty sponge onto the clay to keep it moist. "Just play." She smiled encouragement at Marti and then turned abruptly as a young, bearded man entered the room.

Marti noticed the man's expensive leather shoes and trim fitting pants. She was surprised to see the girl halt the other spinning wheel and hurry over to him. Marti saw him light a cigarette and smooth his oiled hair. They talked in hushed tones and then ducked out of the large workroom. Maybe he was Silvia's boyfriend, Marti thought.

Marti went back to her task. She happily worked the clay up into a column that promptly collapsed, while Janice clicked a few photos to document her progress. Marti gathered the tumbled tower of clay into a ball and started over, training her hands in cause and effect with this new medium.

"I think I'll sit outside for a bit with the dog," Janice told Marti, who was too engrossed in her play to do more than give a nod and a brief okay. Janice grabbed her water bottle and her poncho and headed into the courtyard.

Inside the cool adobe building, Marti soon became frustrated. *Really,* she thought, *if they are supposed to be giving pottery lessons, why do they just disappear? That's not very good business. I need some instruction.*

She got up from her metal stool, wiped her hands on a rag that had been haphazardly tossed at another station, and followed the voices into the next room.

The young man was shaking Silvia as Tomás stood nearby wringing his hands.

"I beg your pardon," Marti said. "Just what is going on here?"

The young man released the girl and turned away from the group. He pulled out his cell phone and ignored the others.

"No worries, *Señora.* Is okay," Tomás reassured her, rushing over and taking her elbow to direct her out of the room.

Sniffling and daintily wiping her nose with the sleeve of her embroidered blouse, Silvia said, "*Sí,* it's okay."

Marti's eyes swept the room, taking in the situation. On a crude wooden table sat several clay pots in various stages of work. Some looked very amateurish. But others were quite good, probably Tomás's work, she thought. A few sat near pots of paint and brushes. Others appeared to have been painted and ready to be fired. Marti caught a glimpse of a few pots of a slightly different, lighter color resting inside a crate with wooden shavings, at the end of the table. The young man moved toward that end of the table and stood in front of the crate, blocking it from Marti's view.

In a nearly unaccented voice, he ordered, "Go teach the lady, Tomás. This is not her business."

Tomás glanced back at Silvia, who nodded. "Come, please," he said.

Marti resisted. Should she leave this situation? This really was none of her business, but surely something wasn't right.

Without a word about what had just taken place, Tomás took Marti's elbow and led her back to her pottery station. He picked up a new piece of clay, forced a smile, and sat at her wheel. "See," he said, as he set the wheel in motion and used his thumbs to make an opening in the spinning ball of clay. As if by enchantment, the ball became a small vessel under Tomás's skilled hands. He adjusted his thumbs and began to create a slightly rimmed edge. Then he picked up a tool from the window ledge and began to level the top of the pot, the excess clay spiraling off the top as he held the tool perfectly still.

"How do you do that so easily?" Marti marveled. "You're amazing!"

Tomás smiled briefly. Then he pulled a piece of wire between the clay and the spinning wheel to free the pot. He lifted it, turned it in his hands to assess it, and motioned for her to take his place. Marti sat down and kicked the wheel again, eager to imitate Tomás's actions.

Eventually, Marti succeeded in creating a bowl of sorts although it was much thicker than the one Tomás had so easily tossed off in his demonstration. It measured three inches across its uneven top and perhaps could be used as a sugar bowl, if it had a lid. Even with its flaws, she was proud of her efforts. "Janice," she called through the open window. "Jan, come see what I made."

But it wasn't her sister that Marti saw in the courtyard. It was the young man who had been threatening Silvia. He was standing near the abandoned well with something in his hands. Marti let the wheel stop spinning as she watched him lean over the edge. The man looked around and then crossed the courtyard to the gate. Marti heard the roar of a motorcycle.

Just then, Janice rushed inside followed by the yellow dog. She loudly praised her sister's craftsmanship, then whispered, "Marti, there is something funny going on here."

In her best high-school-theater-coach voice, Marti picked up the cue. "Thank you, Jan. I worked very hard on this piece." Under her breath, she asked, "I just saw that man at the well. What did you see?"

Janice whispered. "He hid something in it and then he left on a motorcycle. What's going on here?"

Marti slowed the spinning wheel and made a face. "I'm not sure. Let's go check on Tomás and Silvia. Maybe they're in danger." She gathered her belongings and the sisters headed toward the doorway to the other room. The dog trotted behind them.

Silvia stood alone in the finishing room, her hands gently cradling a piece of pottery as she prepared to load it into a wooden crate filled with wood shavings. Marti's head spun around when she recognized what the girl was handling.

"Silvia," scolded Marti. "Where did you get that Moche pottery?"

Surprised, Silvia jerked toward the voice. Her hands lost control of the ceramic vessel she was holding. It slipped from her hands onto the table and tumbled to the floor with a crash. A pile of potshards and red dust was all that was left. Marti gasped.

"*¡Dios mío!* What have I done?" Silvia wailed.

Tomás burst into the room carrying another crate. "*¿Que pasó?*" he demanded.

Silvia ran toward him and threw her arms around his neck. "*Papá,* forgive me, *por favor.*"

Marti saw Tomás's eyes widen. He pushed the girl's arms from his neck and began to shake his head. "*Desastre!* This is a disaster!" He stooped to pick up the scattered fragments and then grabbed the broom and dustpan and nudged away the dog that was sniffing at the remains. Trying to help, Janice pulled the trash can closer to Tomás.

Marti stepped in and looked from Tomás to Silvia. "Can we help, Tomás?"

Silvia shook her head. "You must go now . . . please . . . before he returns. Hurry. . . He will be back soon."

Marti sidled over to the table to peek inside the crate. She gasped, "Oh my goodness! How many are here? These have to be worth a fortune!"

"No look. This no good. You leave now, no charge," Tomás ordered, pointing at the door.

Just then, the mutt began to howl.

"What is it, pup?" Janice exclaimed. "Oh, no, listen! That must be him again."

"He's coming for this pottery, no doubt, this ancient Moche pottery," Marti guessed. "Is that right?"

But neither Tomás nor Silvia would answer as the roar of a motorcycle got louder.

"Hurry," hissed Marti. She shoved both Janice and Silvia ahead of her through the door and into the shadows of the workroom. The dog followed them. Marti watched through the crack where the door met the frame. Only a moment after the three disappeared, she saw the young man burst into the room.

"Is it ready?" he shouted at Tomás. "You said it would be ready."

"*Lo siento, Señor.* Almost ready." The potter shrugged and glanced at the broom and dustpan in the corner of the room.

Marti watched the young man swagger over to the trashcan. He pulled out two chunks of pale terra cotta, both with red engravings on them. His face became dark and he turned viciously on Tomás. Marti stifled a scream as the heel of his hand slammed into Tomás's face.

"Do you know how much money you cost me?"

Marti saw the older man crumple to the floor, blood gushing from his broken nose. She knew this was no act. Tomás was badly hurt.

From behind the door, Marti swallowed the vomit that rose in her mouth. If only she could run. They would have to do something else. She motioned the two women into the darkened pottery room.

Silvia began to whimper. Marti grabbed Silvia's face. "What does this man want?" she whispered. "Tell me."

"It is the smuggled pottery," Silvia whispered back. "He uses my father to ship out the Moche pieces mixed in with the new pieces from our shop. This man, Arturo, promised my father he would sell his pottery to *los Americanos*, but it was a lie."

Marti set her jaw. "Shh, now. We have to stop him." She pantomimed instructions to the two women. Janice gave Marti her poncho and held the dog, but Silvia hesitated, her eyes wide with fear. Marti nodded encouragement, and they all tiptoed toward the lighted room.

"Now," Marti whispered and shoved Silvia into the room. The dog strained, but Janice held its neck and watched.

"Excuse me, *Señor*, we had an accident. I will finish the shipment." Marti saw Silvia flash him a smile then coyly look down.

"You'd better, if you don't want to end up like your old man," Arturo laughed.

The girl moved toward the table and began to place new pots in the crate, covering them in wood chips.

Marti saw Arturo eyeing Silvia. He moved closer and then pressed himself against her back. "Hurry up, *chica*. I have plans for you."

Silvia turned toward him.

On Marti's signal, Janice let go of the growling dog. Marti rushed into the room with the alpaca poncho. As the dog tore into the man's leg, she slammed into his slim shape and deftly threw the rough fabric over his head. Taken by surprise, Arturo shouted, his arms wildly grabbing at whatever he could.

Janice was right behind her sister. She grabbed the largest piece of pottery from the table and slammed it down on Arturo's head. The man fell to the concrete floor, dazed, amidst chunks of pottery.

"Nice throw," Marti said.

"Now what do we do?" Janice shouted.

"Run for help!" Marti yelled. The three women flew from the finishing room, into the courtyard and through the gate. Janice and Silvia sprinted down the hill to the business district, but Marti, gasping for air, stopped halfway down. Her knee bones ground and sliced away at her cartilage with every step.

By the time she reached the gelato shop at the bottom of the hill, Marti was hobbling and gasping for breath. The other women were nowhere in sight. Where had they gone? Marti heard the wail of a siren. A gray police car raced up the hill, its flashing lights illuminating the gate of the pottery compound. Maybe the ordeal was over, Marti thought.

Just as she breathed a sigh of relief, a warm hand clamped over her mouth. Someone dragged her backward into the ice cream store. With the little energy she had left, she managed a muffled, "Help!"

"Stop, stop! It's okay, Marti. Shh. It's okay. They are keeping us safe." Janice turned her sister around and shook her shoulders.

Next to her, Silvia was nodding her head. "*Sí*, this is *mi familia*. They called the *policía*. Did you not hear the sirens?"

Marti's shoulders sagged and she collapsed into a chair set out for gelato customers.

After icing her knee and being talked into sampling a gelato from Silvia's relatives, Marti talked to the police. Silvia had already explained how she and her father had been duped, and with Silvia as the interpreter, Janice filled them in on their suspicions about the valuable pieces being stored in the old well. The local police informed the *Policía Nacional de Peru*, who alerted Peruvian customs authorities and were tracking Arturo and any possible accomplices.

There was nothing new for Marti to share, only a confirmation that her sister had broken the two-thousand-year-old Moche vessel over Arturo's head, knocking him out until the police arrived. The police officers informed her that smuggling pre-Columbian pottery was a serious offense in Peru, but luckily, breaking it in the course of capturing a criminal was not.

That evening, after a quick visit with Silvia and Tomás at the local clinic, Marti and Janice waited in the dusk at the bus stop to catch the last bus back to Huaraz. Huascaran loomed above the sleepy town in the purple haze of twilight, and Janice captured a shot of her sister posing in front of the snow-capped vista.

"Next time when you say you're bored, remind me to stay home," said Janice. "This was not what I imagined when we set out this morning."

"Next time you want to go on a volunteer vacation, remind me to have my knee fixed first," moaned her sister. "When it comes to running away from criminals, I'd prefer to pass."

"Well, at least I can say I know how to throw a Peruvian pot," Janice chuckled, as the empty mini bus rolled to a stop and opened its door.

Graffiti and Street Art
Stephen Terrell

Graffiti and Street Art—those often brightly-colored words and images that adorn walls, schools, street signs and railroad cars—are often used interchangeably. Others see a distinction.

One difference between graffiti and street art is permission. The Herron School of Art website states that there are "strong differentiations between the two forms of expression as well as the types of people that create them." Graffiti is usually the product of quick, surreptitious action—a late night location, a quick look around, and a flash of spray paint. It is often an act of vandalism, sometimes a gang demarcation, and sometimes simply youthful expression.

But in the late 1970s and 1980s, a new type of graffiti appeared. The work of self-trained Jean-Michel Basquiat and Al Diaz appeared under the name SAMO. Their work gained immense popularity. Basquiat's work made its way into galleries, and he became one of the most celebrated artists in the New York art scene until a heroin overdose took his life. Other street artists and commercial successes followed, including Banksy, the subject of the 2010 movie *Exit Through the Gift Shop*; Morley, a classically trained artist; and Retna, an L.A. artist who works with an alphabet of his own creation.

No longer is street art simply a quick act of vandalism with a spray can or the refuge of frustrated unemployed graphic artists. It is often well-planned, complicated art that is put together in advance, and then erected in locations by permission. There is even a museum of street art in Brooklyn and an annual conference in Atlanta called "Living Walls: The City Speaks."

Street Art

Stephen Terrell

The first body was found on one of those warm days of early spring. The kind of day that makes you glad to be alive.

I got the call at my desk just after my first cup of coffee. I headed to the scene near the old Muncie Central Trade School in my city-issued, six-year-old p.o.s. Chevy that I still had to drive due to budget cuts. At forty-nine, I was the second most senior detective in the Muncie Police Department, but I still was stuck with a car that was best described as two-tone, sun-faded blue over rust.

Alexis James, a petite patrolwoman in her early thirties, met me at the scene just off 8th Street. She seemed swallowed up by all the gear attached to her utility belt, but if the weight was a burden, it didn't show in her manner. She worked the midnight to eight swing shift where we crossed paths occasionally on domestics, bar fights, and periodic homicides. She was ex-military and still carried herself with military precision. She didn't bother with pleasantries. Joe Friday would have liked her.

"Detective Rigsby, I found the body over in that deserted parking lot," she said, pointing. "Hispanic male, probably mid to late twenties. From the tats, likely a gang member. Looks like a double tap to the back of the head."

"When did you get here?"

"I caught the call just before the end of my shift. Arrived at the scene at 7:58," Alexis said, consulting her notes for accuracy. "Found the body a few minutes later. Didn't take long. The 911 caller pretty much said where to find it."

"Who called?"

Again she consulted her notebook. "Anonymous woman called from a pay phone. 911 center showed it was in front of Frank's Bar. Dispatcher thought the caller sounded drunk."

The look on my face must have betrayed my thoughts.

"There are still a few pay phones around, sir," Alexis said, without a trace of a smile.

We walked across the broken pavement and shattered glass

that had once been a parking lot for perhaps two hundred workers. After the Chevrolet assembly plant closed, there was no more need for the parts manufactured at the factory, and it shut its doors. It was like the whole damn town. The jobs were gone to Mexico, or China, or who knows where, leaving behind the rusted factories and deteriorating cities that were once the lifeblood of America—big-shouldered tool makers, hog butchers, and stackers of wheat no more.

The body was face down, head slightly turned, arms splayed wide. Drying blood collected around what appeared to be two small caliber holes in the back of the victim's head. Except for the blood, the man looked as if he was asleep, bothered only by a troubling dream.

I pulled a pair of latex gloves from my jacket pocket and snapped them on. Using a thumb and forefinger, I eased a wallet from the victim's back pocket and flipped through it. The driver's license was for Miguel Zayas, age twenty-nine. It listed an address on West Adams, an area now populated by Mexican immigrants, mostly illegals with fake green cards, earning below minimum wage and living eight to a room in houses long ago fallen into disrepair. I was surprised to find more than six hundred dollars in cash still in the wallet. The Little Mexico community operated mostly on a cash basis and apparently Miguel's bank was his back pocket.

"Doesn't look like a robbery," I said out loud.

"Excuse me, sir?" Alexis said.

"Not a robbery. Guy's got almost two hundred dollars in cash in his pocket." Out of the corner of my eye, I noticed that crime scene techs had arrived. As I walked toward them, I slipped four hundred dollars into my pants pocket.

* * *

Nearly an hour later, just as we were getting ready to remove the body, I heard an all-too familiar and unwelcome voice call out from the edge of the parking lot. "Hey, Hammer, whatcha got?"

My given name was Patrick Rigsby, but most called me Hammer, a nickname earned as an all-state linebacker in high school. The annoying voice belonged to Tess White, the crime and court reporter for the local newspaper. In her mid-thirties, she survived the newsroom cutbacks, most likely because she was at the low end of the pay scale. Her hair was dyed fire-engine red and hung in a stylish cut that was long in the front and tapered severely toward the back. She was a pert fireplug, slightly over five feet tall with thick legs and hips and large breasts. She carried some extra pounds, but it wasn't unattractive on her. She always dressed in snug clothes that emphasized her breasts, which may have been another reason she survived the cutbacks in the male-dominated local newsroom.

I walked over to Tess, knowing that if I ignored her, she would traipse into the crime scene to ask her questions. "Male Hispanic," I said, preempting her question. "Tentative ID is Miguel Zayas, age twenty-nine. Address we have is Muncie. But none of that is official yet, so hold off until we get a positive I.D. and notify the family." While I wasn't fond of Tess, experience taught me that she could be trusted not to publish a victim's name before family notification.

"Sure," she said, making notes on the tablet computer she held in her hand. She confirmed the spelling of the victim's name. "Shooting?"

"Yep. Two shots in back of the head."

"Robbery? Gang? Drugs? Any idea?"

I self-consciously let my hand feel the bills in my pocket. "Doesn't look like robbery," I said. "Victim has what looks like a gang tattoo. I'm going to check with Lacy Ringger in the gang unit. We really don't know. And before you ask, no witnesses that we know of."

Tess looked over my shoulder and nodded as if to point past me with her chin. "What about the painting on the wall? Is that connected?"

"What painting?" Before the words were out, I was cursing under my breath for being so stupid.

"That graffiti on the wall over there. Looks like someone painted the murder scene. Is that what that is?"

I turned, still cursing. Maybe eighty feet behind the body on a pockmarked, brown brick wall, there was a graffiti mural in vibrant purple, orange, green, yellow, and white. It was a gruesome, cartoonish image of a man on his knees falling forward, his face contorted in agony and terror. Blood and brains exploded from the back of his head. Smoke curled from the barrel of a handgun held in a black-gloved hand.

"Shit." I said it to myself, but it was loud enough that Tess heard.

I looked back and there was a smile on her face. "Didn't see the forest for the trees?" she said.

I ignored her comment and started walking back toward the painted wall. Behind me I heard her giving instructions to her photographer, telling him to get a photo of the graffiti with the body in the foreground.

* * *

The next morning, I sat at my desk talking with Lacy Ringger. Tall, athletic and with midnight black skin, Lacy was an imposing presence. For the past four years, he had headed the department's gang unit. He was effective in building relationships in black and Hispanic gangs and the communities where they thrived, but the growing white supremacist gangs on the city's East Side were beyond his reach. I showed Lacy several photos of the victim with close-ups of the tattoos on his neck, chest and arms.

"Miguel Zayas," Lacy said after flipping through the first three photos. "Small-time drug dealer with the local branch of LRN—La Raza Nation. That's a Hispanic gang out of Chicago."

"Any thoughts on why someone would want him dead?"

Lacy shook his head. "Who knows? Zayas wasn't a big time player. He sold a little dope, small time thefts. There was street talk that he did low-end enforcement for LRN, making sure people pay up. I think he did a little time. But he's not someone that gets targeted. He's not worth it. That doesn't mean he couldn't have pissed someone off. Obviously he did. But just may have been a bad drug deal, or maybe he messed with somebody's woman. No way of knowing."

"Keep your ear to the ground. Let me know what you hear."

As Lacy got up to walk away, the phone rang. "Rigsby," I answered.

"Detective Rigsby, this is Alexis James. I'm the officer who caught the call on that homicide yesterday morning."

"I know who you are," I said. "Call me Hammer. Everybody does."

"Uh, Hammer," her voice was a bit uncertain. "I did a little snooping around on my shift last night. Went down to Frank's Bar. That's where the 911 call came from. Seems there's an old hooker who comes in there sometimes. Name's Annie Waldron. She was in there night before last getting trashed. Told Frank that she saw a guy get killed. I guess Annie is prone to exaggerating when she's drunk, and most times she's drunk, so Frank didn't take it too seriously. Might be worth checking out."

I thought for a moment, then asked, "Any idea where I can find this Annie?"

"Frank said she's a regular. He doesn't let her hit on his customers, at least that's what he says. She comes in and drinks before she hits the streets, and then sometimes after she's turned a trick or two. Best time to catch her is between seven and nine, or after midnight."

I made some notes on a scrap of paper. "Thanks Alexis," I said. "Good work."

* * *

I found Annie Waldron just after 8:30 that evening, sitting by herself at the end of Frank's well-worn bar. Even in the dim yellow light, the hard-life lines on Annie's face were evident. Her hair was a dull drug-store bottle blonde with inch-long gray roots. It hung to her shoulders in unwashed tangles. She wore a flimsy stained shirt open to just above her naval, revealing several inches of a white bra. Her black mini skirt rode up nearly to her crotch as she sat on the barstool. She reeked of cigarettes, body odor, and cheap floral perfume.

Annie finagled a double shot of house whiskey from me before she told her story. She downed the drink in a single unflinching swallow, then ordered a second. I held up my hand toward Frank. "Not until I hear the story."

Annie took a deep breath. Her voice was thin and raspy, her words slightly slurred. "I had this new john. Don't know his name. He picked me up on Madison there by where that old hardware store used to be. He drove me to this deserted spot over by the trade school. It's a place I've used before." Annie spoke with the matter-of-fact casualness of a clerk describing the sale of a pair of shoes. "Gave him a blow job. He paid me and let me out, then drove off."

I wanted to ask how much someone like Annie could get on the street from someone desperate enough to use her services, but I let the question go. "What time was that?"

Annie shook her head. "Don't know. Maybe midnight." She broke into a small smile that showed a line of broken, yellowed teeth. "Don't punch a time clock."

"Just answer the questions," I said sternly. "What happened then?"

"After he drove away, I needed a drink. Clear the palate. Ain't that what they say on those fancy cooking shows on TV?"

I barked a short laugh, but tried to cover it with a cough. "Go on. Just tell me what you saw," I said.

Annie stared up toward the row of whiskeys behind the bar. "Girl gets kinda thirsty talking this much," she said. "Hard to talk with a dry mouth."

I signaled Frank and he brought another shot glass filled with amber liquid.

Annie took it down in one swallow. Then she continued. "When I got over by the old Thomas Machine plant, I needed to pee. So I found a few bushes and crouched down. That's when I seen 'em. This guy was down on his knees, and another guy was standing behind him, holding a gun pointed right at his head. They was talking. I mean, it sounded like the guy on his knees was really upset. But you know it ain't my business. I watched just long enough for me to pee. I was pulling up my panties, and I heard this 'pop, pop.' I looked over and the one guy was sprawled out on the ground. The other guy was standing over him holding the gun."

"What did the guy with the gun look like?"

"It was dark. There ain't no lights out there. He wasn't very big, but that's all I could tell."

"White? Black? Young? Old?"

"Don't know. Couldn't see. I just got the hell out of there as fast as I could."

"If you saw the guy again, would you recognize him?"

"Shit, he could sit down right next to me and I wouldn't know him."

I continued to ask questions for another ten minutes, but Annie didn't have anything else to offer. I signaled Frank, who brought a third drink, and called it a night.

* * *

The second body was found in mid-July, just after I returned from vacation. This time it was an overweight black woman in her mid-twenties discovered on the northeast side of the city. An elderly black man discovered the body at mid-morning as he was walking from his apartment in a nearby senior housing project to a Dollar General Store. The body was lying in a pool of blood behind a long-closed K-Mart.

This time, when I arrived at the scene, I immediately saw the graffiti. Across the whitewash blocks of the abandoned building was a spray-painted, cartoon-like image of a big, black woman, her back turned, getting her throat slashed by a knife held by a black-gloved hand.

"Looks like you got another one, Hammer."

I turned to see Joe Marcum, a career uniform officer I had known since my first day on the force. He stood with his thumbs inside his belt, his cap tipped back. "Gonna be a hot day to be working a stiff," he said.

I nodded a greeting and asked about his upcoming retire-ment. While we talked, the photographer and crime scene techs arrived. I told Joe where to set up the crime scene perimeter, then pulled on a set of latex gloves. The body lay in a near-fetal posi-tion two feet in front of the wall painting. Her throat had been sliced deep enough to expose her cervical vertebrae. Blood cov-ered her oversized yellow T-shirt and tight spandex shorts, form-ing a now-sticky river where black flies were feasting. Where the skin wasn't covered in blood, there were large, blue-ink tattoos. I wasn't sure any of the marks were gang related, but I knew who would be able to tell me. I called Lacy Ringger.

I kneeled and took a close look. Even in the distortion of death, I could tell that I knew this woman. I couldn't remember from where or how, but I knew our paths had crossed.

Lacy showed up a half hour later as the crime scene techs continued their work. It took him only a single glance at the body to know who it was.

"Bren Taylor," Lacy said. "She's connected with the Broadway Killaz. She's got a short record—hooking, shoplifting, possession, that type of thing. Nothing violent I know of. Got three, maybe four kids. Lives in that new public housing across from the Hoffer Center, if I remember right."

The name clicked somewhere in my distant memory, but I still couldn't place her. I kept trying to sort through my mental files to find the connection, but was pulled out of my thoughts by a too-familiar voice.

"Another victim of the Graffiti Killer?" Tess White yelled from behind a yellow crime scene tape barrier.

"No comment," I shouted over my shoulder.

"Looks like the same style. You can't deny that this is connected to the murder you had a couple of months ago."

I turned and looked directly at Tess. "What part of no comment do you not understand?" I then walked over to her, strides long and purposeful, my jaw set and eyes focused directly on her. "And I don't want to read something in that rag of yours that says I did. Understand?"

I didn't wait for a response, just turned sharply and walked away.

* * *

Late the next morning I sat at my desk, drinking coffee and eating a second cream-filled Long John from Concannon's Bakery. Powdered sugar from the pastry lightly dusted the murder scene photos that were scattered in front of me. My phone buzzed with the distinctive sound made by internal calls. When I picked it up, Police Chief Brad Smith was on the line. He was not happy.

"Have you seen what's in the paper this morning?"

"No," I said. "I don't read the paper."

"Maybe you should," Smith said sharply. "Big front page story by Tess White. Says we got two killings that are connected. She writes about these paintings left at the scene. She's calling it the

Graffiti Killer. Says there's a suspicion that they're gang related."

I fought not to let out an obscenity. "Chief, I didn't say a word to her. Not a damned word."

"Well I've got a half dozen calls already this morning about this, including from the mayor and two council members."

"We're on it, Chief," I said. "I'm sitting here right now going over the photos. But there's just not a lot to go on yet."

"Work it some more," Chief Smith barked. "If the mayor and council start thinking I'm not doing my job, I'm going to start thinking you're not doing your job. I don't want any more stories on the front page. Get it solved!" The phone at the other end of the line slammed.

Seething, I spent the rest of the morning snapping at lab techs and medical examiners to speed up reports. It was nearly one before I took a break for a quick sandwich. As I walked out the door into the sweltering mid-summer heat, Tess White fell into step beside me.

"Anything new on the Graffiti Killer?" she asked.

"The what?"

"The Graffiti Killer. That's what we've termed the guy who's killing people then drawing pictures of it. Pretty catchy, huh?"

I kept my head down and increased my stride. Beside me, Tess forced her short legs to move even faster to keep up. "You should talk to Portia Henshaw," she said.

"Who?"

"Portia Henshaw. She's in the art department at Ball State, but she's an expert in graffiti. Street art, she calls it. Even wrote a book about it."

I stopped and turned, looking directly at Tess. "Why do you think she could help?"

"She knows this stuff. She can identify gang styles. Sometimes she can even identify individual artists from just looking at a piece of graffiti. I know she could tell you if it was the same person. Might be able to tell you if it's from a black, white or Mexican gang member."

"How do you know about this?"

"Did a profile story on her last year when her latest book came out. It was all about graffiti. She thinks it's among the most important art being created today. Something about it being the only form of art actually reflecting our current society. She's knows her stuff."

I stood silently for a long moment. "You really think she could help identify someone by the painting?"

"It's worth asking, isn't it?"

"Thanks, Tess," I said reluctantly.

"Hey, I live in this town too," Tess said quietly. "I want to see this guy caught." She gave me a wink. "Besides, it will make a great story when you catch him."

* * *

Two days later, I was in a crowded office that smelled of old wood and dust on the third floor of the Arts Building at Ball State. Books were strewn haphazardly in scarred, dark walnut bookcases. Magazines were piled in stacks on the floor. The desk was cluttered with papers and what appeared to be unopened mail. A glass and chrome table next to the desk seemed out of place with its organized neatness. The table held a laptop computer, a single note pad, and what I took to be a portable scanner.

Portia Henshaw was in her early fifties. She was tall and lean with a runner's body and a ruddy complexion that I had often seen on people who spent a lifetime outdoors. She wore well-worn jeans and an orange and yellow cotton shirt, open to reveal a white tank top underneath. Her hair was medium brown liberally streaked with gray, pulled back in a ponytail. She wore no makeup.

I outlined the situation and she seemed eager to help. She immediately asked to see the photos of the graffiti from the crime scene. I sat, letting my eyes roam around the cluttered office while she studied the stack of photos. She took her time, silently examining each in turn, then placing it face down. Only when she was finished examining the photos did she speak.

"There's no signature or tag, but I have no doubt the same artist did both of them." She spoke with just a trace of an accent that I couldn't identify. Maybe Wisconsin, maybe New York, but definitely not a native Hoosier. "The bold colors and basic spray paint art style are the same in each. He uses dark edging lines.

The facial details are much finer than in most graffiti art. The use of sharp angles and strong lines is not common in street art, but it's present at both scenes. I'd have to look at the originals, but it looks like parts of these images were brush painted, some with very fine tip brushes. That's rare in graffiti art."

"Is it gang related?"

"A lot of street art is connected with gangs. That's how most street artists get their start. Graffiti is used to mark off territory, sort of like a dog pissing on his side of a tree. It's also used to show gang pride. But nothing in these is consistent with any gang in Muncie, or any gang I've studied for that matter. Can't rule it out, but I don't think it's gang related."

"Tess White said you can sometimes actually identify the specific person that did the graffiti. Can you do that here?"

"I can link the work. I can point out similarities and identify with some degree of probability that the same artist was responsible for different pieces of work. But just to look at something and say who did it, no, I can't do that, at least not with these paintings."

I held out my hand for the photos. "Well it was a long shot."

Portia placed her hand across the photos. "Do you mind if I hold on to these? I make a habit of going around to the common graffiti sites when I have time. I take photos of anything I find interesting. I've used them in my books. I'd like to go back through the photos I have and see if I can spot something that might look like the same person. Would that be okay?"

I pulled my hand back. "Sure," I said. I fished out one of my business cards from my wallet and handed it to her. "Just call me if you come up with anything. Anything at all."

Portia called back about a week later. "I may have something," she said. "This isn't definite, but when I went back through the photos that I've taken around Muncie, I found several pieces of graffiti from about seven years ago that have definite similarities in style. These earlier pieces aren't as complex or as bold. I could see this as being from a younger version of your artist, or maybe from someone who learned from him."

I could feel my pulse quicken, but tried to keep my voice calm and steady. "So you're saying this is the guy?"

"No," she said firmly. "I'm saying there are similarities. It could be the guy."

As I was writing notes, Portia continued.

"This earlier guy, he signed his work with a symbol. A crescent moon with a tear drop falling off the bottom point. From what I can tell, he painted for about a year, then disappeared. But I have no idea what his real name is, or even his street name."

I thanked Portia and hung up. If the case wasn't difficult enough, it now seemed that I was chasing a ghost with a spray can and a brush.

* * *

The third body showed up on a cold, drizzly, early November afternoon. A nosey elderly woman driving back from a trip to the grocery had noticed what she thought was a bum taking a nap outside a long-abandoned truck terminal building off Meeker Avenue on the south side of the city. She called 911, telling the dispatcher that such people shouldn't be free to run around the city sleeping wherever they wanted. It was nearly two hours later when a patrol car drove by, the officer no doubt hoping that whoever it was had woken up and moved on. But someone was still there. It took the officer only a single glance at the graffiti painted wall of the terminal to know this wasn't a drunk sleeping it off. His call to dispatch was immediately forwarded to me.

The scene had become all too familiar, the process too routine. A body lay crumpled on a long-abandoned concrete pad once used for truck parking. The nearest wall of the aging block building was painted with a ten by six mural. This time it showed a man's head exploding in vivid colors of red, pink and white as he was hit by what looked like a metal pipe held by a single, black-gloved hand.

The victim was a middle-aged male, dressed in a dark suit and a stylish, full-length navy overcoat. The back of his head was deformed, struck multiple times by a blunt object. Rain rinsed blood in a thin sheen across the gray concrete.

I knelt beside the body and with a gloved hand, gently turned the face. I had long ago given up being shocked at crime scenes, but now, crouched in the rain, my mind slid into numb disbelief.

It was Rob Kendall.

Our paths had crossed on many occasions during the eight years Rob served as a deputy prosecutor. Now he had his own law firm. Talk around town was he would run for prosecutor in the next election, and he would likely win.

This wasn't someone who had spent his life dealing in drugs, shoplifting and prostitution. No tattoos. No gangs. This was a successful businessman, a politician, a local man of influence. Crouched there next to the body, my entire working theory of the Graffiti Killer washed away in the chilled November rain.

I took a few steps away and called Chief Smith. "We've got another one," I said, my voice grim. "And it changes everything. It's Rob Kendall."

"Shit." That was all Smith said. There was a long silence and then he hung up, undoubtedly to call the mayor. Politics before family. Notifying Kendall's wife would have to wait.

Thirty minutes later, as the crime scene techs went about gathering evidence, I saw a familiar car arrive. Tess got out of the driver's side and made a beeline toward me. Her face seemed drawn and pale. She had none of the excitement of a front page story in the making. "Is it true what I heard? It's Rob Kendall."

I nodded but didn't say anything.

"This is getting real ugly," she said, shaking her head as if in disbelief. "This isn't just gang bangers and druggies now. People are going to get scared."

I couldn't think of any response. I shrugged, then turned and walked back toward the body.

The next day's newspaper led with a four-column headline: "Graffiti Killer Claims Third Victim." I had to give Tess credit. The story didn't push for the sensational. But it didn't have to.

It didn't take long for Chief Smith to barge into my office, yelling at me about the news story and the serial killer panic sweeping through the city. An hour later, the mayor himself told me, "Get off your ass and solve this." At two that afternoon I was summoned to a meeting in the Chief's conference room. The Chief established a multi-agency Graffiti Killer task force. He named Chief Deputy Ted Clark as head of the committee, but Clark's job was to coordinate efforts with the FBI, State Police, and other agencies. To my surprise, I was still in charge of the field investigation.

Federal and state crime labs evaluated and analyzed every trace of evidence, then evaluated and analyzed it again. A dozen investigators interviewed every person connected to the victims, then different investigators re-interviewed them. Rob Kendall's current client list was examined, and his case files from his time as a deputy prosecutor were scrutinized. Detectives tracked down every violent felon and gang member. Some were still doing time. Several had moved to other parts of the country. A few were dead. All were quickly ruled out.

The crime techs could not come up with anything useful. Attempts were made to track all local spray paint purchases, but with the volume of sales and the lack of records on such sales, it was a futile effort. I went back to Lacy to talk about the gang angle, but he convinced me that it was a dry hole. I went back to Portia Henshaw, and she confirmed the graffiti image at the latest murder was done by the same person, but she still was no closer to identifying the artist.

After two months of intensive work, there wasn't a single solid lead, so the investigation sat at a frustrating standstill. That changed with a late night call on a bone-chilling night in mid-January.

* * *

It was after midnight. I was sitting at the Fickle Peach, a downtown bar specializing in craft beers. I was working on my fourth pint of the evening. Or maybe it was my fifth. My cell phone rang, but the number was blocked. I answered with a curt, "Yeah?"

"You're the guy handling those graffiti killings, aren't you?"

"Who is this?"

"I ain't givin' my name. But if you want to solve those murders, you need to get down to the Cardinal Trail."

"Who is this?" I repeated. My voice was adamant, but I became aware of a slight thickness to my words.

"You know where the trail crosses Jackson Street between the old wire mill and that deserted Brodericks factory? There's something going on there. If you show up now, you might break this thing."

I drained what remained in my glass and sat it back on the bar. "I'll call it in. We'll get a car down there to take a look."

"No." The voice at the other end of the phone was sharp. "You want to find who's doing this, you come now. Just you. Anybody else comes, you'll see bodies stacking up so fast you won't be able to count them."

The phone went dead.

I knew it was a crank call. Someone was pulling my chain, wanting to see a cop traipsing around on a frigid night. It was a perverted version of an adult snipe hunt. But what the hell? There was no one waiting for me back at my apartment. Not even a damned cat.

I threw two twenties on the bar to cover the tab, slipped on my winter coat and gloves, and headed out to my car.

Ten minutes later, I pulled into a small parking area near the trail. Once a railroad line that carried rust-belt products to the rest of the world, the Cardinal Trail was now a paved path for walkers and bikers, extending nearly seventy miles from Marion to Richmond. This time of night, with the temperature no more than fifteen degrees, it was deserted.

I turned the engine off and sat in silence, feeling the effects of the alcohol swimming in my head. This was a bad idea. I was in no condition to go walking down a dark trail. I should call in for some patrolmen and let them investigate. I reached for my phone, punching in the number to the dispatcher. "This is Rigsby," I said when my call was answered. "I got an anonymous tip on that Graffiti Killer case. Can you send a black and white to back me up while I check this out?"

"Sure thing, Hammer," the voice said. "Where are you?"

I gave my location.

"Bobby Hoffman and Alexis James have just finished up an OWI arrest. They should be there in ten, maybe fifteen, minutes."

I gave my thanks and hung up. I sat in the cold, listening to some late-night talk show babble on my car radio. I was tired and the alcohol was making me drowsy. I nodded off for a few seconds, jerking myself awake. If I didn't get out, whoever showed up would find me asleep in my car. "Screw it," I said out loud. "They can catch up with me." I got out of the car.

As soon as I started down the trail I saw a soft glow ahead. The paved path bent to the right and disappeared under a bridge for one of the few still-operating train lines. As I followed the bend, I saw the source of the light. A battery-powered camping lantern was suspended from an overhanging bare branch just past the underpass.

As I walked between the ancient concrete bridge supports, something on the left side caught my eye. Among the decades-old graffiti that covered the concrete, there was an area of fresh, brighter paint. I stood directly in front of it. Even with the alcohol, I could tell it was done by the same person as the murder murals.

The colors were muted in the dim light, but the image was clear. A man stood in the underpass, arms flailing wide, his back arched. A disembodied gloved hand was driving a knife into the man's back.

But there was one difference. A sheet of paper held by duct tape covered the face. As a matter of habit, I reached for my latex gloves, but I didn't carry them in my jeans. With my heavy winter gloves, I reached out and pulled off the tape. The paper fluttered down revealing an anguished face.

My face.

Maybe if I wasn't dealing with the effects of the beer I would have heard a sound behind me sooner. But I didn't. I only heard the distinctive metallic click of a gun being cocked and felt the chill of the barrel being placed against the skin at the back of my neck.

"Recognize the face?" The male voice was as cold as the January night.

"Yeah," I said softly, trying to keep my voice calm. "But it's not a very good likeness."

"Good enough, though. So, you figure out who I am yet?"

"Is that what this is about? You're afraid I'm ready to break the case?"

From behind me there was a laugh that put me on edge more than the gun at my neck. "You don't even remember, do you? It was right here at this spot. Seven years ago. You busted a kid for painting on this wall. And when you searched his pockets, you found a bit of weed."

I searched my brain. Through the fog of alcohol I couldn't recall what he might be talking about.

"You wanted a snitch. Wanted me to be your spy on the street. Your bitch. And when I wouldn't do it, you threw the book at me. I was sixteen, but you worked with the prosecutor to charge me as an adult. You were going to teach me a lesson. Wanna guess who the prosecutor was?"

"Rob Kendall?" I asked, softly.

"Yeah. And you remember who was your witness? The one who lied and testified against me so you wouldn't bust her for hooking?"

It was coming back to me. "Bren Taylor," I said.

"Now you're gettin' it. Just too bad that son of a bitch judge died of cancer, cause I would have done him too."

"So what's the connection with Zayas?"

"Oh man, you don't know nothin', do you? Thanks to you, I didn't get sent to no juvie. I got sent to Wabash Correctional. And Zayas was there to greet me. Every night he was there to greet me in my cell. And you know what he did to me, don't you?"

I didn't say anything.

"And when I stood up to him, he did this!"

A hand grabbed my shoulder and whirled me around. A young, white man stood in front of me. He was short and extremely thin. The right side of his face was leathery and scarred in a way I often had seen on burn victims. His right eye was missing and only a stub remained where his right ear once had been. Below his left eye was a tattoo—a crescent with a tear drop hanging from the tip.

"Jesus," I said under my breath.

"He won't help you," the man said, shaking with rage. "He didn't help me. I called his name every night, but he didn't help. And all the guards ever did was laugh and ask how I liked it."

In his distracted rage, I saw my chance. I swung my arm up hard. The alcohol slowed my reflexes, but my movement caught him off guard. My forearm hit him hard on the wrist just behind the gun. I saw the light glint off metal as the 9mm went flying out into the darkness.

I never saw the blade.

I felt the steel edge drive hard into my back, penetrating under my rib cage and driving upward. I didn't feel pain. Instead I felt the force of the steel as it ripped through muscle, arteries and organs. I tried to gasp for breath, but my lungs wouldn't expand. Then I felt the knife drive home again. And again. I did not feel myself falling, but my knees hit hard on the pavement.

"Oh, God. No." In the distance I heard the faint sound of an approaching siren. Then nothing.

About the Authors

Joan Bruce: Joan has written several cozy short stories featuring Candi and Mandy and is currently working on a novel about these wacky friends. Joan resides in Morgan County, Indiana as her alter ego, D. B. Reddick, a former newspaper reporter and retiree from a national insurance trade association who has about a dozen short story credits in anthologies with Pill Hill Press, Blue River Press, Red Coyote Press, and Whortleberry Press.

N. W. Campbell: Norm has been a writer his entire adult professional life. He was first a technical writer, then a United Methodist pastor, an adjunct instructor of English at the University of Florida, the University of Missouri-St. Louis, the University of Indianapolis, and Ivy Tech Community College-Indianapolis. He is a summa cum laude graduate of Northeastern University and holds graduate degrees in English studies, divinity and leadership development.

Sherita Saffer Campbell: Sherita practices and teaches a form of guided meditation that she engages in before writing or while searching for new ideas. She was a feature writer for both the former *Muncie Star* and for a weekly paper. Sherita writes mysteries and has been published in Alfred Hitchcock Mystery Magazine, Fate Magazine, Branches, SageWoman, and poetry books from the Humpback Barn Festival. She has had stories published in five Speed City Indiana Sisters in Crime chapter anthologies.

Diana Catt: Diana has fifteen short stories in multiple genres in anthologies published by Blue River Press, Red Coyote Press, Pill Hill Press, Wolfmont Press, The Four Horseman Press, and SpeedCity Press. Her collection, *Below the Line*, is available on Amazon. She's an environmental microbiologist living and working in Morgan County, Indiana.

S. Ashley Couts: Ashley holds a BFA in painting from Indiana University and Herron School of Art and Design. She is a fellow of the Indiana Writing Project. She has worn many hats, from grocery clerk to police dispatcher to middle school art teacher. Her writings in fiction, non-fiction, and poetry have appeared in local, regional and national publications.

MB Dabney: Michael is an award-winning journalist whose writing has appeared in numerous local and national publications. He spent two decades as a reporter in Philadelphia, working first for *Business Week* magazine as a business correspondent and later for United Press International and the Associated Press. As an editor at *The Philadelphia Tribune,* the nation's oldest continuously published African -American newspaper, Michael earned national and state awards for his editorial writing. He lives in Indianapolis with his wife, two daughters and dog, Pluto.

Marianne Halbert: Marianne is an attorney and author of dark fiction. She has had over thirty short stories published in magazines such as Necrotic Tissue, ThugLit, and Midnight Screaming, as well as in anthologies by Blue River Press, The Four Horsemen, Great Old Ones Publishing, Grinning Skull Press, Evil Jester Press, Pill Hill Press, Wicked East Press, and more. Her collection, *Wake Up and Smell the Creepy*, is available on Amazon. Follow her at Halbert Fiction on Facebook.

Shari Held: Shari is a lifelong reader and a freelance writer from Indianapolis. She loves reading, movies, fine food and fashion. She is a member of Speed City Indiana Sisters in Crime. *Pride and Patience* is her first published mystery short story.

B. K. Hart: B. K. is an avid reader and gatherer of facts which serve as compliments to the writing skill set. B. K. has previously published short stories in three separate horror anthologies and in two Speed City Indiana Sisters in Crime anthologies.

Barbara Swander Miller: Barbara joined Sisters in Crime a few years ago to benefit from the wisdom and experience of more experienced fiction writers. She teaches high school English and also works for the Indiana Writing Project helping teachers implement Writing Workshop practices in their classrooms. *How to*

Throw a Pot is based on her experiences in Peru during a Lilly Teacher Creativity Grant project. . . . Well, except for the criminal parts.

C. A. Paddock: Carol wrote her first mystery, *Mystery Adventure of Jimmy Hashburger,* as a first grader. Although it was never published, the story was featured during the classroom reading hour. Carol earned a BA in Speech and Spanish from Butler University and a certificate in Translation Studies from Indiana University. She holds a CMP (certified meeting professional) designation from the Convention Industry Council. She has worked in advertising, communications, meetings, event management, and leadership development for corporations and nonprofits. *The Making of a Masterpiece* is her first published fiction story.

Claudia Pfeiffer: Claudia wrote in her youth and teens, then quit for nearly fifty years to work in her husband's law office. Now a widow, she bought a computer and began to write mystery, romance, and juvenile fiction. She has been published in two Speed City Indiana Sisters in Crime anthologies.

C. L. Shore: Cheryl has a Bachelor's Degree and a PhD from Indiana University. In between, she earned her Master's Degree in Nursing from the University of Iowa. She is a Nurse Practitioner and practices in a rural clinic for the underserved. She has authored multiple academic articles about family coping with epilepsy. Her mystery novel, *Seeker of Truth,* was published in 2011, and *Titania's Suitor* was published in 2014. Cheryl is published in two Speed City Indiana Sisters in Crime anthologies.

Andrea Smith: Andrea holds a Bachelor's Degree in journalism from Northern Illinois University and a Master of Arts in novel writing and publishing from DePaul University in Chicago. She managed corporate communications for companies such as Eli Lilly and Co., Kraft Foods, and Ameritech. She owned two Subway restaurants and was an adjunct professor of English. Andrea has published four short stories featuring Chicago Police detective Ariel Lawrence. She has been published in the Mary

Higgins Clark Mystery Magazine, Alfred Hitchcock Mystery Magazine and has short stories in five Speed City Indiana Sisters in Crime anthologies.

Brenda Robertson Stewart: Brenda has a Bachelor of Arts degree from Indiana University. She is an editor, mystery author, painter and sculptor. She raised horses for many years and was an accomplished original doll artist. Her forensic mystery series features Lettie Sue Wolfe, a forensic sculptor. She has many published short stories and has co-edited four anthologies. Brenda is also a forensic artist specializing in clay facial reconstruction on skulls and has been known to work on Egyptian mummies.

Stephen Terrell: Steve is an attorney and member of Speed City Indiana Sisters in Crime. He is the author of *Stars Fall,* a legal thriller; *There and Back, Journal of a Last Motorcycle Ride*; and *Visiting Hours and Other Stories from the Heart.* Steve contributed two short stories and multiple factual inserts to this anthology.

Janet Williams: Janet has been writing her entire life, first as a child making her own books and later as a journalist for newspapers in Pittsburgh and Indianapolis. She has always believed that journalism is, at its heart, strong storytelling. Today, she uses her experiences covering courts, crime and politics to create her fiction. Since retiring from a corporate job in 2015, Janet has been writing and hanging out with her dog, Roxy.

Other Publications by Speed City Indiana Sisters in Crime, Inc.

Racing Can Be Murder, Blue River Press (2007)—a collection of nineteen stories written by some of today's best mystery writers. It revolves around the Indianapolis 500 Mile Race and the festivities that take place in Indianapolis each merry month of May.

Bedlam at the Brickyard, Blue River Press, (2010)—a collection of fifteen stories written by some of todays best emerging mystery writers. This delightful collection revolves around the Indianapolis Motor Speedway's 400 Mile stock car race and the festivities that surround it. Each story is separated by a historical narrative or statistical chart to enlighten as well as entertain the reader.

Hoosier Hoops and Hijinks, Blue River Press (2013)—It's only a game, you say? Don't you believe it. After that final buzzer, these stories reveal, it may be the games are only beginning. When it comes to Hoosier Hijinks, not everyone plays by the rules. And that's what makes it irresistible—From the Introduction by Hank Phillippi Ryan.

Decades of Dirt, SpeedCity Press (2015)—Take a journey back in time with this collection of fifteen mysterious tales of historical fiction. Experience a Native American mystic solving a murder, a foiled presidential assassination attempt, a violent case of mistaken identity, the evils of racial discrimination, strife on the Indiana frontier, a killing during the heyday of the jazz era, and nine other compelling short stories.

M. Travis DiNicola has been the executive director of Indy Reads for ten years. Indy Reads is an Indianapolis organization that provides free, basic tutoring for adults who are struggling with reading and writing and adults whose second language is English. Travis has been responsible for the overall management of the organization, has written columns about authors for NUVO newsweekly, and has co-hosted and produced The Art of the Matter on public radio and television. He served as president of the Indianapolis Museum of Art's Contemporary Art Society and vice president of the Indianapolis School of Ballet's board. Travis has a background in theatre, dance, and art.